Praise for the novels of Lynn Hightower

Fortunes of the Dead

"Perfect."

—*Chicago Tribune*

"One of Hightower's best works to date."

—*Midwest Book Review*

"Instantly believable and touching."

—*Publishers Weekly*

Satan's Lambs

"A superior thriller—filled with characters I cared about and a riveting story line that kept me turning pages."

—Jonathan Kellerman

"Lena is one of the most fully realized characters I've encountered in detective fiction. I can't visualize a single barrier to [Hightower's] ultimate success."

—Andrew Vachss

"There's never a dull moment in *Satan's Lambs*. Good characters and a plot that moves."

—Tony Hillerman

"Crisply written. . . . Offers not only a nicely twisting plot but also memorable characterization. Best of all is Lena Padget, a new departure in private detectives, who thrives on junk food and the problems of abused women and children. In sum, *Satan's Lambs* is a devilish good book."

—Ross Thomas

"Lena Padget is a very welcome addition to the ranks of fictional private eyes. She is witty, tough, and always a woman. A cast of entertainingly odd characters, a truly original plot, and the ability to keep the story going without a lagging page or jarring sentence make Lynn Hightower's first private eye novel a delight. I look forward eagerly to Lena's return."

—Stuart Kaminsky

Flashpoint
"Tautly plotted, engaging story, enlivened by crisp dialogue."

—*Booklist*

Eyeshot
"Sharp, shocking, and shamelessly satisfying."

—Val McDermid

"A cracking tale told at a stunning pace."

—*The Mail on Sunday* (London)

The Debt Collector
"There are plenty of reasons to admire Lynn Hightower's Cincinnati police procedurals. Along with style and substance, these stories have heart."

—*The New York Times Book Review*

"Powerful. Hightower is a pro who knows how to get the job done."

—*Los Angeles Times*

"[Hightower's] absorbing, fast-paced narrative thrives on its own high-powered energy, plumbing dark recesses in her central players and startling readers with plot twists."

—*Chicago Sun-Times*

"Explosive."

—*Miami Herald*

"Keeps us turning the pages."

—*The Washington Post*

High Water

"A dynamite tale of family fallout, mystery, and intrigue, southern-style. Demands to be read in one all-night page-turning frenzy."

—David Baldacci

"Lynn Hightower is a skilled and wonderful writer, and *High Water* is a lyrical, compelling novel about secrets, family, and even love."

—Lisa Scottoline

"This intensely involving study of family dysfunction . . . is distinguished by its driving prose, lyricism, and psychological nuances."

—*Publishers Weekly*

when
secrets
die

Lynn Hightower

POCKET BOOKS

NEW YORK LONDON TORONTO SYDNEY

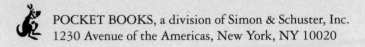

POCKET BOOKS, a division of Simon & Schuster, Inc.
1230 Avenue of the Americas, New York, NY 10020

Library of Congress Cataloging-in-Publication Data

Hightower, Lynn S.
    When secrets die : a Lena Padget novel / Lynn Hightower.—1st
Pocket Books trade pbk. ed.
        p. cm.
    ISBN-13: 978-0-7434-6391-1
    ISBN-10:   0-7434-6391-9
  1. Women private investigators—Kentucky—Lexington—Fiction.
  2. Munchausen syndrome by proxy—Fiction. 3. Children—Death—
Fiction. 4. Lexington (Ky.)—Fiction. I. Title.

PS3558.I372W47 2005
813'.54—dc22   2005047646

First Pocket Books trade paperback edition September 2005

10 9 8 7 6 5 4 3 2 1

Manufactured in the United States of America

For information regarding special discounts for bulk purchases,
please contact Simon & Schuster Special Sales at 1-800-456-6798
or business@simonandschuster.com.

For Rachel, my sweet wild child.
Headstrong, kindhearted, and fierce.

ACKNOWLEDGMENTS

My thanks to Patricia Patrick for technical advice and medical insight.

To Jon Brock, for his wonderful stories.

To Alan, Laurel, Rachel, and Rebecca, for all the usual reasons.

And last but not least to Robert, for enough reasons to fill another book.

The retention of human body parts at postmortem examinations without consent from next-of-kin has caused consternation in New Zealand and overseas. Discussion of these incidents is dominated by legal considerations and the role of informed consent. Further reflection reveals the broader issues surrounding the availability of human material for research and teaching, and inconsistencies in the manner in which the use of such material is regulated. The retention of tissue at postmortem is examined in the light of the regulation. . . . What emerges is the need for ongoing control against a background of ethical awareness, based on an understanding of why human tissue should be treated with dignity and respect.

In February 2002, it was revealed publicly that up until as late as 1996, Green Lane Hospital in Auckland had been retaining children's hearts following postmortem examinations without parental consent. . . . A variety of scandals have also come to light in the United States, involving anatomy departments, tissue banks, nonprofit and for-profit private biotechnology companies, and more recently, crematoria. . . . While commercial pressures skew some of these American cases, the underlying drive remains the centrality of human tissue for research, therapy and teaching. Even more broadly, there is a global traffic in human organs, which is now being widely acknowledged. . . . It has been evident for very many years that the uses to which any society will allow human material to be put is relative to that society's moral values . . . there is no automatic right to use human material for research or teaching purposes.

—Professor D. Gareth Jones and Dr. Kerry A. Galvin,
Retention of Body Parts: Reflections from Anatomy

when
secrets
die

LENA

Chapter One

I have often thought that my sister knew she was going to die. I don't mean that she had psychic dreams; I don't mean she was pessimistic. I think she evaluated the odds of her situation, and, in her heart and her mind, she had faced the outcome. Whitney was seven months pregnant when my ex–brother-in-law killed her, my little nephew, and, by default, my unborn niece.

Whitney always knew how dangerous Jeff was—after she married him, she knew. Yet she had one child with him and conceived a second. There were times, many times, when I wanted to strangle her for this stupidity. Easy for me, on the outside looking in. When Whitney looked at Jeff, she saw the person he could be; she saw the best in him. And when she realized (finally, and much too late) that everything good about Jeff was heavily outweighed by everything bad, she cut him out of her life.

But she always knew that the odds of keeping him out weren't so very good. My sister knew that she might not win, but knowing that never seemed to make a difference. She didn't have to know that she would win before she did what she knew was right. That's brave. It's powerful, too. It means you are free and clear of the kind of manipulations that can sear your soul.

Emma Marsden was like that. She was a lot like my sister in other ways too. She had that same inner vibrancy, a tuned piano full of music. She was ready for the next thing, a wary half smile on her lips, and in her eyes you could see that she was expecting something interesting to happen.

Her likeness to my sister made me vulnerable to her, according to my one and only, Joel Mendez. It was what made me believe in her. It was what made me work for her, and stick with her, when the rest of the world was ready to burn her at the stake.

But I think Emma Marsden brought out the best in me, because to me, Emma Marsden was like that elusive Christmas back home when everything goes right. Just being around her eased the nostalgic homesickness those of us who have lost family always carry in our souls. I guess because she was so much like my sister.

It's all about taking sides. Life, I mean. That's what it comes to if you're honest. Right, wrong, revenge, forgiveness . . . you take a stand. That's what Emma Marsden did. She took her daughter's side. Everything she did was for Blaine, her fifteen-year-old girl. Even when Blaine lost her way. Maybe that's why women are so much better at taking sides than men are. Maybe it plays on the nurturing and mothering instinct—my child first, no matter what.

Which is why, when I met her, Emma Marsden's life was a nightmare. Because she'd been accused of Munchausen by proxy, which, as you know, from watching those television movies of the week that you refuse to admit you watch, means a mother is so reprehensible, and so disturbed, that she will make her own child sick in order to get attention for herself.

I can imagine the hell a parent goes through when they lose a child. But I have no children of my own, so I can only imagine it. To be accused of killing that child, for motives of personal narcissism, was, according to Emma herself, the tenth circle of hell that is reserved for women who have the temerity to thwart the medical system.

The first time I met Emma Marsden was in the Main Street office of her attorney and ex-husband, Clayton Roubideaux. It was a small office, behind a brown door in a townhouse-style building. Roubideaux clearly kept an eye on the overhead. He may have been one of the most successful litigators in Lexington, Kentucky, but there were none of the oversized conference rooms, heavy mahogany furniture, or hushed discomfort you find in large law firms where billable hours are considered an art form.

No ankle-deep carpeting—a status symbol of the past, along with the office fireplace in the center of the room. None of the shiny new hardwood floors preferred by the edgy firms in entertainment law, none of the creaky old wood floors found in the hallowed halls where the business of making money is sometimes confused with social significance.

Roubideaux's office had Berber carpet, the wealthy man's form of indoor/outdoor: practical, pricey, ugly. The front desk was small and the receptionist clearly limited to answering the telephone. Marsden worked with two other attorneys, and there were no cubicles or horseshoe work areas for legal secretaries, researchers, paralegals, or the amazing and generally underpaid legal creature who does all of the above.

There was a receptionist, aged twenty or twenty-two, and as it was five fifteen and Friday she was happily putting away the pencil that was the only clutter on the tiny oak desk behind the kind of partition one usually finds in a small doctor's office or veterinary clinic. She pointed me to a small hallway on her way out the door. I followed the sound of a man and woman who were laughing in the way people do when they are in a waiting room somewhere, anxious about the appointment ahead, and trying to keep their spirits up.

I understood from Clayton himself that he and his wife—ex-wife—hadn't been divorced that long. A year at most. I was wary about being in the office with the two of them, but the only tension I could sense arose when I walked through the door. I wasn't used to being dreaded.

Clayton Roubideaux stood up the minute he saw me, but the first person I noticed was Emma Marsden, who sat with her legs crossed in a high-backed maroon chair. She wore blue jeans and a black sweater and worn, dirty Nikes. We were dressed just alike, except I wore high-topped Reeboks, which were white and new. Her hair was clean, but pulled back in a rubber band, and she hadn't bothered with makeup. She looked like she hadn't had a good night's sleep since the last presidential election. Many of us hadn't.

Emma Marsden was thirty-seven years old, and her hair was already threaded with gray. Her forehead was ridged with worry wrinkles that were startling but not unattractive on such a young face. She had the look of a woman who has forgotten how to be beautiful.

She looked at me over her shoulder, steadily, without smiling. Her ex-husband, already on his feet and waiting for my attention, shook my hand across the oak veneer desk.

"Lena Padget? Clayton Roubideaux." His grip was firm, his smile toothy. "This is my wife . . . ex-wife, I mean. Emma."

Her hand was ice cold, fingers slim, nails cut short, a tall woman whose hand dwarfed my own.

"Please, sit down," Roubideaux said.

I took the other wingback chair and sat all the way back in the cushion so that my feet did not quite touch the floor. I didn't feel ridiculous. I'm used to my height, and the posture had exactly the effect I wanted. Emma Marsden smiled and loosened up, settling back in her own chair. She wasn't rude enough to laugh out loud, but the vision of me with my feet dangling over the edge of the seat clearly amused her.

"We appreciate you coming in after business hours," Clayton said.

I nodded. Why lose credit by explaining that I set my own business hours, that I had slept late that morning and had plenty of time to drink coffee, read *USA Today,* and peel the threadbare indoor/outdoor carpet away from half of the little screened-in porch in the cottage I shared with my significant other?

The old carpet had been evocative of many faded but die-hard layers of ancient cat urine, an odor that is as hard to kill as a cockroach, although it does not run away. But I had soaked in my claw-foot tub, and changed to clean jeans and another of the black sweaters that make up a significant portion of my wardrobe. I was clean and crisp and smelled only of the vanilla lotion I buy from Bath and Body Works. I was ready to go to work.

Clayton Marsden looked at his ex-wife, who looked back at him. "Emma, do you want to start, or do you just want to interrupt me later?"

Great.

"Go ahead," she said.

She had an interesting voice, a little scratchy, like she was recovering from laryngitis.

Roubideaux looked at me. "Lena, do you have any children?"

"I have a cat."

He didn't smile. Neither one of them did. Cats, clearly, did not count, although I was not being flip, and I absolutely love my cat.

"Emma and I had one child together. She also has an older daughter. Her youngest child, our son, died two years ago, while being treated by Dr. Theodore Tundridge at Fayette Hospital. Tundridge is a pediatrician and the director of the Tundridge Children's Clinic."

Clayton and Emma exchanged looks.

The faint music of "La Bamba" drifted into the room from somewhere, the hallway maybe.

"How old was your son when he died?"

"Right at two and a half."

A toddler, I thought. "What did he die of?"

Emma Marsden looked at her feet, and Clayton ran a finger along the edge of his desk. Their silence interested me.

"His liver failed," Clayton said.

Neither of them met my eyes, but pain seeped like acid through their self-containment. They weren't looking for sympathy, they were looking for help. They were looking for somebody to be on their side.

I wondered why they wanted me.

Marsden leaned back in his chair and placed his fingertips along the edge of his desk. He seemed absorbed in placing those fingertips in some kind of preordained and essential alignment, and to manage this he wasn't able to look at me while he talked.

"I don't know if you know this, Ms. . . . Lena. But in this day and age, if you give permission to have an autopsy performed on a family member who dies in a hospital, or if, as in the case of our son, an autopsy is required, that's pretty much license to plunder."

He looked at me.

I looked back. "What exactly do you mean by that? Plunder?"

Emma Marsden faced me. "What it means is that they stole my son's internal organs; kept some of them for research, and donated others for profit."

"Technically, it's not for profit," Clayton said.

Emma looked at him the way I had looked at the urine-scented carpet on my screened-in porch. "Their 'fee,' my dear ex-husband, is simply a *non-profit* way of saying *profit*. Creative accounting. The not-for-profit medical profession makes the *corporate* profiteers look like small-timers. You know this, Clayton, and she's not going to sue us, she's not wearing a wire. Stop dancing around and say what it is."

"My dear ex-wife is right," Clayton said.

I slid forward in my chair, feet on the floor. Their habit of calling each other "dear ex-whatever" was annoying; also, I didn't like being called "she" when I was actually in the room.

"Are you telling me the hospital took your son's organs without permission?" I asked. I found it hard to believe.

"Not the hospital," Clayton said. "Dr. Tundridge's clinic. They treated our son when he first got sick, and Dr. Tundridge was in charge when Ned was admitted to the hospital."

"Tundridge was head of the *committee* of doctors who treated my son," Emma said. "It's an assembly line these days, don't you know? Each specialist looks at one small part, and nobody's really looking at the whole."

"But . . . you're saying they did all of this without your permission?"

"That's what we're saying," Emma said.

Clayton made a tepee of his fingertips, which I was ready to cut off, every single one, since he paid them so much attention and refused to meet my eyes. Odd, for a courtroom litigator. Why was he so uncomfortable with me? It made me think he was up to something. Of course, Joel says I always think people are up to something.

"It's a fuzzy area," Clayton said. "There's a blanket permission form you have to sign when someone is admitted to a hospital. On the other hand, it is so broad and vague that it really doesn't stand up. In addition, because there is very little choice about signing—which means, sign, or forget having your child treated—it could definitely be argued that it amounts to duress."

"We shouldn't have signed it," Emma said.

"We didn't have a choice."

Clayton Roubideaux looked at Emma, and it was such a look that I was embarrassed to be in the room. He wasn't up to anything other than trying to distance himself from the pain of losing a child. I felt ashamed, because I was so judgmental. Just because I was happy these days did not give me an excuse for forgetting what it was like for people who were going through the dark times.

It's strange that happiness does that to you—makes you just a little less compassionate, a little less willing to listen, because you don't want it to intrude, that darkness, you don't want it spilling over into your life and shadowing your relief and peace of heart. I think it is an instinctual and primitive reaction—like a fear of infection. Sometimes it's easier to be effective in my line of work if you're depressed before you interview the client.

"How do you know?" I asked. "Or is that what you want me to do—to find out?"

Emma Marsden shook her head. "We know already, believe me. We know because someone from the clinic *called* us and notified us that our son's heart was not buried with him, and what did we want them to do with it. It was like a . . . a *storage* issue. They let us know they were going to be billing us. And then we called back—"

"I called back," Clayton said.

"Does it really matter who called back, Clayton?" Emma said.

"It might."

She looked at me. I shrugged. It might or it might not, but I wasn't getting in the middle until I was ready. I was planning to take sides, I just wasn't sure how many there were. We had started with two, but watching the both of them made me wonder if there weren't going to be three. Of the two of them, Clayton Roubideaux probably had the money to pay my fee, which meant his was the most practical side to take, but that fingertip thing was putting me off.

"Okay, so you're telling me that the clinic actually informed you that they had your son's, Ned's, heart. That they'd . . . kept it? How did they explain that?"

"Research," Clayton said. "They explain everything with that one word. It's the medical-legal version of diminished capacity. It means they think they can do anything and everything they want, and so far, since the eighties anyway, the courts have concurred."

"So what happened when you called? Did they back down? Tell you it was all a big mistake?"

Clayton shook his head. "Not at all. They did say there was a mistake, but it wasn't that they didn't have the heart, but that they had . . . other things too."

Silence settled while I thought this through. I looked at Emma Marsden. "What other things?"

"Spleen. Liver. Both corneas. His . . . tongue."

I took a breath. "You know this for sure, or that's what they told you?"

"I went there. After they called. I went there to pick them up. I didn't know what to put them in. I just took some bags that were in the drawer in my kitchen. Sloane's bags, Sloane's Grocery? I probably should have taken a cooler, but I didn't know what the hell to do."

I nodded, chewing my bottom lip.

She looked at me, and her eyes were tight, her voice hard, but her hand, of which she seemed unaware, was clutching the neckline of her sweater and squeezing it in her fist.

"When I got there, they showed them to me. The girl who worked there . . . she was new, and she showed me where they were kept. Down in the clinic basement. It was very clean, very well lit, lots of fluorescent lighting. Bright white floors. Did I tell you how clean it was, Clayton? It made my shoes squeak. I was embarrassed because it . . . my shoes looked so worn out and dirty on that floor. And I'm standing there with my plastic grocery bags, wondering if I ought to have brought a cooler, thinking about *Tupperware*, for God's sake, wondering why the parts weren't being released to some . . . undertaker or something. And then she changed her mind. That girl. She'd left me there for twenty minutes, and she came back, and obviously she was in a lot of trouble, because she was just red in the face, like she was embarrassed or something, and she said I would have to leave and they would call me later. And so I . . . I asked to talk to her supervisor, some man named Mr. French, and while she went away to go get him, I put everything marked MARSDEN AGED TWENTY-NINE MONTHS in my grocery bags and ran out of the building and into the parking lot and got in my car and drove away."

She looked at Clayton, who reached across the desk and squeezed her hand. He was still in love with her, and she knew it, but she didn't care. But she felt sorry for him, and it was his eyes that filled with tears, and it was he who could not speak and finish the story.

"Forty-eight hours later I was called by Child Protective Services and informed that I was being accused of Munchausen by proxy in the death of my son Ned. They refused to give me any further information, except that the complaint had just been filed by the physician who treated my son—Dr. Theodore Tundridge. They said they were investigating, and wanted to *offer me the option* of voluntarily releasing custody of my daughter, Blaine, to the state. That if I did so, and that if I admitted that I was guilty of the charges, of making my own son sick enough to die, they would let me have custody of my daughter back after I had taken a prescribed list of parenting classes. But that my daughter would have to be examined periodically by Dr. Tundridge, who would oversee her health care and make sure she was not suffering from any form of abuse or induced illness."

I felt it rising within me, the anger that fueled my job. Like a helium balloon in my chest. And I got that feeling that I usually get when I go to work—I really wanted to help, meaning I was ready to take sides. Their side.

Clayton looked at me, eyes shrewd. "Can you imagine it?

The *power* this doctor and this state organization have when they work together?"

"Sounds like they've done it before."

He nodded. "I thought of that. But there's legal precedent in several other states, not just here. It happens everywhere."

"You mean this kind of deal making? Pressuring mothers to back down off of medical complaints, or they lose their kids and face criminal prosecution? It goes that far?"

"Yes, it does."

"And did you agree?" I looked over at Emma Marsden.

She stared at me, hard. "No, I did not."

"Good for you," I said. Wondering how she'd found the strength to be so brave, so smart, and so wise.

Emma Marsden wiped tears out of her eyes, making them go red. "I need a minute," she said, and left the room.

Clayton Roubideaux opened his handkerchief, blew his nose, folded the handkerchief over one more time, and blew again. "This is hard," he said.

I nodded. "Clayton, do they have any reason to suspect Emma had anything to do with your son's death? You said liver failure. That's . . . broad."

"They don't know what killed him," Clayton said. There was no anger in his voice, just something that sounded bereft. "He was so sick. He would have these attacks, they were so . . . they were horrible. Pain in his stomach, high up, and vomiting, violent vomiting that went on and on and on, he just couldn't stop. We'd take him to the emergency room. They'd do blood work, and his liver enzymes would be sky high, nine hundred when they were supposed to be forty. And then they'd come back down. And they'd do all kinds of tests, and nothing made any sense. And then he'd be okay. And then it would start back up again. They'd rerun every medical test, Emma kept food diaries, we had the paint in the house analyzed, my God, we tried everything. There just didn't seem to be any rhyme or reason to it."

"What did the autopsy say?"

"You know, they never actually gave us all that much information. Just that the liver had lesions, but was in better shape than they thought it would be."

"That's it?"

He nodded. "I should have asked. Asked more questions. But he was gone, and Emma and I were falling apart. Ned was my son, my only child. And Blaine—she was Emma's daughter from her first marriage. I said . . . something I said made Blaine think that I loved Ned more than her and that the wrong kid died, and Emma asked me about it. And I told her the truth. That I'd never said anything like that to Blaine, but that Ned was my real son and . . . and Emma asked me to leave that day and filed divorce papers that week."

He looked at me. "I did love Blaine. I still do. Very much. And maybe I did love Ned more, but so what? It's hard to be straight about that kind of thing when you go through something like this. And Blaine—she's a good kid, but she likes to play victim. Kind of an aggressive martyrdom, which is a scary thing, let me tell you.

"You know, we had a good marriage. Emma's first husband was a piece of shit. And I was good to both of them, to Emma and Blaine, and all I did was try to be the best husband and stepfather and father I could possibly be."

I wondered if he was aware that he'd separated out his role to Blaine and Ned right there. *Stepfather* and *father*. If that was his worst sin, he was probably a pretty good guy. Of course, there were two sides to every story. Two sides at least.

"Okay, then. I'm interested. But what exactly do you want me to do?"

Roubideaux's voice went crisp. "Information gathering. Take a look at this doctor. See if he has a record of any other unusual deaths on his watch. Anything that takes the blame off Emma and puts it somewhere else. Look into his clinic. See if any other parents have had him keep back, you know, parts."

"So what you're looking for is proof that Dr. Tundridge, and maybe others in the clinic, or that he associates with professionally, have accused your ex-wife of Munchausen by proxy in retaliation because she objected to, and is causing trouble over, their use of . . . their retention of your son's . . . organs."

"Yes, that's it exactly. You'll help me build a case for Emma, and against them, if it goes to court. I'm not sure it will. I honestly think our best bet is to work with them. Emma says hell no, but Child Protective Services has enormous power in this kind of case. They can take Blaine into protective custody just on the word of the doctor alone, and I think the only reason they haven't is because of how old she is."

"And how old is that?"

"She's fifteen." He drummed his fingers. "You can't make an omelet without breaking eggs."

I looked at him. "Trite but true. What point are you making that I'm missing?"

"About Emma. I want you to take a sort of devil's advocate role here. If you look into her side of it, and find nothing, then I can be sure the Commonwealth Attorney's Office will have nothing too."

"Are you asking me to investigate your ex-wife for her role in the death of your son?"

"In a roundabout sort of way."

"Would you have asked me this if she was still in the room?"

"No. I had planned to call you, to talk about this end of the . . ."

His voice trailed away because I was standing now.

"Mr. Roubideaux, I'm turning you down."

"You just said you were interested."

"I was, until you asked me to look into the possibility your ex-wife is guilty. And because you made sure she was out of the room when you asked me."

"So? I don't think she is guilty of anything but being a pretty wonderful mother, I just want it proved. Give me something I can take to court."

"Am I working for you or her?"

"Both of us. Except that I'm paying your bills."

"What you mean by that, Mr. Roubideaux, is that I'm to tell her I'm working for both of you, but in actuality I'll be working for you. That is a deceit."

"That's not a nice way to put it."

"There isn't a nice way to put it. I won't play both sides against the middle. And I think you're a shit. Good-bye, counselor."

"Good-bye." His voice was faint and the expression on his face reflected a mild shock and a deep offense.

I didn't much care.

I shut the outside door pretty hard, making the bells clatter. Emma Marsden was sitting on the hood of a battered BMW Z3 Roadster that was parked on the curb right out front. The car was a silver convertible with a black cloth roof. The driver's side had taken a hell of a blow just past the door, but it was still a BMW, and a Roadster, and a beautiful thing. The parking meter had expired, but Emma Marsden didn't have a ticket on her windshield, and it was after five now, when parking was free. She sat cross-legged, and she was smoking a slender black cigar. She couldn't have looked less like a grieving mother.

"Smoke?" she asked.

I was tempted to take one, but I shook my head. It made me like her more, though. I liked women who smoked cigars. I was smoking them some myself these days, so it made me feel validated, even though I'd come to the practice so many years after it was fashionable that it was probably unfashionable again.

"Forgive the drama back there. I don't know why it hit me

like that, so hard all of a sudden, and I don't make a habit of crying in front of strangers."

"You've got reason. It must have been a nightmare, down in
that basement."

She looked up at me. "It makes you want to go down there,
doesn't it? To take a look?"

I rocked back and forth on my heels. Clients often unloaded
their anger by being combative. It was usually best to deflect.
"This sort of thing can't be legal."

"I'll think you'll find that it can be. I'm sure Clayton
explained." She flicked ash onto the pavement. "Do you need
anything else from me? Information or details or some kind of
release form where people can talk to you about my son's medical
history?"

"No, actually. I'm not taking the case."

She frowned, and rubbed a bit of bird crap off the paint job. I
made a mental note not to shake her hand. She looked up at me,
speculative, not particularly friendly.

"Too tough for you? Or too depressing?"

"Neither."

"Then why?"

"Because I don't like clients who lie to me, and I don't get in
the middle of feuding divorced people, and because I don't like
being made party to a deceit."

"Wow. What the hell does all that have to do with me and
Clay?"

"Pretty much everything."

"Uh . . . what did he say to you, anyway?"

"Privileged."

"Why? You said he's not your client."

She had me. I looked away. The sun was waning, and sunlight striped the pavement, sending shards of blinding light into
the eyes of drivers. And the temptation was more than I could
resist. I didn't like the guy, and I was dying to tell her.

"He asked me to investigate you. To his credit, he said it was in the role of devil's advocate, so that he'd know the worst if things wound up in court. But he wanted me to tell you I was working for you, when I was really investigating you, and he justified it because he implied that it would be for your own good. Then he reminded me that he would be paying my bill."

She took the cigar out of her mouth and stared at me. "Would you mind very much staying right here for just five minutes?"

"I'm cold."

She handed me the keys to the car. "Get in and warm yourself up. Heater works like a little oven. I won't keep you waiting."

But she did keep me waiting.

She was right, the heater worked great, and so did the CD player. I listened to some kind of mambo dance music and tried hard not to like knowing that when people walked by they thought I owned the car. Even with a dent in the side, a BMW Roadster was impressive, at least to a poor person like me. I even smoked one of the cigars I found in the glove box. It was mild and sweet and expensive, and I didn't inhale, but I watched the people walking by on the sidewalk (there weren't many of them), and I turned heads. I looked interesting. I even felt interesting.

When Emma Marsden came out of her ex-husband's office, she slammed the door.

She motioned for me to roll down the driver's side window. "You ever been to the Atomic Café?"

"It's a personal favorite."

"Will you let me buy you an early dinner? I'd like to talk some more."

I considered turning her down. Clearly, it was good old Clayton who could afford my fee. But I didn't like good old Clayton, and I thought Munchausen by proxy had about as much merit as the old repressed-memory craze, and I figured Emma Marsden was getting screwed over from more directions than one. That, plus my talent for poverty even in economic boom times, made me say yes.

"It's just around the corner. Why don't we go in my car. You may as well drive, you're in the seat."

I didn't object.

She ordered the *ropa vieja,* which is a sort of Cuban pot roast, and I had the jerk chicken, with a side of black beans and rice. We drank Red Stripe beer and munched on sweet potato chips while we waited for our food. The restaurant was just this side of deserted. A guy in khakis and a black sweater read *Ace Magazine,* ate Jamaican pot pie, and drank something with an umbrella in it. I admired the umbrella. I admired the man for ordering something so playful when he was alone. Then I realized the man was familiar, very familiar in fact—my ex-husband, Rick. Not that big a coincidence, as his office is practically next door. He looked up as a stunning blonde walked past the bar and right up to his table. She was breathless, tall and built, with enough flesh to get her through a cold winter. Her hair was short and thick, and she wore a pair of reading glasses shoved up atop her head. Her trousers were black silk and had likely cost the earth. She also wore a sweater, French blue and cashmere, and boots that made her even taller.

A goddess.

Rick stood up, smiled at her like he used to smile at me, except more worshipful, then bent her backward and gave her a full-on tongue kiss. Clearly he'd seen me. Little beast.

Judith took the kiss in stride and sat down across from him, then, at a word from him, looked over her shoulder at me and waved. Her eyebrows were raised, and I knew she was on the verge of inviting us to join them, but I gave them both a sort of casual but dismissive wave.

Business? Judith mouthed, and I nodded. She blew me a kiss and turned back to Rick, who was watching me a little, and Judith a lot.

"Someone you know?" Emma asked me, turning to get a look.

"Old friends." I held the squat beer bottle in my hand and took another drink, trying not to fill up on the chips. I was completely unable to resist.

"The first thing I want to tell you is that Clayton isn't my ex-husband, because we were never actually married."

I raised an eyebrow. "Then why—"

"All that gag-gag 'my dear ex-wife' crap? Clayton started telling people we were married when Ned was getting so sick. He got tired of all the last-name confusion, and in spite of his many lectures on the idea that marriage 'isn't necessary to a relationship,' the truth is, that's just a load of crap. Although I think, at the time, he believed it, and so did I. It was only when things got dicey that he went traditional and felt better saying he and I were married. It smoothed things out, with the hospital and later when we went through the funeral arrangements and all that stuff."

"And you went along with it?"

"Yeah."

"Why?"

She shrugged, and looked away. "I didn't like it, instinctively. But not enough to take a stand in front of people. I had to think about it to realize how mad it made me."

Our food came. Hers looked good, and made me second-guess my own order. The roast looked tender, thick with gravy over a bowl of rice, but I cut into my chicken, took a small bite, and sighed inwardly. Definitely the right choice.

"So why aren't you still together? The grief thing?"

"The grief thing? Oh, you mean how you go through the death of a child, and it screws up your marriage because you aren't the same person you were before it happened?"

I stared at her.

"Survivor group counseling. No, that wasn't it."

I ate chicken, listening to her reasons. She swore it wasn't the death of their son that had driven them finally and completely apart. She called it a three-part breakup, very analytical.

Part one was, indeed, the stress of losing their son.

Part two had come the evening Clayton Roubideaux had been foolish enough to make his true feelings known—that in comparison to his love for his blood son, his feelings for her daughter, Blaine, were a poor second best.

Part three was the way he told people, while Ned was sick and even after he died, that they were married. They weren't. He was divorced, as were most men her age who were available for a committed relationship, and she could understand not wanting to get married again. But she could not understand saying you were when you weren't. So all of his crap about "not needing the paper" etc. was just that, crap. He thought marriage *was* important, but just didn't want to be married to her. And he had a need to legitimize his grief, his choice of mother for his son, and the time they spent together with the lie that they were, indeed, married. It was knowing how much he valued the vows, coupled with the knowledge that he did not think enough of her to commit to her and to their life together, that convinced her to end the relationship.

"Clayton and I weren't destined to make it. He didn't love me enough, you know? If I hadn't gotten pregnant with Ned, I don't think we'd have moved in together. Or, I don't know, maybe me getting pregnant made us get serious too soon. Although, sometimes I think this sloooow-drip courtship trend is an excuse for people to dawdle around in relationships. I don't know. I just screw relationships up, don't listen to me."

I laughed, trying not to sputter beer.

"But it would have been stupid to stay with a man who didn't love me enough to commit to me, even though I'd had a child with him, which, from my standpoint, means I made all the commitment and he gets off scot-free. Which is fine, because who wants a reluctant committer?"

"No one."

"And what makes me actually hate him, is he told my daughter that he'd wished she had died instead of Ned. That alone—"

"He actually said that to her?"

"Not in those words, but believe me, he made it clear. I was there, I saw it."

I mixed sour cream and salsa in the black beans and rice. Messy and delicious. I took a bite, thinking, as I listened to her, that there were, as always, three sides to every story. Listening to him in his office, he had been an ideal husband and father. Of course, he hadn't been a husband, which made his story suspect.

"He's not a bad guy," Emma said. "At least, not horrible. I think you've seen him at his worst."

I took another bite of beans. So far, I was reining in my opinions, at least verbally. I was thinking mean thoughts, though, as usual.

"I'd still like to hire you. To investigate the doctor, and if you want to investigate me, go ahead, I don't care. But I don't want you reporting in to Clayton. I want him out of the mix. I do want to know what those people think they have on me."

"What people?"

"The doctor. The Child Protective Services people. The *law*. Because I think the accusation is just a blackmail thing."

"Extortion. If you mean that they are threatening you with legal action if you don't back off in regard to what happened with your son and his remains."

"That's exactly what I do mean. And if you think I am guilty—"

"I don't believe in it."

"In Munchausen by proxy?"

"That's right. I think it's just another way of society controlling uppity women. Why, do you?"

She held her fork, midair, head cocked to one side. "I think
it's probably rare, but yeah, I believe it. I wish I didn't. But I do.
But I guarantee you I'm not one of them."

"Did you ever consider the possibility your ex-husband,
excuse me, ex-whatever, might be?"

"I thought it was only women."

"I'm sure that's what they'd like you to think."

She put a slice of Caribbean cornbread on her plate and broke
off a piece with her fingers. She chewed, a small thread of coconut
on her lips. "There's no way Clayton hurt Ned. I promise you, he
didn't. I know him that well at least. He truly loved Ned more
than anything in the world. He'd have laid down his life, happily
and without hesitation, if it would have taken one hour of suffering from our little boy. I have no doubts about Clayton in that
way. He loved Ned like he loved his life. He needs to have more
children. But he'll never be the same. He wouldn't let me box up
any of Ned's things until he moved out. Then he boxed them up
and took them with him."

"Was that okay with you?"

"It's not like he asked." She wiped her lips and the coconut
disappeared.

"Do you think he seriously suspects you of having something
to do with Ned's death?"

She shook her head. "I don't think so."

"Really? Even after tonight?"

"You'd have to know the guy, Lena."

It was funny the way she said my name. It reminded me of
the way my sister used to say it. Other things about her were
reminding me of Whitney. Her confidence. Her air of knowing
what was what.

"He's just trying to cover every base and stay in control of
something that scares him shitless. I can understand it. I can let

it go. But I want you to work for *me*. What I need to know is how much you charge. And what you think this case will cost, in the long run."

"I charge fifty-five dollars an hour and pay my own expenses unless something really unusual comes up, or we start getting into travel and airline tickets. Then I'd discuss it with you first."

"Unusual like what?"

"Usually the money starts flying out the window when you hire consultants—attorneys, doctors, forensic experts. And I guess if you needed me to fly to, say, Paris, France, or something, I might need you to help out with the airline ticket. Paris, Kentucky, is on me. As to how many hours, it's hard to say. They add up pretty fast. I can always work to your budget—as in, stop when the money runs out. Limit my areas of inquiry."

"I have a proposition. How about I give you my car?"

"The BMW?"

"Yep. And in return, you spend a lot of time following up every possible area of inquiry, and if the case takes weeks or months, you work it. And you take care of all expenses no matter what comes up, including Paris, France."

"You mean the BMW?"

"Yeah. I can sign it into your name tomorrow, if you want to meet me at the courthouse."

"Sounds like I'm being overpaid. Or is there a lien I have to pay off?"

"I own it free and clear. There's no way I can get a good resale value out of it with that big dent in the side. And I don't have any kind of cash available. And I expect to get a lot of work out of you. It would be nice for me to know no matter how expensive it gets, I'm paid up, and I don't need to get Clayton in the middle of it."

"What are you going to do for a car?"

"I have a '94 Jeep Wrangler I was saving for my daughter. It's paid for. I can keep banging around in that. It's what I was driving when I met Clayton. The Roadster used to be his, then he decided to get a new car and the dent took a lot out of the trade-in value so he just gave it to me. And you can sell whatever you're driving now, and keep that money to cover your expenses."

I didn't tell her that would net me about one thousand dollars, if I was lucky.

She shrugged. "Think about it. Have another attorney look over this document." She passed an envelope across the table. "There is a confidentiality thing in this agreement, wherein you agree not to divulge the gist of the conversation the two of you had. You and Clayton."

"I wouldn't do that anyway."

"You did to me."

"That's true. But I wouldn't to anyone else."

"Clayton is what you might call anal. And he can't draft an agreement where he doesn't get some kind of concession. Like you said, he's a lawyer. Also, I had to let him put that in there so he'd draw up this fee document, between you, me, and the BMW."

"I'm seriously tempted."

"I can throw in some free dance lessons, if that would help."

Chapter Two

Lately I have taken to smoking cigars, a habit I clearly share with Emma Marsden. It is a terrible habit, especially considering that I can only afford cheap cigars, the kind that will bring everyone in the room to harmonious agreement—be they Democrats, liberals, Republicans, warmongers, pro- or anti-choice, for or against the death penalty—the agreement being that the kind of cigar I can afford is disgusting. If I were smelling it instead of smoking it, I would be disgusted too.

On the other hand, I appreciate that the cigars have wooden tips, and are slim and black and slightly sweet. Nothing so good as chocolate, but still good. And although they pollute my lungs and the atmosphere, and add certain intriguing elements to the more feminine aspects of my personal scent—vanilla lotion and Escada perfume—they do not have calories, they do not make my abdomen swell so that my jeans are tight, and are for these reasons much better than chocolate. This is how women think, and I am a woman. If you are a woman or you know one who is honest, you are not surprised.

Cigars are good for people like me who eat for three reasons: hunger, boredom, and the need for distracting stimulation, which is different enough from boredom to have its own category, but still close.

I think it is the ritual of smoking cigars that I like, as well as the rebellion. I had a very southern upbringing, which means that beer and cigars are not the norm if you are female. In my family, even beer was unusual. It was bourbon and cigars, but that was for the men. Mixed drinks were highballs. My sister and I drank beer in college to annoy our parents and prove something, but our parents were fascinated and encouraged us to order beer whenever they took us to dinner. My dad would order a beer too, and my mom would taste ours but didn't like it. For Mom it was Diet Pepsi or nothing, which is much worse for you than beer, which at least has B-12.

I was quite delighted when Emma Marsden insisted on me taking the BMW home for the night, so long as I was willing to drop her off at her house. We made an appointment to meet at the courthouse before lunch the next day to transfer the title of ownership from her to me, and for us to sign the letter of agreement in regard to my services.

Her house was out of my way, but driving the car was what I wanted to be doing. It was a 1999 Z3 Roadster, automatic, with antilock brakes, a CD player, and a power convertible roof. There was a small slit in the plastic rectangular back window, right along the crease where the plastic folded when the top was down. I didn't much care. We drove out Main Street, away from town, until it became Richmond Road, and we followed it through the strips of restaurants, dry cleaners, and apartment complexes, past Lexington Mall and Home Depot, past the Man of War intersection that led to Homburg Place, where Emma Marsden taught ballroom dance at an independent studio, past the highway access to I-75, past a Waffle House, a Holiday Inn, and the Solid Gold Men's Club, to Athens, Kentucky, where Emma had her house.

There was something about it. A bit tumbledown, but solid,

red brick, with a thrusting front porch (yes, there was a porch swing) and lights in the window. It reminded me of my little place in Chevy Chase (the lesser end of that neighborhood), and her place, like mine, clearly needed work. Still, for pure potential you couldn't beat it. I had realized, after living in my cottage for a while, that some people look at old houses and see what is there (mold in the corners of the ceiling, cracks in the plaster, hardwood floors that have been loved into scratches and dents, linoleum floors that need to be peeled up to reveal the heart of pine underneath). I see what the house can be. I see it so clearly I forget what it really looks like, which makes me slow at renovation work, but content with what I have. I would rather have a run-down old cottage that is seventy years old and needs a shitload of work than a brand-new house that is bigger. I'm not sure why that is, except that it seems to me a matter of presence, and charm, and happiness in the details. An arched doorway that leads to ten-foot ceilings and cracked walls and an electrical system that is nothing short of dangerous is my idea of home. Perfect drywall, carpet instead of battered wood floors, and tiny little twig trees just starting to grow have less and less appeal to me the longer I stay in my house.

As soon as I pulled into the gravel driveway, the front door opened and a teenage girl stood behind the screen door, watching.

"That's my daughter, Blaine. Would you like to come in and meet her?"

What I really wanted to do was see the inside of the house. Now that I am working on my own, I like to see what other people are doing with theirs. I hesitated, but the teenage girl walked out onto the porch. Her face, lit by the outside light, was heart-shaped and breathtakingly beautiful—or would have been if she'd had a more pleasant expression. She tapped her wrist like she was pointing to a watch, though she was not, in fact, wearing one. She gave both of us a stern look.

I glanced over at Emma. "Out past your curfew?"

She laughed. "Clearly. Come on in, she doesn't bite."

"No, thanks. I need to get home."

"If you change your mind about the car, and taking the job and everything—"

"I won't."

"See you at the courthouse tomorrow."

I waved at Emma's daughter, who waved back but did not smile, and heard her say "Who *is* that, and why is she taking your car?" as soon as Emma was on the porch. I backed out of the driveway without looking back, feeling that *you-are-in-so-much-trouble* sensation I hadn't had since I was a teenager myself.

I put the top down at the first stoplight, even though it was cold, and turned the heat on full blast to keep warm. I caught two teenage boys looking at me from the front seat of a Camaro.

"Nice car," they said, heads bobbing to the thrum of music.

I smiled. And hit the accelerator as soon as the light turned green, leaving them two car lengths behind. I have always loved a powerful engine.

CHAPTER THREE

In the best of all possible worlds Joel would be just walking up the sidewalk to the front door when I pulled into our narrow driveway (paved, to Emma Marsden's gravel, but who's keeping score?). He wasn't. Second best, he would have been sitting in his favorite chair in the living room and getting up to glance out the window. But no, he wasn't home. He'd *been* home, though, because somebody had turned out all the lights I'd left on when I headed out late that afternoon. It's a fate thing—light-leaver-on-ers always do seem to mate up with light-turner-off-ers.

I hate coming home to a dark house.

My cat was right at the door when I came in. The days when I would have had to snatch him up by the tail as he raced outside to a world forbidden to indoor cats are long gone. John Maynard Kitty is about as old as the economist he was named after.

He nudged his head at my calf, and croaked. His mews deepened into croaks about three years ago. I picked him up, gently with old bones, and turned on the foyer light. He blinked and dug his claws ever so delicately into my shoulders. He did not like being left in the dark.

I turned on the lamps in the living room. The maid service

had come, not Joel. They had turned off all the lights, not even leaving on the smallest lamp for my kitty. And they'd rearranged the furniture in the living room again, which pissed me off. I did not like cleaning *crews*. I much preferred the lone cleaning professional who likes to be paid in cash, takes longer to do the work but does a better job, and who doesn't wear a uniform. But Joel is in charge of the cleaning service, and we have other things to argue about. If it was left up to me, we wouldn't have one. Of course, if it was left up to me, we wouldn't clean.

I don't mind a clean house, if only people would *let my stuff alone.*

I moved the furniture back where I wanted it, because, yes, I had actually put it that way for a reason, and picked Maynard up and carried him into the kitchen. He can walk, of course, but these days he prefers being carried, so long as it is me who is doing the carrying.

I poured dry kibble in a bowl and mixed it with real tuna fish—StarKist, white tuna, packed in oil. Maynard has started losing weight, and it worries me. The vet says his teeth are okay, but he really scarfs down the tuna and I am trying to fatten him up. I am waiting on the result of blood work to see if he has a thyroid problem. He has lost way too much weight, especially since he eats a lot of junk food, courtesy of me, and should therefore be pudgy. Maynard and I have long been crazy about potato chips (salt and vinegar my favorite, sour cream and onion his). The vet visit turned into a senior wellness checkup, long overdue I guess, but the bill came to two hundred and thirty-five dollars. Which would not have been a problem if I had gone to work for Clayton Roubideaux, instead of Emma.

On the other hand, that *was* a BMW in my driveway.

I had a new CD of Brazilian music, which I put in the player. I felt so good that I started up the gas grill outside, and headed for the laundry alcove off the kitchen. The hamper was overflowing. And, if left to Joel, it would take days to get it done. One thing you can say about me is that I am efficient. Whereas Joel would sort the laundry into seventy-three little piles that were not even allowed to touch each other, much less be washed together, I just washed everything in cold water. I opened the top of the washing machine, stuffed in a full load, and set the dials. What took Joel at least eight to ten loads, I could do in three. Sometimes two, if there weren't a lot of towels. Was Joel ever going to be surprised.

He was late—around eight-thirty, and he hadn't bothered to call, which he usually did, but I wasn't mad. We both have those kinds of jobs. Cops don't work regular hours, and neither do private investigators. And Joel, moving up in the rank of detectives, often worked late to clear the paperwork from his desk. He likes to leave a clean desk before he leaves the office. I find this odd, since it'll just get messed up again the next day, but there is no need to be critical.

Dinner was ready by the time I heard Joel's key in the lock. One load of clothes was in the dryer, the other sloshing through the wash, and I was curled up on the couch smoking one of the cigars I had found in Emma Marsden's glove compartment. I mean, *my* glove compartment. I had planned, when I saw them, to return them to her tomorrow, but later I had gone out and brought them into the house. I thought that Joel and I could have a celebratory smoke after dinner.

He didn't say hello when he came through the door, but I was used to that. Joel isn't overly vocal, and he comes home looking grim until he transits from the world of work to the comforts of home.

"Hey, baby!"

He stood at the edge of the living room, blinking. Well, the lights were bright. I tend to turn all of them on.

He only glanced at me and frowned, and I realized he was looking for the owner of that beautiful car in the driveway. He didn't know he was looking right at her.

"Who's here?"

"Just me."

"Just you?"

"Me and Maynard Kitty."

"Then whose car is parked in our driveway?"

"Mine."

"Lena, there's a BMW sports car in the driveway, are you totally oblivious?"

Actually, he didn't really say "are you totally oblivious," but clearly he was thinking it.

"I know, I know, it's mine! Ours! You can drive it whenever you want, I'll share it. Isn't it beautiful?"

"You bought a car?"

"Right, with the jingling change right out of my pocket. Or did you think I got a loan? And who in their right mind would loan me money?"

"Is this something where the dealer lets you drive it home to try it out?"

"I don't think they let BMWs off the lot like that."

"Well, this one is obviously . . . used."

"You mean that big son of a bitch dent beside the driver's door? I don't care, Joel. How else am I ever going to afford a car like that?"

He walked over and gave me a kiss, and just looked at me, waiting for an explanation. He looked tired. Not a good day. He is dark, hair and skin tones. Eyes deep brown. He has lost most of that air of world-weariness he used to carry around like the hump on a camel, but there is something sad in his eyes that will never go away.

"It's payment, from my new client."

"New client? If they can palm you off with a BMW, they can afford to pay you cash."

"Palm me off? Joel, you make me feel like that character in 'Jack and the Beanstalk,' coming home with magic beans."

"You mean Jack?"

"I do if he's the one who gets the heat for screwing up."

"Nobody ever gives you money, Lena. You always come home with magic beans."

"What's wrong with that, so long as they're magic?"

"It's just not . . ."

"Sensible? The norm? What, Joel?"

"Practical."

"Speaking of practical, I cooked. And don't even start to get that look on your face. It's my kitchen too."

"Is it corn casserole?"

To his credit, his tone was pleasant. But I never cook corn casserole for Joel anymore, he just doesn't appreciate it like me and Maynard. It's an easy dish, creamed corn with potato chips crumbled over the top, baking time a scant twenty minutes.

"Grilled chicken, dirty rice, and peas."

"Sounds good. I'm starving."

"We're out of wine. But I do have cigars. Good ones—Portofinos!"

"As always, Lena, you surprise me."

CHAPTER FOUR

Headlights arced in through the living room blinds, a car in our driveway, sometime around eleven o'clock. Then the doorbell rang, which was awkward since we were naked, entwined on the couch, and smoking those Portofinos.

"Lena, you are so restless. Can't you be still for five minutes?"

"The doorbell rang."

"Did it? Probably a wrong number."

"You couldn't hear it over your snoring. See? Your cigar went out."

I stood up, pulling on my jeans.

"Always bouncing around these days. You used to be so restful, Lena."

"You mean depressed."

"I found it attractive."

I couldn't find my bra or my sweater, so I grabbed Joel's shirt, buttoning it up quickly. Whoever it was, I'd get rid of fast. Weirdly late for someone at the door.

"I'm too tired for bad news," Joel said.

"Maybe it's a mortgage lender wanting us to refinance. They're getting so aggressive these days."

I opened the door. The air outside was chilled, the first blast of fall, and a trio of leaves blew in when I opened the storm door to admit my ex-husband and his woman.

"What a wonderful time to drop in," I said.

"Lena, you didn't look through the peephole." Rick gave me two kisses on each cheek.

Judith hugged me. "*Sorry.* I know it's late. But Rick insisted."

Rick waved a hand. "Oh, please, Judith, it's never too late for family."

"Or never late enough," I said.

Rick paused. He was still wearing the black sweater and khakis, and a pair of fake eyeglasses. "What does that mean?"

I shrugged. "Don't analyze it, Rick, just accept the insult."

"Aren't you going to ask us in? Or are you giving Joel time to get his clothes on?" Rick grinned at me and pointed to the shirt, which was buttoned seriously out of sequence, causing obvious bunching along the midsection. He raised his voice. "Are you decent yet, Joel? Are you wearing her shirt since she's got yours?" Rick covered his eyes and wandered into the living room.

"I brought you something," Judith said. She'd changed clothes. Levi jeans that fit her loosely and a white work shirt. Her work shirts were always white, and always smudgy looking since she worked with metal and oil paint for a living. "Come look, it's in the trunk. We brought your car back, by the way."

"My Miata? You didn't have to do that."

"Yes, we did. The neighborhood association has been sending us notices about you leaving it on the front lawn."

"How picky. It's a commercial area."

"I know. And I thought it could wait till morning. The truth is Rick saw you drive away in the BMW and then not come back for your car and he was antsy about it."

"Why didn't he call?"

"He did."

"Oh. That's right, the phone did ring. I must have been . . . doing the dishes."

She just grinned at me, then opened the trunk of her 1968 Caddy convertible. Solid white, red leather interior. "I have a wedding present for you."

It was a fireplace screen, heavy, the metal intricately worked in baroque curlicues, and it had been painted chalk white. "I'm getting tired of black and I'm painting things. I just put a lavender one in our bedroom. I somehow thought—for your living room—pure white. To offset the red walls."

It took my breath away. "I love it, Judith. I'm honored." I gave her a hug.

Judith's metal works were so highly in demand that it would take years for her to fill every order that came her way. Her solution was to work only on what interested her, since she swore that anything else stifled her creative process. People took her to task for that—some of them other artists who wrote articles about her in the newspapers, along the lines of artists have to work in order to eat, or they are being unprofessional. Her usual reply was that it was *her* creative process, so fuck off.

Judith being Judith, the projects she chose would have no relation to what brought in money. Only, since Judith was Judith and one of those magic people, they did bring in money, and a lot of it. She and Rick were rolling these days. It couldn't have happened to a more perfect woman. Too bad it didn't happen to Rick when I was married to him.

She put a hand on my shoulder when I reached in the trunk to pick it up.

"That's man's work, honey. Let's go inside and have a drink. They can figure out how to get it in later. I just wanted you to see it. Sure you like it?" And she grinned. She knew I did.

I followed her through the door. "Wait a minute. Did you say *wedding* present? Because Joel and I—"

"Shhh, don't say that word so loud in front of the men. They'll spook."

"This isn't one of your psychic things, is it? Or are you just messing with me? Joel and I haven't even talked or even thought or—"

I stopped, because for a minute I thought Joel did have on one of my shirts. But it was his, only smaller.

"What happened to your shirt?" I asked him.

"It was like this when I found it. In the dryer."

Rick put a hand to his head. "Oh, my Lord Jesus. Don't tell me you let her do laundry?"

Joel looked sadly down at his jeans, which were gaping open because they could not be fastened. "With Lena, it's never a matter of *letting* or *not letting.*"

There must be something wrong with the washing machine, I thought. I said, "There must be something wrong with the washing machine. Judith? Beer?"

"Please," she said.

"Wine if you have it," Rick said.

"Beer then."

I went to the refrigerator, smiled fondly at the dirty dishes on the countertops, pleased that I had gotten Joel out of the kitchen *before* the dishes were done, though I've never known any man to refuse what Joel had not been able to refuse either. I like it when men are predictable.

There were chilled beer flutes in the freezer, thanks to Joel, who was more of a homemaker than I'd ever be. But I didn't want to add to the considerable mess I'd made cooking dinner, so I took the beer out in bottles. I checked the washing machine on my way back through. Definitely on cold water. I wasn't stupid, for God's sake.

I made two trips, handing round beers. Joel had gone upstairs to slip into something a little more comfortable, and came back in his favorite pair of paint-splattered sweatpants just as Judith was lighting up a cigar.

"Sooo bad for you," Rick said.

She smiled and blew smoke his way, then handed it to him across the room so he could take a puff. He inhaled deeply and looked so much like a man enjoying good sex that Joel and I exchanged looks. Rick was doing it on purpose, of course.

Rick waved a hand, and made a sad little face when Judith took it away from him. "Those sweatpants look inhumanly comfortable, don't you dare let Lena get near them."

I peeled at the edges of the label on my beer bottle. "I don't know what happened to the clothes, Rick, but it wasn't anything I did."

"No, of course not, dear. Juvenile delinquents broke into your laundry room and shrank them while you and Joel were deep in . . . discussion, there on the couch."

"What's with the glasses, Rick? You don't have to be in character here. Take them off."

My ex is an actor. He runs a debt rescue service now, where he fends off creditors for people in financial distress. The name of the business is You're In The Right Place, and he's good at his job because he used to *be* a debt collector, to his everlasting shame. Which is what he used to do between acting jobs, which meant he did it a lot. I know most of his "characters" and their props because I was there in the old days when he created them.

"Those are real," Judith said.

"Real?"

"Just reading glasses, Lena Bina. And don't try and change the subject. Shall I tell them how you did laundry when we met?"

"No, you shallent."

He took the cigar back from Judith and puffed away. There was no point in offering him his own. He and Judith always smoked together, a small intimacy I somewhat envied and admired. Rick had loved me very much, way back when, but he was absolutely mad for Judith. Well, we all were. She was just that kind of person. If I had to choose between her and Rick, naturally, I'd have to choose her.

Rick looked at Joel. "Lena Bina used to leave the washing machine lid up, as a matter of course, and just shove her clothes in right after she took them off, then dash naked across the apartment to get dressed. After the washing machine was full, she'd dump in twice the soap required, then wash the clothes on HOT water, with the water level on low. Then she'd forget about them and by the time she got them into the dryer, they'd had a good two or three days to stay wadded up and wet and get nice and sour smelling, which is something you can't always wash out."

"Rick, that only happened one time, and it was an experiment to see if the no-trouble system would work. I just didn't happen to check the water level."

Rick dismissed me with a wave of the cigar, which he handed over to Judith. "The lesson is, Joel, don't let her near a washing machine."

"Rick, do you know how annoying it is that you always tease me like I'm your sub-intelligent little sister?"

"Lena, considering that we were married, don't you consider that remark . . . I don't know, vaguely incestuous? Even for Kentucky?"

"Depends on what you mean by vaguely. As in too vaguely . . . or not enough?"

I saw Judith give Joel a look. They knew we couldn't help it.

"Oh oh oh there he is my little Maynard Kitty."

That was sure to piss Joel off. Maynard loves only me and Rick, no matter how much Joel makes up to him.

Maynard struggled to jump into Rick's lap. "Oh, baby," Rick said, scooping the cat gently up. Rick looked at me sadly. Maynard was getting very old.

He settled the cat into the "meatloaf" position that Maynard favored, then tilted his head up and raised an eyebrow. "What's with leaving your car in my front yard and driving away in a BMW? Have you come into money or something?"

Joel laughed unkindly and muttered something about magic beans.

"It's my fee for a new case."

"Lena Bina, do you never ever get paid in actual dollars? Even euros would be—"

"Rick, I don't remember asking for your opinion or advice. Or yours either, Joel."

Rick looked at Joel, who refrained from making the comment he no doubt wanted to make.

"What makes any of you think this subject is open to discussion?" I said. "Because I promise all of you, it's not."

Rick just gave me the mysterious smile. It was quite mysterious, so clearly he'd been working on it.

"What's the case?" Judith asked. "Is your client the woman you were in the restaurant with?"

"Yes. Her name is Emma Marsden. She's the one you've been reading about in the papers."

I noticed that Joel was sitting up a little straighter.

"The Munchausen Mama?" Rick said.

"I don't believe in Munchausen's."

"What is it, anyway?" Judith asked.

"Oh, you know, the one where the mother makes her child sick so she can get attention." Rick raised an eyebrow at me. "Lena, of course, will predictably think that the entire syndrome is made up by evil men to keep perfect women under their thumb."

I nodded. Rick, as usual, had nailed it.

"Except it does happen," Joel said.

I looked at him.

"I've seen it, Lena."

I shook my head at him.

"Videotapes, made in hospitals, where the mother actually

injected the child with something, air bubbles. Or put a pillow over their face to suffocate them."

"Are you telling me this is common, Joel?"

"No, rare. More accusations than proof, and I'm aware of at least three other incidents where this particular doctor made an accusation that didn't stick."

We all turned to look at him, Judith, Rick, and myself.

"You seem very up-to-date on the subject, since I just talked to the woman today and took her case a few hours ago." And awfully forthcoming with information, I thought, but did not add, because I did not want to impede the flow.

Joel stared at me. "There will be something in the newspapers tomorrow. Maybe on the news, concerning Emma Marsden."

"Which naturally you can't tell us about," I said.

"No, it was leaked to the media on purpose, by the Commonwealth Attorney's Office, so there's no reason I can't leak it to you."

I clenched my fist. Joel had a mournful air that did not give me a good feeling about the future of my client.

"There's a videotape," he said.

"No no no."

"It's not what you think," Joel told me. "It's a tape of Emma Marsden in the parking lot of a local restaurant having sex with her ex-husband."

Rick leaned forward. "Have you seen it?"

"Bits and pieces. They were playing it in one of the interrogation rooms."

I sighed. "What does that have to do with Munchausen's, Joel?"

He shrugged. "Nothing. Except it was taken on her child's birthday, the first birthday after he died. She and the child's father—"

"Clayton Roubideaux," I said.

"They'd evidently gone out to mark the occasion, and wound up in his car."

"So she's guilty of what? Sex?"

Rick took the cigar from Judith's reluctant fingers. "Well, Lena Bina, you have to admit, on the anniversary of her child's death—"

"Is there anybody in this room who *hasn't* had sex in a car?"

I saw no hands. Certainly not my own.

"Joel, is she going to be charged?"

"On the basis of the tape? No, as far as I know she's not. That's why the information is going to the media, instead of before a grand jury."

"Trial by public opinion?" Judith said.

"The doctor who treated the child is raising a lot of fuss," Joel said.

"What have you guys got on her?" I asked him.

Joel shook his head at me. "That wouldn't be what I was worrying about, if I were you."

"And what would you be worrying about?" I asked him.

"Who took the videotape. From what I understand, it came in anonymously, through the mail, to the office of the Commonwealth Attorney."

"And you guys just take it on faith?"

"It's not my case, Lena, but the guy working it takes nothing on faith. If I know Jack Linden, he'll be trying to establish whether or not it really is Emma Marsden in the tape, as the letter states—"

"Oh, so it came with a letter," Rick said.

"Yes, but you'd need a court order to look at it."

Rick looked at me and rolled his eyes, but even though Joel and I were constantly dealing with professional boundaries in flux, this was one I knew I had no chance of crossing.

"Joel, I assume you don't have a problem with me letting Emma Marsden know?"

"No—if the media knows, I see no reason for her not to."

"It's mean not to go to her first."

"I won't argue the point." He glanced at the clock. "It's late, though."

I bit my lip. "I know. But better now than first thing in the morning when she picks up the paper or turns on the news. She's got a teenage daughter, you know." I turned to Rick and Judith.

"Would you guys want to know?"

Rick nodded.

"Call her," Judith said.

CHAPTER FIVE

Emma had gone through all the motions. She had done everything required. She'd cooked Blaine's dinner and cleaned up the kitchen. Read the newspaper and stayed up late watching a movie about Joan of Arc, and now she could not sleep. She got up out of bed, padded into the living room, which was almost icy cold now that the air outside had cooled, and the earth and foundations of the little worn-out house no longer released wave after wave of heat. The window air conditioner hummed away on the lowest setting.

At first the noise of it had driven her mad. But now she didn't think she would ever sleep without it, provided of course she ever slept. It was white noise, her background, her comfort. Part of the cocoon of the little house she thought of as a sanctuary. The little house that had belonged to her great-aunt Jodina, the little house that now belonged to her, legally, all the papers signed, a hug and a gruff kiss from the tall woman who was afraid of everything except responsibility.

Emma went to the kitchen, poured herself half a glass of white wine from the jug of Chablis. She didn't mind drinking wine from a jug. A box, that bothered her. But the jug of heavy glass had the right feel to it, and definitely the kind of price tag she needed these days.

The wine was cold. She took her glass into the living room and curled up on the worn fabric of her couch, set the glass on the coffee table she had kept since her mother died. It had folding edges with hinges that could go flat or stand up, making a box out of the surface. She sat cross-legged and stared at the wall and the framed cover of the 1929 edition of *Fortune* magazine. Red background, the picture of a leaping stag with arrows whizzing through the air in pursuit. Not unlike her own life. She had bought it for eleven dollars at Wal-Mart and had carted it with her, move after move. The glass in the frame had broken two moves ago, and she'd just emptied it over the trashcan, then hung it on the wall. She ought to replace the frame and told herself she would, but knew in the back of her mind she probably wouldn't. One of those small, easy, inexpensive tasks she never took care of.

As always, the presence of her son rode the backwaters of her every thought. Emma smiled at him, her little baby boy, wherever he was. She took another sip of Chablis. Said a small prayer of thanks not just for wine, but for cheap wine.

She missed her car already. She was not likely to own a BMW again.

There were worse things.

When she saw a homeless person, her first thought was always, *When.* Not *Poor thing,* not *Get a job,* not *There but for the grace of God go I;* she just thought, *When.* Her friends laughed the first time she said it out loud, and afterward, when it became one of her sayings, they just smiled and tuned it out. Dark humor was one of her specialties.

Emma was the last person in the world they would suspect might actually have such a fear. But Emma knew things that so many people don't know. She knew how close she was to the edge financially and, frankly, emotionally. She knew how alone she was in the world. She knew that some of those people who wound up on the streets had started out with more than she'd ever had, achieved more than she ever would, and had more family and friends who loved them than she did.

She was not a very good poor person. She would never forget her aunt Suki grimacing in genuine disillusionment and telling how she had gone with the church group to deliver Thanksgiving baskets to the poor families. She could still hear her aunt's contempt for the way the children in one of those families had dug through the basket right there in the middle of their living room floor and actually opened the dessert and ate it right there—not waiting to eat it properly on Thanksgiving. Everybody in the family had shaken their heads in sorrow at the inappropriateness of some poor families, and Emma had thought at the time that she would not want to be a poor person and follow the poor person rules. And she'd been right. She did not like poor person rules. They ground her up on the insides. She figured that a lot of poor people had ulcers. She certainly had one. A big fat angry ulcer, or whatever it was that woke her up at night and made her throw up.

Once you've had *the fear,* it changes you. Makes you aware. Appreciative. And sometimes, late at night, or when the bank account is overdrawn, it makes you afraid. Emma had learned years ago that fear was useful. Look it in the eye, and don't waste time trying to convince yourself nothing is going to happen. Your subconscious will not let you sleep until you make a plan. That's all it wants, the subconscious. A little notice and a plan to stick in the back pocket of the brain to handle the contingencies. People could save a lot of time and money spent on that last glass of wine, that Vicodin, that joint, the shopping trip that was unaffordable, the late nights on the Internet betting on football, if they'd make a deal with the subconscious. That's all it would take for the people who were just trying to sleep—the ones who were into vice for the enjoyment were still free to dance in the dark.

Emma was eighteen pounds over the weight on the charts given out by insurance companies. She didn't worry about it. There were a lot of things she didn't worry about. Her hips were rounded, her breasts were large, and she was tall. Besides, the weight charts did not have a category for voluptuous women who liked all sensuous things, including eating, and she never gave it a third thought. A second thought, well, yes. She was after all a woman raised in a culture that served guilt with every meal.

One thing losing a child did, though, it swept all the crap right out of your life. It gave you perspective. The people who talk out loud about the good that comes out of tragedy are the ones who never had any—tragedy, that is. Of course, if you actually agreed, and brought up one possible good part, they enveloped you with an undertow of accusation for not grieving properly—a fog of judgmental disapproval that lurked darkly beneath the surface like a stage-four cancer. Next up came the conversation that began with "It's a good thing it didn't happen to me because I would have just not been able to handle it . . ."

Ending with either "You are so strong," *or* "brave," which really meant *You are an insensitive woman who just doesn't have the depth of feeling and sensitivity that someone like me has, and likely God knows that, which is why it hasn't happened to me and won't happen to me . . . and I wonder what you did to deserve this. . . .*

Or *I'm sorry it happened to you, but would you mind pretending it didn't so that I don't have to feel bad, I have enough stress in my life already. I'll acknowledge your grief by staring at you when I think you're not looking so I can SEE your grief, and make sure it is there, and suddenly stopping mid-sentence in case the remark I made was insensitive and not allowing you the face-saving option of pretending you didn't notice and that what I said didn't hurt, or worse, actually not noticing and not being hurt.*

Emma's new perspective didn't please people. She was supposed to rave over sunsets—and hell, yes, they were nice, and yes, she'd take a moment and look at one if the opportunity came up at a convenient time and not during *Jeopardy!*—but life wasn't about sunsets. It was about breathing in and breathing out without a great deal of pain. It was about having a place to live—better still, one you actually liked. It was about having a job. It was about being able to feed your kids, and maybe even not sweat when you stood in line waiting for the grocery store total, balancing what was still on that slow-moving black rubber belt with the continuously rising total on the screen that was ever so conveniently turned your way. It was about curling up at the end of the day with a good book or a television show you actually liked, about affording cream to go with the coffee, about not worrying about having your utilities cut off, about not making funeral arrangements and healing healing healing. Fuck healing. Best not to mention that she was currently of a frame of mind that almost made it a pleasure to be cussed out by her teenage daughter because she was still by God alive, very much so if you judged by the level of dust the child could kick up. It meant that Blaine was there, alive and well, and that she was grieving, which was something she was going to have to do not to be in the unbearable pain that sibling loss inflicts. Emma was wise enough to have finally figured out that some teenagers grieve by torturing their mother. Because a mother was supposed to protect you. And it was a hard lesson—finding out your mother couldn't protect you from everything.

Emma had only one child to protect. Not two anymore, and the thought stabbed her in the mid to right quadrant of her stomach, way high, right where the liver was. She'd looked it up in an anatomy chart just because it seemed more logical for a pain like that to hit in the heart. Oh, God, little Ned. Two years and five months old, with a hold on her heart and soul and a smile that defined irresistible.

And that somersault of thoughts that she would not think about. What had really gone wrong? Did the doctors do everything they should have? Why had she accepted such a vague diagnosis? What could she have done?

Emma took deep breaths, enduring the rising panic, breathing her way through. It wasn't as bad as it used to be, the state of her heart. People said it a lot, sweet sadness. She had always wondered what it was about sadness that could possibly be sweet. She knew now. It was thinking about something that makes you unhappy because it made you happy a long time ago. Sweet sadness had always seemed to her a term of indulgence. But it wasn't an indulgence if you were careful not to overdo. It was all about balance, really. Some sadness, some memories, but not too much sadness, and not too many memories. Too much would move you from nostalgia to a mood disorder.

Clayton had told her to start going to church again. He'd told her to go to mass regularly until the business with the Munchausen's accusation was over and done with. And she did, she did go to mass. But somewhere where she was not known, not in her own church, where people would be watching for her. She would go in private, for a religious need. Not in public, to make a statement.

As always, the more she looked for answers, the more questions she found.

What, for example, does one do with the sweep of anger, the sudden spin into rage, the very improper show of grief?

Emma had not forgotten the sheer pleasure of looking at a blank wall. A blank wall, a blank mind. But she found, with surprise, that she no longer needed either. She did not feel bad about feeling good, and by God no one was going to get away with making her think that way. She wasn't going to *act* grieved. She was grieved. She wanted peace of heart, she wanted to get better, she did not think it a sin or a betrayal of her son to heal. She would not conform, she would not pretend; she would not because to do so would be to deny her very real grief, to disrespect her very real strength, and to pretend that the spirituality and, believe it or not, happiness she had achieved by going through this terrible loss was somehow a wrong thing, when she knew it to be so right. She would teach her daughter, by example, the only real way to teach, how to handle the terrible things that life will throw your way, and survive to enjoy the very wonderful ones that make it all worthwhile. She had no patience for people who got mad at God when the horrors took over their lives, who threw grieving temper tantrums because they were petulant, childish, arrogant, and selfish enough to think they were immune.

She had to laugh. Because there she was, doing exactly what she hated, judging the way someone grieved, and disapproving all to hell. Shit, she was just as stupid and intolerant as everybody else. The grief halo needed to go out with the rest of the garbage in the kitchen.

She was asleep on the couch, balancing the half full glass of wine on her chest, when the phone rang. It took her a few moments to wake up. She almost didn't answer. But she could never quite pull that off.

"Yes?"

"Emma? This is Lena Padget."

The name was familiar.

"You hired me today? I have your car."

"Oh. Right." Emma sat up. Awake, now. "You mean *your* car. Or have you called to tell me you've changed your mind?" Her stomach went tight. She would be all alone and in trouble, as usual, if this woman turned her away.

"Not at all. No, I've got your back."

What an extraordinary thing for the woman to say. And what a wonderful feeling it gave her.

"Look, I'm sorry to call so late, but I wanted to warn you about something."

Emma glanced down the hallway to Blaine's bedroom,

thinking she would like to check on her daughter, just to see she was safe, and she'd do so as soon as she was off the phone.

"Someone has sent a videotape to the Commonwealth Attorney's Office."

"The commonwealth attorney?"

"It's like the district attorney. They're the ones responsible for filing criminal charges."

Emma set the wine glass down. "Criminal charges? You mean for the Munchausen's? Am I going to jail?"

"No, not as far as I know. Let's just say that there has been a leak to the local media about some kind of videotape with you in it."

Emma chewed her bottom lip. "But what kind of tape could they have? Me scrubbing the bathroom toilet? Teaching mambo? I don't do anything very interesting." But what she thought was, *I am not going to jail, not yet, not ever.* Should she and Blaine run away? From their house that was all paid for? Move Blaine yet again to yet another school because some doctor stole her son's heart?

"The date of the tape is February twenty-seventh."

Ned's birthday, Emma thought.

"It starts out with you and Clayton Roubideaux at some restaurant parking lot."

"Oh. Oh, right, we had dinner together. It was our son's birthday. We thought it would be nice to sort of make it a special day, so we had dinner. In spite of us arguing in his office this afternoon, we're still friends. And we both miss our son. Is that against the law? Did I spill food or talk with my mouth full? Who made this tape anyway, were the police following me? Was I staked out?"

"As I understand it, it was mailed in to the Commonwealth Attorney's Office anonymously."

"Weird." But her stomach felt like it was curling up, and the small of her back had gone cold. Who would do such a thing?

Tape her eating dinner in a restaurant? And on that night. The night that marked the birth of her son who had died so sadly and so young. She hadn't seen him, whoever he was, this creep with the video camera.

"Most of the tape was filmed in the restaurant parking lot. When you and Clayton Roubideaux were . . . in his car."

The air went right out of her.

"I just wanted to warn you in advance. In case there was something in the newspapers. Or on the news."

"Right." Her throat was so tight. She felt like she was choking. "Thank you."

"I'll look into this. I'd like to know who made the tape, for one thing. I'm going to—"

Emma made very little sense of the words, but felt grateful that for once she did not have to think or take action because she wasn't sure she would ever even find the strength to get off the couch. She was remembering, as best she could, what might be on that tape.

"Look, I need to go now," she said, and hung up.

Emma put her head down on her knees so that Blaine would not hear her crying and wake up.

Oh, God.

She had smoked a cigar and drunk too much wine and stuffed herself with an expensive dinner and a rich dessert—this to celebrate the birthday of her dead child? This had not been a celebration of life, it had been the bravado of a disgusting woman. The Commonwealth Attorney's Office had it all on tape, herself sitting at the skinny rectangular table, the edges of the ironed white tablecloth just brushing her thighs across the slit in the silky black dress where the slippery material pressed against her nipples and outlined them for everyone to see. The slender spaghetti straps slid sideways over her shoulders and she was too buoyed up by the wine to care about pulling them up. She had been seductive, she had worn dark lipstick, overlaid with moist and heavy gloss, and left an imprint on the side of the glass. She had been a glutton. She had eaten a steak, she had drank a bottle of wine, she had smoked, and kissed her ex-supposed-but-not-really husband in the parking lot. She had felt the night wind on the back of her neck when she lifted the hair off her shoulders.

And the evening hadn't stopped there. Oh, no. She'd just been getting started.

She had gotten out of her car and walked over to Clayton's, had leaned her hip up against the door handle and drummed her fingers on the top of the side-view mirror. She had parted her legs and given him the look, and he'd opened the car door immediately and put a hand on her knee.

"Just my knee?" she'd told him, but had taken hold of his wrist when his fingers slid upward. She let him touch the black lace top of the stocking, then traced the garter and satin strap with his forefinger, and told him, in a whisper, to put the seat back.

And he had.

He'd have signed away his retirement, he'd have cut off his right arm, he was caught in the glare of her desire and intent. It was unlike him not to take the lead, it was unlike him to take orders, and it was unlike him to enjoy doing both.

The car seat glided way way back and he frowned but seemed definitely intrigued when she'd strapped him into the seat belt. It wasn't that she had a plan or a fantasy she was acting out, it was just that she was wide open to obeying the urge wherever it took her. And it took her places that night.

It is a wondrous thing, the endless stream of orgasms a woman can have when she is hot and slippery with desire.

She had stood within the embrace of the open car door, and pulled her dress up to her waist. Held up a hand when he reached for her, and said *wait*.

She liked the way he watched her every move. She liked the way his eyes followed her hands as she peeled the little snippet of panty down over her legs and let them hang about her ankles. She was sweaty inside her dress, and the night had cooled and felt amazing against her legs. She still wore the garter belt and the stockings, but she was bare everywhere else and the feeling excited her.

Once he was strapped tightly into the seat, she unbuckled his belt, undid the trousers, and pulled them down below his knees. She'd kneaded the erection that pressed tightly against his briefs and rubbed a finger across the damp spot that topped the arc of his flesh against cotton. She'd kissed him through his underwear, and he had moaned, and closed his eyes, and said her name over and over again.

Damn right.

And then she'd peeled the briefs down and faced him, knees tight against his hips, rubbing herself up and down but not allowing him inside, putting his hands on her hips, and letting herself slide wetly up and down, pressed against the hard erection, just taking her pleasure against him. It felt amazing, and she closed her eyes, but not before she saw that he had a ferocious little half smile and that the more she enjoyed herself the harder he got.

You like that? he'd whispered.

I do.

And when she'd come, the first time, flesh throbbing gently against him, he'd groaned and kissed her, and she liked the wine and tobacco taste on his tongue.

She took his finger and placed it gently in her mouth, running her tongue up and down the side, and he thrust himself at her but she just smiled and dipped her tongue in and around the crevices on either side.

You're killing me.

Enjoy it.

She pulled the dress down beneath her breasts and guided his mouth to her nipple.

Gently, she told him. *Then hard.*

I remember how.

And while he sucked at her breasts she balanced herself right over the tip of his erection. He tried to pull her down, tried to thrust himself inside, but he was strapped pretty tightly by the seat belt and stopped when she told him to behave.

Just a little ways down. Halfway. He breathed hard and his head went back and he groaned and closed his eyes very tight.

You could think of baseball.

She pulled off, then was back up again, sliding slowly down until he was deep deep inside her.

Be still, she'd told him. *Be still.*

She'd bitten him gently on the side of the neck, then ran her tongue in and out of his ear.

And then she pulled herself off him, slowly of course, and somewhat regretfully, and moved off his lap, and over to the other seat, where she could take him into her mouth without interference from the steering wheel.

She knew exactly how to get him where he wanted to be, but first she let him enjoy the feel of her mouth all around him, moving slowly up and down, her tongue flicking from one side to the other. She did not want to hurry him. She wanted him to enjoy.

And pretty soon she had a rhythm going, a rhythm that was literally making him curl his toes inside the expensive leather shoes, because he'd honored her tonight by dressing in his very best.

And once the rhythm was going just so, she did that little thing that he loved, where she tugged ever so lightly at the base of his erection with her bottom lip, creating just the right whisper of friction, while her mouth slid up and then down. It had the desired effect, as she knew it would.

Blaine touched her shoulder and made her jump; she hadn't heard her daughter get up, hadn't heard her come into the living room.

"What's wrong, Mama, did somebody die?"

Emma looked at her daughter's tense little face and sighed. She'd have to tell her.

"It's not good news, honey."

"What?"

"Okay, first, nobody died."

Blaine nodded but did not look relieved, and she sat down on the couch next to her mother.

Emma did not go into the details. She watched her daughter's face for shock, disapproval, and disgust. But Blaine had tossed her head and snorted.

"How dare they, Mama? Those assholes! Sex isn't sinful, it's an expression of love between two adults who have a deep and lasting relationship."

Emma hiccuped, then grinned at her daughter.

"That's what you told me, right?"

"Right."

"They have no right to do this." Blaine patted the edge of the couch. "Come on, Wally. Come up. See, Mom, she's upset because you're crying."

The dog scrambled up onto the couch beside Emma, looked soulfully at both of them, and belched loudly. Emma and Blaine both laughed right in the middle of their drama.

"Hang on, Mom."

Blaine returned quickly, lugging a blanket, a box of tissues, and her secret stash of chocolate.

Emma thought she should stop her daughter when Blaine picked up the phone and called Great-Aunt Jodina—but she knew she needed help. And Blaine hung up and told her with a smile that Aunt Jodina would come as soon as it was light enough to see, and that no, they hadn't woken her up, she had heard a noise and was sitting in her living room loading her shotgun when the phone rang.

And then Blaine refilled Emma's wineglass and poured herself a glass of milk. How healthy of her daughter, Emma thought. Look how she does not take advantage. They sat together on the couch sharing the Cadbury's Milk Chocolate bar, and Emma started to feel a little bit better. Not a lot, but definitely a little. Especially when Blaine had hugged her and said, "Oh, Mom, this is so unfair. You've been through so much." It was nice to be understood, even for a little while. And in the mom chamber of her heart she was pleased to see that she was raising such a fine little girl.

CHAPTER SIX

Tired—the word nailed him. He was too tired to stop on the way home from work for toilet paper or cashews or the dark robust Belgian beer he favored. He was too tired to cook, too tired to go out, and too steeped in professional experience to be attracted by the neon lure of fast food promises that littered the drive home. He spent a significant portion of his work time observing the slippery globules of weighty yellow fat that padded the interiors of the men, women, and children who made the detour to his stainless steel tables on their final road home, revealing their innermost privacies to his swift, benevolent blades.

No, thanks.

The other pathologists, the techs who worked with him at the state lab in Frankfort, Kentucky, would have been surprised by the description of Dr. Marcus Franklin as tired. Punctual, maybe; workaholic, definitely. Precise to the point of rudeness, brusque when preoccupied, a distant boss whose face lived in a frown. A brilliant man with a stick up his butt. None of these descriptions would have given his coworkers pause.

The exception, of course, was Lucca, his secretary and younger sister. He'd pulled strings to hire her, broken a few of the rules he usually followed, and had expected a lot more kick from the staff and management than he'd gotten. Nepotism was business as usual in the South, and Kentuckians were as good at it as anyone else.

There could be no question that Lucca was more than qualified for the job—not with an MBA from Northwestern, experience running the fencing business she started with her ex-husband and signed away in a divorce, and a personal warmth and charm that was a direct contrast to her brother's distracted brusqueness.

As it turned out, nepotism or no, the staff in Franklin's pathology department would have died on the hill to keep Lucca running the admin end of the department. If anyone had rolled their eyes or worried about her competence when she was hired, they'd never admit it now. Lucca could do the job standing on her head. She had a good work ethic, organization was her specialty, and her ease in lifting the load of minutiae from the staff, combined with the sheer fun of having her around, made her the department darling. She humanized Franklin, kept on her desk a preschool-era picture of the two of them dressed in Halloween costumes—Lucca as a pig, Franklin as a cow. She treated her brother with offhand affection and casual insubordination. She referred to his directives as suggestions and turned into an instant tornado if they were not couched in tact. Whenever Franklin's preoccupation with the job got in the way of his recognition that he was dealing with a staff of human beings, she called him on it, but always in private between just the two of them.

On the other hand, anyone who was unwise enough to speak critically of Franklin in earshot of Lucca received the immediate brunt of her personal fury concerning this one subject where she had no sense of humor. You could never call his sister shy.

Lucca was the other person who knew Franklin was tired. You couldn't see it in his walk—not the way he went down the corridors like a man on the road to salvation. And not in the way he pursued prosecutors and/or defense attorneys when he thought they were on the wrong page. Not from his tireless court appearances, and his house brand of peculiarly ferocious politeness that masked the rage that washed over him when dealing with a litigator who was trying to spin the science.

But the energy, the fizzle, it wasn't there anymore. Lucca had gotten used to him not looking happy. But now she did not think her brother looked well. His skin was tinged red, he looked flushed more often than not. He'd put on weight, and he looked puffy—the wristband of his watch straining around the swollen joint.

Nothing new in his eating habits. No breakfast, peanut butter crackers and Sprite for lunch, if he didn't send out for something. His face was taking on a worn look, as if he didn't sleep well, though when she'd asked, he'd said he slept too well, and was having trouble getting up.

Not that he'd see a doctor. Marcus had a horror of hypochondria, and always seemed convinced that no one believed him when he complained. Since he was rarely sick, but usually deathly ill when he was, this worry made no sense. But that was Marcus, and had been since they were little. Lucca remembered him bellowing at their mother when he was eleven about being hauled to the ER to get stitches in a cut on his head. He'd had a severe concussion, his pupils had contracted to pinpoints, and he was bleeding like a pig. Still, he was sure the doctor would think he was making a big deal out of nothing.

So Lucca did not bother to suggest her brother see a doctor. If he got miserable enough, he'd go. Maybe he just needed some sleep, or better still, a long vacation. Her diagnosis was emotional exhaustion and not enough fun. No surprise, with a job like his.

Marcus had no idea who she was, this woman who'd called him up at seven-thirty, well past office hours, and who did not seem surprised to find him working late. From her voice he could tell that she was old, from the accent that she'd grown up in the coal mine regions of eastern Kentucky. She knew his name, the number of his private line, and talked to him as if they'd just resumed a conversation that had been interrupted but was still on track.

"Ma'am?" he said.

The flow of her conversation slowed and eased away, like she'd gently applied mental brakes.

"I didn't catch your name. Did you say Calhoun?"

"I did, sir. Jodina Calhoun. I met you seven years ago when my daughter died. You remember when that ambulance got hit at the railroad crossing?"

The image was instantaneous, a flashback launching the posttraumatic stress that had haunted him more and more these last years. A flicker of images moved through his mind like pictures rotating on a Rolodex, until he was in the middle of the memory, and he was once again listening to the crunch of his boots on the snow and ice.

A deputy led the way with a flashlight, the cone of illumination jittering as the man's hand shook. It was a long walk, because they had to approach from the back of the train and thread their way past sixteen boxcars. The intermittent rotation of emergency lights lured them toward the wreckage. Every police car in the county was there, as well as a fire truck, and two ambulances—one on its side, crumpled like a wadded ball of tinfoil, the top of the ambulance sliced open and lying upside down in the snow. And still the lights from the roof flashed, and the glow of red played against the frozen road, as if the ambulance were a living creature, dying slowly now, only able to light the way to disaster.

The deputy was muttering something that sounded like a prayer. There were none of the swift and mumbled pleasantries common between professionals at disaster sights, the familiar and worn groove of surface-friendly greeting used to separate the worker bees from the victims, their way of assuring themselves that their world was still intact.

There were no macabre witticisms or dark dirty humor, because no one ever indulged rude humorous tendencies in Franklin's presence more than once. Kentucky was a small state, professionally speaking, and word had gone out fast. Marcus Franklin was infuriated by disrespect to civilians, in life or in death, and words came to him like bullets when delivering a reprimand. That part of socializing he found effortless.

The professionals hadn't liked him the first years—the cops, the doctors, emergency techs. He wasn't good with people. His world had settled heavily on his shoulders before he'd taken the state medical examiner's job. He was awkward with people he didn't know well, resigned to the shy and out-of-place feeling that had dogged him from birth.

Gradually the friction had worn smooth. Too many people had a friend or a family member who remembered Marcus with sober gratitude. He returned their phone calls. He answered awkward questions. If you wanted to know how much your loved ones suffered, what it was that really killed them, he would be honest and as easy as he could. He returned the suicide notes after an investigation closed, and no juicy details got out of his office with any degree of regularity. Anyone on his staff prone to gossip didn't last. Reporters were treated with terse civility, guilty until proven innocent, but if they were careful with their words and more so with their facts, he'd open up a little if he could; otherwise they might as well not exist.

A lot of the patrol officers didn't like him. The ones who did had been the few who had been unable to control their physical reactions to mayhem, and found not humiliation but steadiness, tolerance bordering on actual kindness, and a strong presence that made them confident, as if the good guys were still in charge.

His presence made everyone stand up straighter and watch their language, but it also gave them the lift of spirit and sense of relief one feels when the cavalry arrives. He inspired confidence, if not affection. Marcus knew it and accepted the responsibility, and it rode him hard, like all the other responsibilities that kept his chin close to his chest and his shoulders slightly hunched.

The sheriff had told him that an ambulance had tried to beat a train, a tragic decision that had cost the life of the patient they were trying to save, as well as the entire crew. That's how it looked, in the beginning. Later they would learn that the crossing arm had been torn away and the signal lights had not flashed, though the bell had rung. The train was part of the coal line, running without lights and no scream of the horn as it crisscrossed the countryside, so as not to disturb the handfuls of houses and farms in the area. Near the interstate it was another story, with lights and noise and as much commotion as possible. But the trains ran constantly out in the rural areas, and the locals did not appreciate listening to the horn day in and day out. The ambulance driver had never known the train was there. Not until impact, when the roof of the ambulance was ripped off, the driver decapitated. The attending tech and nurse in the back of the ambulance, bent over the woman whose heart was refusing to start, were thrown sideways and crushed. The conductor applied the brakes as soon as he saw the first flash of light, but the train had been going in excess of forty-five miles per hour, and he didn't see the ambulance until the train was upon it. The metal apron of the engine caught the edge of the metal gurney where the patient lay and dragged her three hundred feet down the track. When the train finally stopped, her head and upper torso were still wedged into the side of the train, the gurney had shattered, and Marcus Franklin had to insist that the track and the ground around it be gone over again and again until every mutilated piece was found.

The woman was named Karen Calhoun Mattingly, she had

been fifty-seven years old, a widow, and the grown daughter of Jodina Calhoun. She had suffered a massive heart attack forty minutes before the ambulance crew arrived to try and revive her. The nurse and tech were both intent on bringing her around to the best of their ability, and were aware of nothing but their patient when the ambulance collided with the train. Three seconds after impact the tech was dead. The nurse, infused with a stubborn life force, lingered four and a half minutes before her brain bowed to the impossibility of keeping the body alive. There would be no open caskets at these funerals.

As Marcus made his way along the track, he noticed a slender woman standing near the engine. She had been swallowed whole by a big green barn coat, the kind you might buy at a feed store, and she had her back turned to the wreckage. As he got closer he realized that she was watching him. The glare of working lights set up by the deputies made her eyes look black, her face worn and seamed. She was, in fact, seventy-three years old, the night of the accident, and she was Karen Calhoun Mattingly's mother. She had been following the ambulance in her Chevrolet Impala because there had not been room in the back of the ambulance truck for her to ride along. She had not seen the train until it knocked the ambulance sideways and had slammed on her brakes, looking away as the top of the ambulance was sheared off and the driver decapitated. When she looked back up, she had seen the metal flash of her daughter's gurney as it was caught up on the apron of the engine, had seen the white sheet that covered Karen blown backward. It happened so quickly that by the time her mind processed what she saw, it was over. But that thing wrapped around the right side of the engine had been Karen—there was no mistaking that quick glimpse of her daughter as she was caught midsection and lifted, her head tilted sideways, the hair streaming in the violent thrust of the wind.

It wasn't the first time Marcus Franklin had been called to a death scene only to deal with the living before he could get to the dead. Jodina Calhoun had been ice cold and blue with shock by the time he made it to her side. It had taken him three days before he'd been able to call and reassure her that Karen had unequivocally been dead before impact, that she had not been aware, that she had not suffered when the train caught her body and mutilated her so badly that even her mother could find nothing that was familiar in what was left.

Before the scene had been cleared and the bodies buried, the battle between the families of the dead and the bureaucracy began. The initial blame that landed on the driver shifted to the chasm created by questionable accountability. The signal arm had been torn away before the accident, and the driver had no warning that a train running the coal line at speed and without lights was headed straight for him. The state was responsible for the roads and road safety, the railroad company partially responsible for the upkeep of train signals, and the county responsible for communication between the two. The battle had splashed through the state newspapers with numerous follow-ups for the first two years, and by that time the families of the nurse and the emergency tech had each reached a settlement with the insurance companies. The nurse, who had two children, was in her early thirties, and was well on her way through the training required to become a surgical nurse. She was valued at a figure over seven million. The emergency tech, unmarried, had a price tag of five.

Three more years passed while the ambulance driver's valuation was complicated by the discovery of an out-of-wedlock child he had fathered before he'd joined the army after high school, and the mothers of his children, one high school sweetheart with a ten-year-old boy and one wife of four years with stair-step babies, one and three, a boy and a girl, had battled furiously and settled separately, the former for two million, the latter for six. At this point the only newspapers reporting the remaining threads of the story were the local publications in eastern Kentucky.

Seven years after the accident, the only one who had not settled was Jodina Calhoun. She was not holding out for more money. Just the opposite. She wanted nothing to do with the process of cashing in on the horror of seeing her only child torn to pieces before her very eyes. The insurance companies were frustrated. In spite of being provided with documentation by Dr. Franklin that Karen Mattingly Calhoun had been dead before the accident, it was their opinion that Jodina Calhoun had a strong lawsuit, and their stockholders agreed. The decision was made that she had to be paid something, and though she protested, wrote her congressman, and appealed to Dr. Franklin himself, they issued her a check for one half million dollars.

And just as Jodina Calhoun predicted, the local papers put her picture on the front page with the story of the settlement, and she knew it was only a matter of time before she was murdered in her bed, or wherever she happened to be, by some local cretin who would want to search through her house on the chance that she had some of that money lying around. As far as Jodina Calhoun was concerned, the insurance company had refused to let her mourn her daughter in peace for the last seven years, and then tidied up their books and consciences by sentencing her to a violent death. She had always been nervous, alone in her house. She lived remotely, on her son-in-law's farm, and she'd slept up at the big house ever since the story came out.

More than anything she wanted to go home and sleep in her own bed, because no matter how nice Craig was, no matter how much she loved those grandbabies, you're just more comfortable in your own home. The insurance company had taken her home, her peace of mind, and sooner or later her life, and she still didn't understand how someone could make you take money if you didn't want to.

Marcus became slowly aware that there was silence on the other end of the phone. "How are you doing, Mrs. Calhoun?"

"Nobody has killed me yet, but I figure it's just a matter of time. My son-in-law run two men off the farm last Monday night, and I figure they was after me. Don't forget your promise."

"If you get murdered, Mrs. Calhoun, I'll do the autopsy personally."

"And you'll hound the state police till they track down the son of a bitch that snuffed me out?"

"I'll make it my personal crusade."

"Thank you."

"You're welcome."

"But that's not why I called."

Marcus rubbed the ball of his thumb on the edge of the desk. "What's on your mind, Mrs. Calhoun?"

"It's pretty delicate. Hard to explain on the phone. Plus who knows who might be listening?"

Franklin heard a rustling noise, and he pictured the woman looking over her shoulder. He heard the murmur of female voices in the background. He closed his eyes. He was hungry, and he was tired, and there was nothing worth eating at home in his house. He was too shy to eat at a restaurant by himself.

"Dr. Franklin, have you had your supper yet?"

"Oh, I'm okay."

"Now, look here. I just fried some chicken, and I'm getting ready to put in some buttermilk biscuits. You ever had biscuits cooked in an iron skillet?"

"No, ma'am." Would an iron skillet matter unless you were anemic? He'd acquired a taste for biscuits since he'd moved south.

"Why don't you come on by for a bite of supper? I got a blackberry cobbler cooling on the stovetop, and corn pudding in the oven."

"Mrs. Calhoun, I don't have the time to drive three hours even for a dinner as good as that."

Jodina Calhoun made a hissing noise. "Well, I'm not at home, am I?"

"I don't know, are you?"

"No, sir, I'm staying here in Lexington with my little grand-niece, and you could get here in forty minutes driving slow. I need your help, and I got somebody I want you to meet."

He was tempted. But he would lose his appetite in a room full of strangers, plus he had to get up early for court. And he was too tired to drive that far.

"I'm a pathologist, Mrs. Calhoun, and unless you need my help in the capacity of my job as a—"

"I *know* who you are, and it involves body parts and organ stealing, and the safety of little children, so who else am I going to call?"

Franklin puzzled over the question. "The Marsden case?"

"You know about it?"

"I've been following it. How are you involved?"

"Emmet's my little grandniece, isn't she?"

"Emmet?"

"Emma Marsden, sir."

He hated it when she called him sir. It was like she was putting herself in her place on his behalf. Like she was saying he was more important and his time was more important, and he'd been raised well enough to flinch when a woman very much his senior in age called him sir. He could see his mother folding her arms and shaking her head at him ever so slightly.

"Now, if you don't want to drive over for dinner, we can come to your office, if you don't mind us showing up there some-time. You just say when."

Marcus scratched his chin, looked at the stack of files in the chair by the door, the papers in the in-tray. The ashtray was grimy with ashes and cigar butts and the fluorescent light over his head had been going from dim to bright at regular intervals since early that afternoon, driving him crazy. He needed to get out. He needed something to eat other than the heel of potato bread, black bananas, and questionable salami he had in the kitchen at home.

"Give me your address," Marcus said.

"Hot damn, he's coming." Jodina's voice came through muffled, like she was holding her hand over the receiver. "Do you drive slow or fast?"

"Why?"

"I'm trying to time the biscuits, ain't I?"

He closed his eyes for one moment, striving for patience. If she hadn't been his elder, he might ask her why the hell she thought he had any idea what was in her mind. "How long does it take to cook them?"

"A good twenty minutes, if the oven's hot."

"I'll call you on my cell when I'm twenty minutes out."

"Huh. If they'd had cell phones when I was a young woman, it would have saved my husband a lot of burnt biscuits."

Franklin had a change of heart as quickly as he'd made the decision to take the invitation, but the phone clicked in his ear. Apparently when Jodina quit talking, that was the end of the conversation. Franklin's mind wasn't on biscuits. It was on body parts, organ stealing, and the safety of little children. He wondered why in hell he'd said yes and how he was going to get out of it. He checked the caller ID, but the Calhoun number did not show up as anything but anonymous. That was one thing he did remember now, how paranoid the woman was. Maybe she'd gone over the edge and planned to poison him with those biscuits.

But in his mind's eye he saw a frail old woman who wanted nothing more than to bury what was left of her daughter in peace and anonymity, and he knew that she might joke but she was genuinely afraid and it was a hell of a world where an insurance company can force a settlement whether the victim wanted it or not. The suits ruled, and although they'd only wanted to clear

Jodina Calhoun from the books, and the businessman in him sympathized, the human in him did not.

Either way, he couldn't not show up unless he called, and he didn't have her number. He'd drive out there and listen a little, but he wouldn't eat. It embarrassed him to eat with strangers, and he knew it was shyness and stupidity, but that didn't take the discomfort away. He wanted only to go home and be still.

The worst of it was knowing he'd brought it on himself.

CHAPTER SEVEN

It took Franklin a half hour more than he'd figured to find the house because it wasn't actually in Lexington, as Jodina Calhoun had told him, but in Athens, which was a tiny sprout of a place right off the Richmond Road exit. The locals called it "A-Thins" instead of Athens, as in Greece, as in how any outsider might pronounce it, but every place has its eccentricities, and Franklin preferred cities with flavor rather than bland strips of everything the same. Still, he was annoyed because he'd had to wander around figuring out where the hell he was, and he was the type to map out his route before he grabbed the keys to the car. The crunch of leaves beneath his feet sounded angry. He punched the lock button on his keyless opener, and the loud squeal that alerted everyone within fifty feet that the car was now *locked* and *alarm-ready* made the woman in the porch swing look his way. She didn't look any happier to see him than he was to be there, and he paused, shy and embarrassed.

"You look too damn grumpy to be selling something." She was smoking a cigar. She sat on a wicker porch swing, the white paint almost totally chipped away, and her legs, tan, firm, and rounded at the calves, were propped on the porch railing. She took a long draw on the cigar and flicked ash into the mouth of a ceramic frog, then tilted her head sideways.

She was a pretty woman. Really pretty. Face kind of round and inquisitive looking, eyebrows thin and arched and dark, eyes so blue they looked violet. Her hair was dark, and it looked shiny and very soft, which was noticeable in these days of gels and mousse and spray. It hung around her face in a nice way, bits and pieces coming loose from the clip that held it up in some kind of French knot. She wore silver hoop earrings, and her shoulders were bare save the tiny straps on the white sundress she wore. She had a slim neck, and the sundress had a scoop neckline that showed the rounded tops of large breasts that seemed to be holding the dress up, because the straps of the dress had slid over her shoulders.

He could tell she was wearing thong panties, and he could not stop himself from looking where her legs were propped on the railing to see if he could get a glimpse, but she pulled those long legs down off the railing and tucked them up under the dress. Franklin hoped she hadn't noticed his look but she probably had—otherwise why had she pulled those legs up so quick? But she was pretending she hadn't noticed him notice.

"I'm not selling anything. I was invited to dinner." The defensive tone of his voice made him wince.

Her grin was instantaneous. "Yeah? Name, please, and I'll check the guest list."

He felt witty all of a sudden. "Iggy here." Not that she would have the least idea what—

"You like the Iggy movies?"

"Guilty."

"I thought I was the only person in this town who liked independent films."

"I'm only in this town temporarily, so I don't count."

"Oh, you count all right." She relit the cigar, using a wooden kitchen match. "Smoke?"

"Okay."

"Hang on."

She hopped off the swing and reached inside the front door, coming back with a long black cigar. "Portofino," she threw over her shoulder.

"I'm suitably impressed." He sat in the swing, scrunched to one side to make it clear he wasn't so much taking the swing over as sharing it. If she was surprised to find him almost in her seat, she didn't show it. He was surprised, though. He was not one to obey impulses, and here he'd done it already four times in the last five minutes.

She snipped off the end of the cigar with a pair of small purple-handled scissors, handed it to him with the box of wooden matches.

The cigar was a treasure. Five dollars apiece, and he never spent near that much on his own. Not that he cared what it smelled like or that it had been raggedly cut with a pair of purple scissors. He was content just to smoke it with this dark-haired woman who smelled of tobacco and Angel perfume.

She put her hands on her hips and looked down at him. "So are you actually here to eat, or have you come to give us fifteen minutes of your precious time and some lame excuse for not staying to supper?"

He took the cigar out of his mouth. "I wish you'd quit reading my mind, it makes me uncomfortable."

She laughed. He really liked that laugh. It was . . . what would be a good word? Boisterous. Not a tinkly girl laugh. It made him feel good to know he'd made it happen. The truth was, he often had amusing things to say; he just never actually said them.

"That depends on how much trouble I'm in with Jodina. I was supposed to call and tell her when I was twenty minutes away so she could put the biscuits in the oven."

Her smile went soft. It gave her a vulnerable look that was a likely conduit to the delicate woman behind the bravado. It made him want to tell her that everything would be okay, and he thought again of Jodina's reference to the safety of little children and body parts.

Please God let this woman be normal.

"I'll tell her you're here," she said, and the screen door groaned as the spring eased it closed in increments, finally reaching its limit and letting it slam suddenly shut, reminding him of the summer cabins his family had rented back home in Michigan. His father had been dead for seventeen years—dying suddenly and young of a heart attack—and eleven years later his mother had suffered a massive stroke that had smoked over half of her brain cells. Neither Marcus or Lucca had been cruel enough to want her to linger, and they had been happy for her when she'd died three days later without ever waking up. Franklin knew better than most when to restrain the cruelties of life support, and the ER doctor had been as close to a friend as Franklin usually had. His mom and dad had been gone long enough that he could remember them with pleasure, and it was astonishing to realize that during those summers in the cabins, his father had been younger than Franklin was now.

It occurred to Franklin that he'd been letting the weight issue slide, and that his father had been in much better shape those summers than he was now. His dad had seemed pretty old then, but only a six-year-old would consider a twenty-eight-year-old mother and thirty-two-year-old father *old*.

The screen door slammed open, and Franklin noticed that the wood frame was scarred with the exuberant comings and goings of that slender door. Normally he would disapprove and wonder why no one painted that wood, fixed the spring, or replaced the screen that bowed at the bottom; but somehow the whole effect was so comfortable and homey, he didn't think he'd change a single thing.

Jodina Calhoun beat the woman *(why the hell hadn't he asked her name?*) out the door, and they were both moving so fast, it looked like some kind of a race. They were too much alike not to be related. Not in looks exactly, although it was hard to tell, since Jodina Calhoun had to be in her eighties now or close to it. It was more a matter of their personal ambience.

It struck him then—was this woman the grandniece? The Emma Marsden he had been following in the papers?

The years had made their point with Jodina Calhoun, and Franklin knew very well that she had earned every crease in the aged paper-thin skin. Her back had settled in the C-shaped curve of advanced osteoporosis, and when she held out a hand for him to shake, he was gentle with the thick knobby joints of her long, work-worn fingers. He knew without asking that her fingers were stiff and that the joints gave her pain every day—pain that would be as ingrained in her life as breathing. But she was still vivid, not faded in the way of elderly people who have distanced themselves from a future they have no desire to see. Jodina Calhoun, clearly, was still very much in the game.

"I see you met Emmet," Jodina said, and Franklin looked again at the woman whose very presence made his nerve ends tingle.

"The *notorious* Emma Marsden," she said, giving him her tan, slim-fingered hand.

Franklin was not surprised to find her handshake firm, and the skin soft as fresh creamy butter. She looked soft all over, where a woman ought to be soft, and firm where a woman ought to be firm, and he used the handshake as an excuse to move a bit closer and catch another whiff of the present but elusive perfume.

"It's not every day I get to meet a woman who's genuinely notorious."

"Not living, anyway."

Franklin was startled into a laugh, and Jodina folded her arms and frowned at her niece.

"It is just like you, young lady, to try and make a bad

impression on the one man who might listen to us and see our side of things, and I'd like one good reason I shouldn't wring your neck right this minute."

"She's made a fine impression," Franklin said, with complete honesty, then closed his eyes, took a deep breath, and asked what was cooking that smelled so good.

"Oh, my Lord, the biscuits," Jodina said, and Emma held the screen door open as the old woman barreled back through.

Emma Marsden tilted her head and smiled up at him. She was tall, but Franklin was taller. "Masterful," she said, and her right cheek sank into a dimple.

Franklin took a deep puff on his cigar and grinned. He agreed.

The kitchen was hot, and sweat had beaded up on the back of Franklin's neck. He stood stiffly beside the kitchen table, trying to stay out of the way. The kitchen floor was old, yellowed linoleum.

The house did not have central air. He'd seen a window-unit air conditioner sticking its rear end from the living room window. The rest of the house seemed comfortable enough—not ice cold like he liked it, but tolerable. His nose was sensitive. He detected the thread of mustiness common to old houses and elderly ductwork, but the kitchen was a study in aromatic layers.

It was a funny kind of kitchen. The table was yellow mosaic tile and black wrought iron, and it looked Italian. Emma told him she'd got it on sale at Pier One when he'd walked in the kitchen and told her he liked it. The black iron chairs had curled-back tops and soft gold cushions lightly coated with animal hair. The tablecloth was French blue, and the dishes some kind of Italian swirl pattern.

White lace curtains hung across the window on the back door and looked like they'd been there since the turn of the century. The countertops were scratched green Formica, and the cabinets country pine with black hinges and handles that blended well with the table. Emma Marsden kept her spices in a conglomeration of various containers. The economy-sized lemon pepper was Kroger brand. Anise, basil, and bay leaves were lined up in red and white canisters that came from the McCormick Gourmet Collection. The baking powder was the familiar white label, red trim, Clabber Girl brand that his mother kept in their kitchen while he grew up. The bag of flour was White Lily, and it sat in a tuffet of spilled powder that trailed across the cabinets and onto the floor. He noticed that Jodina Calhoun had flour down the bosom of her dress and caked in the creases of her palms. This was a real kitchen, where women who loved to cook and were good at it spent a lot of time. Nothing matched, but everything went together, and the room had the ambience and presence of that little coffee shop or bistro you walk into where the owners run the place to suit themselves. As individualized as a fingerprint.

A glass casserole dish that held a cooled blackberry cobbler sat on the white enamel stove. A matching dish held corn pudding. The biscuits were keeping warm in an iron skillet with a dish cloth over the top, and fried chicken drained on a huge platter right by a stainless steel sink that was overrun by mixing bowls and large wooden spoons coated with dried batter of some kind or another. Dirty glasses lined the countertop near the sink.

Emma poured wine from a huge glass jug of Carlo Rossi burgundy. The wine goblets were huge, and each stem was wrapped with a wine charm made of colored glass. Franklin's glass had a green charm, and Jodina's glass had a blue one. Emma's was ruby red. She winked at Franklin, took a plastic ice tray out of the top part of a refrigerator that was no taller than Emma herself, crammed as much ice as she could into her great-aunt's wineglass, then filled it from a yellow pitcher that sat by the side of the stove.

"Peach tea," she explained to Franklin. "You want tea or the wine?"

"The wine," he said, because that was what she was having, though the peach tea sounded good too.

"You can have both," Emma said.

"Yeah?"

She nodded as if it was a proper request, when they both knew it absolutely wasn't. No pretense in this household.

Just as Franklin noticed that there were four places set at the table, the back door opened and a small, long-haired female walked in, followed by a weighty golden retriever.

Emma smiled at the girl and the dog. "Hi, guys. Hungry?"

The girl looked at Franklin and frowned. Her hair was a thick golden brunette, streaked with pink highlights. The hems of her jeans were too long, and ragged from being walked on. A good six inches of slim young tummy showed between the bottom of a tiny green T-shirt and the waistband of her jeans. Her makeup was carefully applied, almost model perfect. She looked a lot like a younger version of Emma Marsden, without the smile.

She'd only glanced once at her mother, but she stopped long enough to give Jodina a genuine hug.

The dog gave a war whoop and ran straight for Franklin, whose knees went suddenly weak.

"Wally, *no,*" Emma said, and to the girl, "Blaine, get the dog."

Wally was quicker on her feet than Blaine was. She had both front paws on Franklin's shoulders and was looking him right in the eye before the girl could get a hand on her collar. The dog's eyes were brown and intelligent, her muzzle white with age. The animal opened a large mouth, and a pink tongue as thick as a steak fillet hung sideways over the black, saliva-streaked gums.

"Jesus," Franklin said. He was a man used to working around strong, unendurable odors, but this dog had the worst breath he had smelled in a lifetime.

The girl yanked the dog backward. "Off, Wally."

Franklin reached a tentative hand out to the dog's domelike head. "Good boy."

"Wally's a girl," the child deadpanned, and Franklin wondered if the kid was having him on.

Emma looked at the girl over her shoulder. "Put her in the bedroom and get washed up for dinner. But first say hello. Marcus Franklin, this is my daughter, Blaine. Blaine, Marcus Franklin."

The girl looked him over, eyes gone dull and bored. Very unimpressed. Franklin offered a hand. She forced a plastic smile and gave him a limp handshake. In all the articles Franklin had read on the Marsden case, very little if any mention had been made of Emma Marsden's other child. Franklin hadn't expected a teenager.

"Whatcha drinking, baby girl?" Jodina said, and Blaine grinned at her over one slim and tiny shoulder.

"Wine."

Jodina winked and splashed just a little bit of burgundy into another wineglass. There was an ease between the two of them that made the tension between mother and daughter stand out.

The girl had the look of her mother—but she was shorter and more petite, and while Emma exuded *presence,* the girl's energy, undeniably strong, smoldered beneath the surface. The mother would always be noticed. The daughter had learned to tone down the essence and to blend.

Franklin looked up in time to catch the look the kid threw him on her way through the doorway. Keen, intelligent, suspicious. Emma gave Franklin a sharp look, and he was jolted by the defensive and protective air she suddenly acquired. There was nothing friendly or amused in that look, and Franklin realized that if he didn't get along with the daughter, he was dead meat.

"Blaine, put Wally in the bedroom," she said.

"Not on my account," Franklin said quickly.

Emma grinned at him over her shoulder as she fixed two large glasses of peach iced tea and put one in front of his place and one in front of her daughter's. "If we don't put Wally up, she'll sit by your side and beg."

"I grew up with dogs," he said.

"Liar."

"What do you know about it?" he asked.

Jodina Calhoun looked to the heavens. "She knows everything. If you don't believe me, ask her."

The splash of water was noisy from the bathroom, which was evidently right off the living room. The door slammed shut suddenly, then a toilet flushed, and the door opened again.

"Wash your hands," Emma said.

"Mom." The tone, mortified.

Franklin sympathized. The kid looked old and smart enough to take care of her bathroom habits privately without any input from her mom.

CHAPTER EIGHT

Syd sometimes had to reassure herself that everything her husband, Dr. Theodore Tundridge, was doing was completely legal. She was the one who had urged Ted to turn the videotape of the Marsden woman over to the police, and now she was questioning the decision. She had not expected the tape to make the six o'clock news. How had the media gotten hold of it?

Ted, however, was very sure. Sure that he was right about the Marsden woman and the death of her child. Sure that he was right about the research. He had no tolerance for anyone questioning him. The Marsden woman had objected to the pathology lab, and Ted was furious. Syd lay awake at night, wondering if Ted was accusing the woman because she had the nerve to challenge his right to use tissue samples for research. Ted did not like his authority challenged. He was one of those tiresome people who were always right.

He had assured Syd, in a drawn-out and huffy conversation, that there was solid evidence the Marsden woman might have had something to do with her son's illness. Might have. From what Syd could gather, the only evidence was staff suspicion.

The videotape that had so strangely and suspiciously been

mailed to the clinic had ended any sympathy Syd had for Emma Marsden. That kind of behavior, on her child's birthday—it was weird. It made Syd squirm.

But if she was honest, the path lab made her squirm too.

She wondered how far she could push her objections. There was no question she had the upper hand in the marriage.

Syd was usually careful to keep her opinions to herself. Theodore took this silence as approval, and Syd's approval, though he rarely realized it, was integral to his happiness.

Syd did not like her husband. She hid her opinion of him from everyone but herself. She never spoke negatively about him in front of the children. (Girlfriends were a tempting indulgence she was not always able to resist.) Theodore was completely unaware of how she felt. This she also knew. She was not having affairs, not that she didn't have offers. She was fairly attractive, though her husband was not aware of her on a physical level and never had been—there was very little that could penetrate his self-obsession. She had not put him through medical school, so she had no debts for him to repay—financial or emotional. She was not wealthy, not until she became Mrs. Theodore Tundridge, but she did not have a single thread of avarice in her soul. She simply admired his work, and did not wish to disrupt the lives of their four children—all adopted, siblings left orphaned after an automobile accident killed their parents. Syd had adopted the two oldest initially, twelve- and ten-year-old boys. They violently opposed being separated from the others, and it was clear from the outset that the children needed to be together. Syd had planned all along to adopt all four of them, but it had taken time, patience, and a certain manipulation. Being a doctor's wife had many advantages. Eventually Syd managed to convince the family and Child Protective Services to allow her to adopt the two youngest—a little girl of five and a toddler of one and a half, another boy. That had been five years ago, and her children were now seventeen, fifteen, ten, and six. She loved them with all her heart, and felt they were meant to be in her life. She was perfectly able to conceive, and she and Ted had something of a sex life now and then, but she was obsessively and phobically afraid of childbirth. Someone had shown her a Lamaze class film at an early age, and it had made an eternal impression. (Syd thought showing such things to women *after* they got pregnant was the height of cruelty.)

She was perfectly aware that her husband did important work. His research into pediatric liver disease was groundbreaking and lifesaving, and he not only served the usual middle-class and wealthy patients but also devoted a significant part of his clinic to the children of those who could not afford medical care, which, these days, could be almost anyone.

It was a good life, in Syd's estimation, not the least because it was a life she had chosen. She was happy to be able to stay home with her four children, who had needed her so desperately when their beloved mother and father had died on I-75 coming home from a University of Louisville basketball game. She did sometimes miss passion—not the Hollywood version, which, in her opinion, had little to do with any reality she'd ever seen. Those kinds of ideals wreaked havoc with people's general expectations so that they constantly bypassed love for the occasional spark of infatuated lust. She knew what she was giving up, and sometimes it bothered her, but not very often. There had been someone, once, after she'd gotten married, and she often thought that the two of them could have been blissfully happy. But he, too, had been married, and though his spouse had been cold, critical, and controlling, he had after all made his choice and been happy with it before he knew Syd. When it came to having affairs and breaking up marriages, she was the last woman standing. It just wasn't in her.

Syd and her children had a lovely life together, with Ted as a distant, distracted father who spent most of his time working. She took the kids bowling every Friday night. They went to soccer games on the weekends, soccer practice during the week. There were dance classes at Diana Evans School of Dance for the Sugar Babe (officially Renee, but she had always been Sugar Babe to Syd and the boys). Syd allowed no television during meals (except on weekends; then it was a free-for-all) and took them all to Second Presbyterian Church every Sunday, no matter how much they complained and begged to sleep in. Involvement in the youth group, however, remained a matter of choice.

Syd did the tax work for her husband's clinic, as well as keeping an overview of the books, because, in addition to her skill as a mother, nurturer, and homemaker, she had graduated magna cum laude with a B.S. in accounting and a degree in tax law from Emory University. She'd hung both diplomas over the washing machine and dryer. She was not supermom, but she did have a sense of humor. Her weaknesses were romance novels, the thick ones you could really get into as well as the slender quick reads; Pecan Sandies shortbread cookies; and chess, which she played online, no one in her family coming close to being able to give her a good game.

She raised her children in a four-thousand-square-foot house in Heartland subdivision, and because she loved a clean house and hated cleaning, she had a maid come in once a week. She and the maid had become very good friends; she was probably closer to Ginny than to any of her other girlfriends. They exchanged advice on children and husbands. Ginny had one child, and her husband was disabled. They were very much in love and spent a lot of time traveling in their RV now that their son was grown and out of the house. Ginny was fond of Syd's children, and Lucy and Ethel, the two golden retrievers that Syd and the kids had adopted from Golden Retriever Rescue, had cured her of a fear of big dogs. The household included a foul-tempered iguana named Earl, an odoriferous mouse named Casper, and a cat, Mr. Bo Jangles, who had shown up on the back porch one unseasonably cold morning during the kids' Thanksgiving holiday three years ago. Once freed of matted hair and parasites, Mr. Bo Jangles had turned into a sleek beauty who never again bothered to venture outside, preferring to spend most of his time peering down at the dogs from the top of the television set.

Syd knew the doorbell was going to ring before the chimes began bonging. The dogs had jumped from their upside-down paws-in-the-air rub-my-tummy positions and were now circling her legs, preventing her from answering the door in their enthusiasm to let her know there was someone out front and wouldn't it be a great idea if they all went together to bark and take a look? Sadly, the dogs did not seem to respect Syd as pack leader, but held the attitude that she was a member of the gang, albeit an important one. She was, after all, in charge of rides in the RAV4.

Syd looked through the peephole and saw that Amaryllis Burton was on the doorstep, wearing a white lab coat with her name tag and the clinic name stenciled on it in pink cursive. Syd hesitated. Unfortunately, the glass panels on either side of the double door, frosted though they might be, made it clear that someone was there inside.

Syd swung the front door open and tried to smile. Amaryllis, medium height and plump, fair-skinned but plagued by an outrageous number of large brown moles, gave her a big smile beneath eyes brimming with hostility.

"Taking it easy today?" Amaryllis said, showing all of her teeth. She looked Syd up and down, taking in the sweatpants, the sweatshirt that read "The Only Bad Coffee Cup Is an Empty Coffee Cup," the chestnut hair expensively streaked with blond highlights piled carelessly up and held by a comb, and the face clear of makeup. Even in grubbies, Syd knew she outclassed the woman on the doorstep, whose overstretched tan sweater and A-line brown skirt had been worn to the nub. She knew Amaryllis resented that Syd's nails were recently manicured. French tips, though, short and squared-off. Syd refused to consider herself spoiled or frou-frou. Amaryllis could get her nails done if she wanted to, it just wasn't her style. She treated looking dowdy as if it were part of a healthier lifestyle, like buying organic fruit.

Amaryllis glanced down at the novel Syd held splayed against her thigh; the front cover showed a woman stepping into a carriage. Syd was a sucker for Regency romance and collected first edition Georgette Heyers.

"Am I interrupting something?" Amaryllis said, pursing her lips at Syd's book.

"I was just getting ready to walk out the door."

Since she was barefoot, the lie was blatant, but Syd rarely felt it necessary to be polite to a woman who so often and so clumsily put the moves on her husband. Ted was convinced that Amaryllis was in love with him, although Syd thought Amaryllis, to her credit, was mainly interested in his prestige and bank account, in that order. Ted often thought women were in love with him because he was a doctor, and considered it part of the job. Usually he was wrong.

Syd had told him long and often that she would not tolerate affairs and there would be no second chances, but that if he had the bad sense to fool around with Amaryllis Burton she would kill him just for having bad taste. Syd didn't like Amaryllis, but Amaryllis *hated* Syd. Syd had everything that Amaryllis wanted—a prominent doctor for a husband, a house full of children, and what looked, from the outside at least, like a lot of money.

"I won't ask to come in," Amaryllis said, glancing over Syd's shoulder into the house. She offered Syd a thick file. "I thought I'd better drop this by."

Syd took the file, which meant she had to open the screen door, which meant, by the rules of good manners, that she had to ask Amaryllis in.

"You sure you don't want to step inside?" Syd asked.

Amaryllis eyed the dogs. For a moment Syd held out hope, but Amaryllis inclined her head and stepped through the open door, squealing in what was meant to pass for pain—and in all fairness might actually be pain—when Ethel jumped up and pushed both paws against her stomach.

"Bad dog," Syd said halfheartedly. They *were* bad dogs, both of them, and every attempt she made to train them was undone by her bevy of outrageous children, who thought dogs were put on the earth to be spoiled.

Syd led Amaryllis into the living room and saw the raised eyebrow of disapproval. The truth was, Ginny had spent the last two weeks on the road in her RV, and the house was much the worse for wear. The open bag of cookies that Syd was having as a late brunch was set up high on the mahogany and marble antique table so that the dogs couldn't get to them without a lot of effort. The dogs circled Amaryllis, who made shoving motions with her hands that interested them momentarily, but the smell of the cookies was more to their taste, and they settled side by side beneath the table, long strings of drool coming from their maws in anticipation of what those Keebler elves could do. Syd gave them both a cookie, then remembered to offer one to Amaryllis.

"Just one, I guess, I'm starved. We're about run off our feet at the clinic today, so I thought I'd better bring these over on my lunch hour."

Syd flicked the open file: the monthly list of clinic expenses. That was odd. The information was confidential, and one thing Ted was a bear about was keeping the financial end to himself, as in to herself, since she kept track of most of it. She and Mr. French.

"I'm surprised Mr. French asked you to bring this over," Syd said.

Amaryllis, who had been reaching for another cookie, looked up. "I offered."

"Really? And he took you up on it?"

"Oh, I don't mind."

Syd smiled, and Amaryllis smiled back, basking in martyrdom. Syd's smile, however, hid a great deal of anger. She could access this information via her computer. There was absolutely no need for Amaryllis to have the printout, and only she and Mr. French, and Ted, of course, had access. There was no way on this earth that Mr. French would hand any financial information over to anyone who could glance through the file at their leisure on their unnecessary drive over.

Obviously Amaryllis was lying.

Nosy, of course. And always anxious for an excuse to come to the house and stare at Syd as if she were an exhibit in the museum of things Amaryllis desired. Something not quite right here, Syd just wasn't sure what, and she was wise enough not to push until she found out. Which was hard, because she wanted to ask the woman, in that formal icy polite voice that made even Ted nervous, just what the hell she thought she was doing. It might well be nothing more than an excuse to come out to the house, or she might be insinuating herself into the financial workings of the clinic. Amaryllis was envious of Mr. French's authority, as administrator, over the nursing and support staff.

"How are the children?" Amaryllis asked, in that soft sad voice she used to remind everyone that her own child had died a lingering death of liver failure at the age of eight. It was how she'd met Ted—he'd been her son's doctor. One thing led to another, and Amaryllis, who had begun by just hanging out at the clinic to "help," had finally been hired. Ted said she was likely lonely, as her husband, whom Syd had thought might be imaginary until she'd finally met him at last year's Christmas party, spent Monday through Friday on the road analyzing mortgage portfolios for investment firms. She had a brother she was close to, a truck driver, who lived in Sevierville, Tennessee. He and Amaryllis jointly owned a house they'd inherited after their parents died. Syd knew Amaryllis spent at least one weekend a month down there.

"All the kids are fine," Syd said. She used to be kind to Amaryllis, but it was too hard. "Freddie loves first grade, and for the first time I have a whole morning and afternoon while all four are in school."

"The lady of leisure? I'd go out of my mind with boredom."

Syd did not like being called a lady of leisure. She worked her butt off as a mother of four and often was up late taking care of the clinic finances. Nor did she like being dropped in on and insulted in her own living room. But all she said was, "Don't let me take up any more of your time." Amaryllis, disappointed but defeated, followed her to the front door, head swiveling as she took in every detail of the messy and actually quite dirty house, to file away in the nasty wrinkles of her mind. She left with a smug smile of superiority, letting Syd know that no household of hers would ever be allowed to suffer so much slack and neglect, and that she had standards of homemaking and, most likely, motherhood that would leave Syd, literally, in the dust.

CHAPTER NINE

It is my opinion that for every intricately difficult and unfair situation, like that of Emma Marsden, there is an equally intricate and likely unconventional pathway that will get the job done—either by going over, under, or through the problem. All you need to remember is that you don't have to play by any rules other than your own. It is always effective to keep in mind the goals, and fears, of all interested parties.

The hero of this method of living is my ex-husband, Rick, who has always done things his own peculiar way. Which is why I was headed over to see him when the Emma Marsden videotape made the front page of the morning paper. Rick was no doubt busy with other things, but it is my opinion that my Ricky is a bit bored with his job. The problem is that his business brings him too much money and personal satisfaction to slow down. Rick works vaguely with a sort of listlessness at anything that doesn't interest him. Acting was the only thing that fired him up until he started his business.

Joel is not jealous of Rick. This annoys me.

I wasn't exactly sure of how to approach Emma Marsden's problem. I only knew that the traditional way involving lots of research, and legwork, and legal advice, not to mention an actual attorney, ridiculous fees, and months and months duking it out with the legal system, wasn't going to help my client any time soon. And she needed help soon. She had come to the attention of both the Commonwealth Attorney's Office and Child Protective Services, and there were no doubt many terrible things headed her way. We needed to move quickly.

There was actually a parking space in the restaurant lot of the Atomic Café, so I didn't have to put the BMW on the small lawn of Rick's office (and home—he and Judith live upstairs). I hesitated after walking through the front door. I smelled coffee and was considering helping myself to a cup, but it had an over-cooked aroma, and frankly, I would much prefer that Rick make me a fresh pot. Also, there were a lot of phones ringing in the right wing of the building (right if you are facing in). It sounded very busy back there.

Rick's door was shut tight behind a Do Not Disturb sign. I didn't hear anything from behind the door, not even when I put my ear to the wood, but it is a thick door, so there was no telling. In the way of ex-wives universal, I ignored the sign and walked in, making sure to shut the door tight behind me, because once inside, I agreed with the sentiment that Rick should not be disturbed.

He had his feet up on the desk, and he was sound asleep, snoring even. Opening the door didn't wake him up. Rick had always been a heavy sleeper.

I stretched out on the couch, facing him, and watched him sleep. Some of the papers had drifted off his desk, either from neglect, from a strong wind, or from being kicked off while he slept. I wondered how long it would take to let him wake up naturally, and thus be in a better mood.

I myself had slept pretty well, despite Emma Marsden's problems. I felt a little guilty about it, but on the other hand, a little distance is a good professional qualification. I wondered if my life was going too well to make me an effective detective. On the other hand, with a mind no longer clouded by anger and emotion, my thought processes were clearer. I wasn't obsessed with my work anymore, and was content to leave off after a reasonable day's work and slouch around with Joel. He'd scaled his own hours back, or he did whenever he could, and we were turning into a couple of dull but happy homebodies. I remember thinking, quite some time ago, that it was good that he and I were both so ambitious about our jobs, because it meant that neither one of us was critical or unhappy with the other when work got in the way. Luckily, we'd both slacked off about the same time. True love.

"You're awfully quiet over there, Lena Bina."

"Ricky? You're awake?"

"Have been since you pulled your car in outside. Thanks for not parking on the lawn. Although now you have a BMW it's not quite as annoying."

"It just happened there was a spot."

"Did you really think I was asleep?"

"Yeah."

"I was *feigning* sleep. And you—be serious now, Lena—you were totally convinced, *totally,* that I was asleep?"

"Totally. Why do you care?"

"Just rehearsing, Lena. I might eventually need to feign sleep, and it's one of those things I was never good at. I'm honing my craft, as always."

"Once an actor, always—"

"Lena. I'll go back to it eventually. As soon as I get more staff trained and up and running and as soon as Judith and I get married."

"She finally said yes?"

"No, I finally gave her an ultimatum."

"You did?"

"Yes. I am too much in love to accept a half-assed commitment. All or nothing."

"What did she say?"

"She said she'd think about it."

"That's encouraging."

"Sarcasm noted but not appreciated. Do you think she'll say yes?"

I knew of course that she would, she had told me as much last night before she and Ricky left, but I saw no reason to ease his worry. He would appreciate it all the more when she relented. I wondered how long she was going to let him dangle. It seemed a bit cruel of her, but then I am of the blurt-out-whatever-pops-into-your-head category of female.

"Rick, did you worry like this when you asked me to marry you?"

"No."

"Why not?"

"Because you'd already told me you'd say yes. Refreshingly direct, Lena, you always have been."

He pulled his feet off the desk and sat up in the chair. "Well, my dear, thanks for coming by."

"Nice try."

"Lena, there is no point in sitting there trying to get me to do your work for you, I have a business to run."

"Okay."

"Of course, my offer of an office beside mine, an office of your own, where you can work if you will promise to work without bothering—I mean, interrupting me, is still open."

"Thank you."

"But that doesn't mean I'll do your work for you."

"I wouldn't ask you to."

"Yes, you would. That's why you're here."

"I didn't want you to do my work for me, Rick. I just wanted your advice. But you're right, I am interrupting, and I shouldn't keep you from your day."

He nodded at me. I just sat still.

"Okay, what?"

"This business with Emma Marsden. I mean, I know the best thing to do would be to consult an attorney, and read up on the law, and try to figure out what the cops have on her, and see if they have anything even remotely like a case, and maybe she should file suit, and then—"

Rick came up out of his chair and paced in front of the desk, hands behind his back.

"That's quite good," I said.

"What?"

"The pacing. Hands behind the back. Frowny-face. I would call it 'concerned exasperation.'"

Rick's face went a bit pink. "Thank you. And it wasn't all faked. You are exasperating."

I smiled up at him and waited. I felt sure he would tell me.

"Lena, you can do all of that, and you'll get your client tied up in a fight that could last years. Meanwhile, she may wind up conducting a lot of that fight from jail, or under the scrutiny of a grand jury, and she'll run up some god-awful legal fees."

"I'm way ahead of you on that, Rick."

"You . . . then why are you here?"

"Because your computer is better than mine, and you're better at ferreting things out than I am, and I think the first thing we need to do is look into this doctor, this Tundridge, who made the accusation. Especially since he's made three other accusations in the last five years. Also, you haven't heard the best part."

"About the sex tape? I was sitting right there in the living room—"

"That's not the best part."

"Depends on your viewpoint, Lena Bina. What did Joel tell you later? Did he watch it?"

"I don't know. I didn't feel like I could press him on it after shrinking all his jeans."

"I take your point."

"No, the best part, or the most gruesome part—"

"Gruesome? Do not leave out a detail."

"This whole thing started with the Tundridge Children's Clinic—"

"I've heard of it."

"Congratulations, you get a cookie."

"Did you say—"

"I said 'cookie.' Anyway, this clinic, which was started by Tundridge, and I think he owns the major stock in it, but it's kind of a doctors' consortium—"

Rick waved a hand at me.

"Anyway, the clinic called Emma and told her that they had some of her son's remains, that were . . . how did they put it? Retained. Retained after the autopsy. And that she would have to pick them up, or she'd have to pay a storage fee."

"Storage fee?"

"Yeah, evidently she had seen that on her bill and inquired, and then somebody in the office doing the paperwork called her and told her to pay the fee or come pick the stuff up."

"When you say 'stuff,' my dear, what exactly do you mean?"

"I mean the child's liver, his heart, his tongue. And some other parts, I think."

Rick sat back on his desk as if he could no longer stand on his feet.

"Tell me you're making this up."

"No. I'm not."

"And did this doctor have permission to keep all these . . . various bits and pieces? I mean, Lena, honey, this is grotesque. It's bizarre, it's—"

"I *know.* And you haven't heard the best part."

"The best part?"

"Or the worst part. Emma Marsden goes to pick this stuff up."

"To pick it up?"

"Well, Rick, she was kind of in shock and she didn't know

what else to do. She didn't want them to throw anything away. She'd thought it had all been buried with her son, you know, and she wanted to put him all together, so to speak."

"Good lord."

"So when she gets there, they take her down to this sort of basement pathology lab, and then the girl goes and asks management, you know, about a container or something, and finds out she's in a shitload of trouble for, one, calling Emma Marsden in the first place, and, two, almost letting the parts out of the path lab. So she goes back downstairs and tells Emma that there's been a big mistake. But by then Emma has seen her son's heart in a jar—"

"A pickle jar, I bet you."

"No, Rick, I don't think so. So Emma tells the girl to go get her supervisor, and then when the girl leaves, Emma puts everything in a bag and runs out of the clinic with it."

"Lena, that's—that's—"

"Horrible. I know. Can you imagine?"

Rick stared past me to the wall, though there was nothing there to look at. "It's wonderful."

"Rick? Wonderful?"

"It's just the dramatic possibilities. It would make a hell of a play, although God, nobody would ever believe something like that could happen—"

"Rick—"

"A play, Lena. I need to write a play. And then direct it."

"And star in it too?"

"Lena, I'm serious."

"I know you are, and so am I."

"We need to get a line on this doctor."

He turned to his computer, and I stared up at the ceiling and waited for him to spout information.

"I'll make a fresh pot of coffee," I said, but I don't think he heard me. His fingers were moving across the keyboard, though every little while he stopped to make a note. I wasn't sure about the ethics of him writing a play about all of this, but I figured that I could worry about that later.

"I need to see this basement," Rick said.

One thing we agreed on.

While the coffeepot sputtered and steamed, I went into what Rick liked to call my office, a bare room with a large desk, a rug, and a laptop computer that was used by the staff when they overflowed their own desks. I wondered if, like everybody else in the world these days, Dr. Theodore Tundridge had a Web page. He didn't, but his clinic did. I looked at the staff pictures and their bios. There was a family photo, of Tundridge and his wife and kids. Four kids, which surprised me for some reason. The kids looked happy.

They actually had the clinic consent form online, buried in their brochure.

It opened with the statement that patient privacy was a "priority." A preening statement made it clear that the clinic followed federal guidelines (found in the Code of Federal Regulations at 45 CFR §§ 164.500 *et seq.*). I had no idea what *et seq.* meant. It then pointed out, quite reasonably, that health care information would be used for the normal business known as health care operations. I wondered who wrote this stuff.

Health care operations included treatment, *duh,* payment, *no doubt,* and then a repeat of that catch-all phrase, "health care operations." The most interesting part, as far as I was concerned, came under "information we share without your signed consent." There seemed to be quite a few of these instances. I counted twelve. None of them involved treatment or payment. The good of public health was cited, so that diseases and medical devices could be tracked. Then came the protection of victims of abuse or neglect.

The next category was federal and state health oversight

activities such as fraud investigations. I puzzled over that one a minute, then moved on to judicial and administrative proceedings, and then to "if required by law or for law enforcement." Next came the coroners, medical examiners, and funeral directors, and after that organ donation. I wondered if that meant voluntary or involuntary.

Another possible use was to avert serious threats to public health or safety. Evidently, the writer of this list had seen some of the disaster movies on Ebola.

The next entry was creepy. "For specialized government functions such as military, national security, intelligence, and protective service." Did they put this in before or after the government created the Department of Homeland Security?

They'd also fork over the info to Workers' Compensation, if you were injured on the job, and they'd rat you out to your correctional institution if you were an inmate.

It was the last entry that got my attention: "For research, following strict internal review to ensure protection of information."

Under their responsibilities I found the following outrageous statement: "We reserve the right to change privacy practices, and make the new practices effective for all the information we maintain." Under patient rights, I did find that one could request that the clinic restrict how they used or disclosed one's medical information, but that was followed with "We may not be able to comply with all requests."

And even though you were entitled to an accounting of how your medical information was disclosed, excluded from this accounting were disclosures for treatment, payment, health care operations (again), and some *required* disclosures.

You could, however, receive a paper copy of the privacy notice even if you'd already received it electronically.

Generous.

I printed copies of the brochure along with staff pictures and bios and picked up the phone. Rick had several lines coming into the office, and I inadvertently interrupted two phone calls before I got Emma Marsden.

"It's Lena, Emma."

"Have you seen the papers?" Her voice was thick. She'd been crying.

"Yeah. Sorry. It's nasty."

"They ran it on the local news at noon. I probably shouldn't have watched."

"How could you not? Besides, you need to know what you're up against. I question how much use the tape is, anyway. It doesn't mean anything. It really has no relation to the case at all."

"They're using it as proof that I'm a bad mother."

"We'll fight it. The first thing the police have to do is establish that it really was you. But what interests me is that it was taken at all. I don't guess you saw—"

"Do you really think I'd have carried on like that if I thought it was being taped?"

"No. But what about Clayton? Is he the type to—"

"No. He never did anything like that while we were together. And he had no reason to expect anything like that would happen. Who would?"

"Don't beat yourself up, Emma. People have sex with their exes all the time. You had a nice dinner together, you remembered the good things and the time together with your son. It's not so strange."

"It was like that. Like you say."

"The worst thing you can do is apologize. I say admit it was you and brazen it out."

"Like Scarlett O'Hara and the red dress?"

"Just like that. Chin up and all that. So you had sex in a car. Most people have. What I really want to know is who filmed you. Was this before or after Tundridge made his allegation?"

"You're thinking it was him?"

"He could have hired somebody."

"It happened before that business down in the clinic basement, over Ned's . . . parts. It was weeks before he made his accusation. I honestly think he accused me of the Munchausen's thing just to get me off his back over him having retained my son's organs for the chamber of horrors he likes to call research."

"I agree. But there's got to be some reason somebody made that tape. Do you think somebody has been . . . I don't know, watching you? Stalking you for some reason?"

"No, no. No calls, no weirdos hanging out at the shopping centers just when I happen to go there. Really, I'd notice something like that. I have a very pretty teenage daughter, I'm always on guard."

"And you and Clayton. You weren't in any kind of legal tangle, where he might like to have something to discredit you with?"

"Not at all. Clayton isn't nearly as bad as you seem to think he is."

"Few people are as bad as I think they are. Many are worse." Time to move on. "Look, I've got the Web page up, on the clinic. I need to know who you talked to there. And what you know about anybody on the staff. Do you have time tomorrow afternoon to go over this with me?"

"Sure. Maybe I can get hold of Amaryllis Burton. She's on the staff, she might have something for us. She called me already today over the newspaper story. She's sympathetic to the cause. Even to the point of losing her job, if she's not careful."

I looked back at the Web page, scrolling. "Amaryllis?"

"Amaryllis Burton. She's some kind of nursing assistant. She and I are kind of friends. She lost a son too, liver disease, just like Ned. Tundridge treated her child like he did mine, and she wound up volunteering in the subsidized part of the clinic, you know, just to get out of herself and heal from her loss. She coun-

seled a lot of us who lost children. She's been working there for—
I guess it must be seven or eight years now."

"She's not on the Web page."

"She's worked there for years."

"You think she'd talk to us?"

"I know she would."

"Set it up, then, and let me know when she's coming."

"Done. And thanks, Lena."

"Sure." One of the biggest parts of my job is professional
side-taking. Equalizer for hire.

I was checking the balance on my bank account when I heard
Rick call my name. Depressing, really. As soon as the check to
the vet cleared, there would be enough in there to pay the bank-
ing fees, barely. It was no way to live.

"Lena Bina?"

I never come when I'm called. Eventually Rick remembered
this, and stuck his head around the doorframe.

"Interesting things coming up, if you'd care to join me."

"Sure. I made coffee."

"Always an event, when you're domestic."

The printer in Rick's office was clattering away when I followed
him inside. We both had fresh cups of coffee, mine with cream,
his black, and he had that kind of arching-up way of walking he
gets when he feels like he's done something clever. I hoped he
had.

He turned—actually, he twirled—and looked at me right
after he got behind his desk.

"It's all about research with this guy, isn't it? Keeping the
body parts and all that?"

I wanted to make a remark about the twirl, but it would
interrupt the flow of information, so I resisted.

"Lena, are you listening to me?"

"Of course I am. All about the flow of information."

"What?"

"Research, I mean. All about research."

"I found an abstract published by Dr. Theodore Tundridge in the *New England Journal of Medicine.*"

"The *New England Journal of Medicine?* That's so legit."

"This guy is legit. But listen, Lena. And maybe you better sit down."

I sat down, clutching my cup of coffee. It was too hot to drink, so I blew on the top.

"The name of the paper is 'Unusual and Valuable Viral Antibodies.' It describes the blood of patient X, a young male, aged twenty-nine months, who died of liver failure. In analyzing the child's blood to determine the cause of his illness and eventual death, Dr. Theodore Tundridge discovered these extraordinary antibodies. His assumption is that the antibodies were formed to deal with some type of toxin the child was being exposed to, and though the child is deceased from liver failure, he is continuing to run tests on stored tissues."

"Oh, lord, Rick. You think it's Ned Marsden? You think Emma's child is patient X?"

Rick folded his arms and rocked from side to side in his chair. "I went through death notices from the time of the publication, which was eight months ago, and two years before, and then to the present. No other child of that exact age died in Lexington except Ned Marsden. So unless he was treating a child from another state, which is possible, I guess, Ned Marsden is patient X."

"How strange."

"It gets better, Lena. He's patented the genetic material from the blood of patient X."

"*Patented* it? Can he do that?"

Rick nodded. "He sure can. And if he hasn't sold it to some pharmaceutical company for millions of bucks, he will, believe me."

"But why all this crap with Emma? Why accuse her . . . you

think because he doesn't want a lawsuit and a legal investigation when he's in the process of making a deal?"

"Yeah, maybe. Also, consider he might want access to the sibling. Emma Marsden has another child, right? A daughter?"

"Oh, of course. Emma Marsden agrees to take parenting classes for Child Protective Services, and to let Dr. Tundridge do regular exams on Blaine, which will no doubt include tissue and blood samples . . . and maybe she'll have the same genetic materials as her half-brother." I leaned back in my chair. "God, Rick, that's wonderful."

"Why?"

"Why? Because Emma Marsden can sue his sorry ass, that's why. He can't just patent her child's genetic material; it doesn't belong to him. He didn't have permission."

"Lena, she could sue all she'd want, and she'd lose. There's precedent, believe me. Who do you think has Karen Silkwood's bones? You remember her? The antinuclear protester?"

"Somebody has her bones?"

"The Los Alamos lab she was challenging."

"I just read the clinic consent form. It pretty much gives them permission to do anything they damn well please."

"Well, they take the high road. At least they get permission."

I put my head in my hands, thinking. "It's still good, Rick. We can show that Tundridge is not some concerned doctor looking after an abused patient. We can prove he's got ulterior motives."

Rick leaned forward. "I suppose you could go through channels, Lena. I'm sure in two or three years, maybe even several months with any luck, and with the help of a good attorney, Emma Marsden can get Child Protective Services, and the cops and Dr. Tundridge, off her back."

"I don't go through channels, Rick. That's why people hire me. Simple solutions for complicated times."

CHAPTER TEN

I listened for a minute to the engine of the BMW. I loved the way it sounded. I remembered the Mazda 626 I used to have, and the oil leak that no mechanic had been able to repair, and how I had to put a quart of oil in every three weeks, and be careful not to park in the driveways of my friends, so as not to leave large oil stains for them to remember me by.

I told myself that driving a BMW might well be a temporary phase of my life.

I took Man of War to Tundridge Road and found the clinic close to Jesse Clark Junior High, on the opposite side of the street. It was a red brick building, one story, very new, the parking lot freshly paved. The lot was full, with a large section reserved for staff. There were three spaces for doctors, and one of them was marked "Tundridge." A navy Volvo was parked in his spot. So he was there.

I noticed a small gas station and food market next to the parking lot, so I drove over and bought a small disposable camera. I wasn't sure if I would use it, but I wanted to have it just in case.

The reception area was thinly carpeted, and very clean, and

the girl behind the front desk wore a stiff white lab coat with her name, Janet, embroidered on the pocket in pink cursive.

She smiled at me from behind a sliding glass window and pointed to a white pad that listed names. One of those tie-down pens rested near the pad of paper, and a glass cylinder held lollipops of various flavors. I hesitated between cherry and grape and finally went with the cherry.

I glanced over my shoulder. The waiting room was crowded. Mothers, and some fathers, and a heaving mass of small children. Some of them sat in laps, some of them played with a set of blocks, some looked at books. One was rolling on the floor, and another was climbing to the top of a couch. The noise level was impressive.

"My name is Lena Padget, and I'd like to see Dr. Tundridge, if possible."

The smile left Janet's face, and she glanced at the list of names.

I raised my voice. I wanted to make sure Janet could hear me, and if the parents in the waiting room overheard, I didn't mind.

"I'm not a patient—Janet, is it? I don't have an appointment. I'm here representing Emma Marsden. I'm a private detective, and she's my client. You do know who Emma Marsden is? Her child, Ned, two and a half, was Dr. Tundridge's patient. I'm sure you remember Ned. He died of liver failure." I was aware of heads turning behind me, and I heard one woman hushing her child so she could hear. "If you'll recall, Dr. Tundridge accused Ms. Marsden of Munchausen by proxy—that's where a mother makes her own child ill—when Ms. Marsden objected to Dr. Tundridge keeping Ned's internal organs in the pathology lab you guys have down in the basement."

Janet was on her feet, face very pink. "Would you please have a seat, Ms. Padget? I'll have someone out to help you in just one moment. Just sit down, and I'll be right back."

I smiled. My pleasure.

I sat in the middle of a row of chairs, making myself available to talk.

The mother whose little girl was rolling under the chairs scooped her daughter up and sat down beside me.

"Excuse me for butting in, but I couldn't help but overhear what you said up there. Are you saying that Dr. Tundridge keeps children's organs in a lab down in the basement?"

I had the attention of every adult in the room.

"That's right. You can imagine how my client was very upset when she got a call from the clinic asking her to either come get them or pay a storage fee. She had no idea at all that the organs had been removed from her child's body. You can understand how she felt."

A man and a woman scooped up their toddler and headed to the reception desk. The man crossed a name out on the list, and the three of them left the office.

Janet appeared in the doorway. "Ms. Padget, could you come with me?"

I stood up and followed her down the hall.

I went slowly, looking at the line of examining rooms, studying the faces of the staff as they walked by.

"This is Mr. French," Janet said, and left me at the door of a small office where a large pear-shaped man sat behind a walnut desk. He stood up when he saw me. He wore a white lab coat, and like Janet, his name, Mr. French, was etched in pink thread.

"I'm Mr. French," he said, shaking my hand. He was a big teddy bear of a man with rectangular glasses on the end of his nose and a lot of curly brown hair. "Now you just sit down right there." He pointed to a leatherette armchair. "And you and I can have a talk."

I sat.

"Oh, where are my manners. Do you want some coffee, or maybe some herbal tea?"

"No. Thank you."

Mr. French did not seem the least bit hostile. This puzzled me.

"Now you, Miss Thing"—he shook a finger at me—"have been out in the waiting room causing trouble."

I didn't deny it.

"So why don't you tell Mr. French exactly what it is that you want?"

Why did I feel like I was talking to Santa Claus?

"I want to see your lab," I said.

"Oh, no, no, that would be off limits."

"And I want to talk to Dr. Tundridge about Emma Marsden, and his real reasons for accusing her in the death of her son. His real, financial, genetic-material-patenting reasons."

He tapped a finger against the arm of his chair. "Yes. Yes, that's a sad, sad case. Poor little Ned. We were all very upset when he died. He was one of the really sick ones. It tears me up, the whole thing. To hurt your own child—"

"Emma Marsden didn't hurt her child, and Dr. Tundridge didn't make that accusation until she objected to his practice of retaining the body parts."

"Mrs. Marsden gave us permission."

"No, she didn't. Not unless you count that ridiculous permission statement you have on your Web site."

"It's perfectly legal, you know."

"It's perfectly ridiculous, you know."

Mr. French took a deep breath. "Personally, Lena, I agree with you. I'd like to see our permission forms get more explicit. I'd like things explained better. It's one of the things I'm working on with Dr. Tundridge as well as the other physicians in this practice. But for now, all I can tell you is that it is legal."

"Dr. Tundridge has made these accusations before."

"Dr. Tundridge is vigilant. Understand this, Lena. I've worked with him for many years. He is a truly dedicated researcher. Between you and Mr. French, his people skills could use a *little* work. He has that doctoritis thing—you know what I mean, don't you?"

I leaned back in my chair. I knew what he meant, I just couldn't believe he was admitting it.

He laughed deeply enough to make his belly shake. "Lena, I have been a nurse for twenty years—from back when men weren't nurses, you know? I've suffered a lot of nonsense from that old bugaboo doctoritis. And I don't like it, not at all, but it's like working with bees, my dear, you're going to get stung, that's just life.

"But doctoritis does not make Dr. Ted a bad man. No, no, it just makes him an arrogant one, and bless his little heart, how could he not be with the brainwashing he got in medical school, and, you didn't hear it from me, a mother that absolutely positively dotes?"

"Mr. French, I'd like to talk to Dr. Tundridge personally. Are you going to let me do that?"

"No, my dear, I'm not, because if I did, then I wouldn't be doing my job of running this clinic. I can't bother the doctors with harassment."

"Perhaps you could give him a message for me then. Could you do that?"

"I could and maybe even would, depending on the message."

"Tell Dr. Tundridge that Emma Marsden will be going to the newspapers with the story of what goes on down in the lab here in the Tundridge Clinic."

"There's not a thing goes on here that isn't legal."

"It may not play well in the court of public opinion."

"Mr. French gets your drift."

"Good. And also tell him that we know he sent the videotape to the police. Maybe he even hired someone to film it. Looking for dirt on Emma Marsden, the patient who had the guts to stand up to him."

"That is absolutely not true."

"Of course it's true. It had to come from this office. Who else knew anything about the details of the case? Nothing else makes any sense."

"Prove it, my girl." The phone rang on his desk and he picked it up. "Janet? They're here? Good, good, send them on back." He stood up. "And speaking of the police."

I heard voices in the hallway, a man and a woman. Two uniformed patrol officers stopped in the doorway. I recognized one of them.

"McFee? That you? Not guarding the warehouses anymore?"

"Hello, Lena." McFee, a big guy with a square fighter's face, saluted. "You know Bonnie Maguire? Patrolwoman Maguire, Lena Padget."

"Hello," Bonnie Maguire said from the doorway. She had red hair, cut short and flipped up in the back, dark eyebrows, and the anxiety of a new hire.

"You know Detective Joel Mendez?" McFee asked her.

"No."

"Well, anyway, Lena is his significant other."

Mr. French tapped the top of his desk. "Excuse me, police people! I want this woman removed from the premises and arrested for trespassing."

"What woman?" McFee asked.

"I think he means me, Chris." I looked over at Mr. French. "You do mean me, right?"

"She's trespassing. Please handcuff her and lead her out."

McFee frowned and turned to face Mr. French. "What do you mean, trespassing? I was walking down the hallway, and all I heard was a normal conversation between you. It even sounded friendly. It sounded friendly to you, didn't it, Bonnie?"

"Yes, Chris, I have to say it did."

"Are you the party who called the police?" McFee asked.

Mr. French folded his arms. "I asked someone on my staff to make the call."

"And what seems to be the problem?"

"I want this woman to leave."

"Did you ask her to leave?"

"No."

"Why didn't you just ask her?"

"She's clearly here to cause trouble."

"If you could explain that to me, sir."

Mr. French picked up the phone on his desk. "Yes, Janet, please come in, thank you."

I crossed my legs. Janet didn't take long. She stood in the doorway, and McFee waved her in.

Mr. French lifted his chin. "Janet, would you—"

"Excuse me, sir," McFee said. "Ma'am. This lady here in the chair. Did you speak with her?"

"Yes, I did."

"What did she say?"

"She asked to see Dr. Tundridge. But she didn't have an appointment."

"No appointment?" McFee said.

"No, sir."

"And then what?"

"She told me she was representing a client named Emma Marsden, whose son used to be a patient here."

"And did you ask her to leave?"

"No, I asked her to wait in the waiting room."

"And what did she do?"

"She waited. She also talked to some of the parents in there."

"I see. And then what?"

"Then I took her to Mr. French's office."

McFee turned to Mr. French. "And you asked her to leave?"

"No."

"You didn't ask her to leave?"

"He offered me coffee," I said. McFee gave me a look.

"Did you offer her coffee?" McFee asked.

Mr. French nodded. "Of course I did. I wanted to keep things smooth until you came to arrest her."

"Sir, we don't arrest people for going to a doctor's office without an appointment."

"She was obviously here to cause trouble."

"It doesn't look like she caused trouble to me. If you had asked her to leave, and she refused, then you might have a point. But you offered her coffee. Mr. French, I don't want to come across as a hard-ass, but the department doesn't like it when people file a false police report. You can get in a lot of trouble. The line of thinking is that even if you think of it as some kind of joke, like a prank, you know? Then officers like myself and Ms. Maguire are distracted answering prank calls, when we might be needed somewhere else. Who knows, someone could be injured or even killed because we didn't get there soon enough because we were here instead."

"This was certainly not a prank."

"Well, you know, trying to have someone arrested falsely, that's even worse."

"Then I want a restraining order so she can't come back."

"Sir, you have to go through the proper procedures for getting a restraining order, and you have to show cause."

"At least make her leave, then."

"You mean, escort her out?"

"That's exactly what I mean."

"But that might embarrass her. And then she could sue the police department, and she could sue you, and she could win. And I don't think any of us want that."

"But what if she won't leave?"

"I suggest you ask her to leave, and if she doesn't, you can call the police. Good day, sir. Lena. See you around."

I waited till they were out of the room, then looked over at Janet and Mr. French.

"Is there something you wanted to say to me?"

Mr. French glared at me. "As a matter of fact—"

"It's okay," I told him. "I'm going."

I waited till I was back out in the parking lot to eat my cherry lollipop. I didn't want to be accused of stealing.

Chapter Eleven

That morning Emma was sick. Wally always came when Emma was sick. Good old Wally. The dog knew. No one else seemed to have figured it out.

She was very sick.

The attack had arrived like the ones before, except it came in the morning instead of the middle of the night. The pain usually came with no warning, waking her from a sound sleep.

The first thing she always did was check the clock. On the average, the attacks lasted three hours, give or take.

The pain hit like a sheath of red light between her breast bone and the edge of her right rib cage. Upper right quadrant, was how the WebMD article had put it. The pain was simple and cruel. No throb, no coming and going, no pressure that could be relieved by shifting position. Just pain, radiating through her; she could feel it all the way to her back. There was no possibility of comfort, but the best position involved sitting cross-legged, left shoulder against the bathroom wall, right arm wrapped around her midsection to support the muscles that ran beneath the area of pain.

It had to be the bathroom wall, of course, because it had to be the bathroom, and she had to be sitting on the linoleum floor in front of the toilet. The toilet lid was up, seat down because sometimes she had to use it to support herself. She set a watch on the bathroom counter, propping it so she could see it from the floor, next to a glass of water for rinsing her mouth. She wet a washrag, wrung it out, and folded it neatly.

This morning she'd forgotten the sweater and the socks. The first wave of intense nausea floated like an oil slick in her belly. She dreaded it—the wrenching vomiting coupled with the pain in her side and the not knowing where it came from or why. The first time she'd thought it might kill her. Then she realized that whatever it was would only kill her slowly, and she'd suffer, so there was no happiness there. She didn't like doctors, or hospitals, or emergency rooms. Well, how stupid, who did? But somehow in the middle of these attacks she didn't care what they might do to her in an emergency room. They could cut her open and remove things and leave angry red scars like zippers in her pale skin. They could drug her and overcharge her and put her in debt. They could be rude, or boss her around, or treat her like she had no choice and no control. Those kinds of things only worried her when the attacks were over. The one thing she could not let them do, and the one thing they very well might do, was take her daughter Blaine off to foster care. They would say she was making herself sick. She was not to be trusted. And that was the one thing she could not allow. You could say she was being paranoid. Or you could say she was being a good and careful mother. You could say she was playing with fire and taking a risk, you could say she was letting them bully her, you could say she was letting them win. You could say every one of those things, and all of them would be true.

But you couldn't really say she had a choice.

She was cold. Shivering. She staggered to the bedroom.

She'd put her arms through the sleeves of an old cotton sweater just as the nausea became impossible to keep down, and she popped her head through the neck hole and ran back to the bathroom, throwing up so violently that she had to balance on one knee and stretch the other leg out behind her, toes to the floor, like a runner's stretch. She held the edges of the toilet bowl so she would not fall. She heaved again and again, managed to catch a breath, heaved again. Kept heaving still after every last bit of food and fluid was flushed from her system, and there was nothing left but the burn of acid in her throat, and the white froth that she threw up now instead of bile. Her body wasn't making bile anymore, and she did not know why, but she was researching it, along with her other symptoms, online. She wasn't going to let whatever this was kill her. She had boundaries.

Pain level eight, she would tough it out. Pain level nine, she would get help, and pain level ten, go to an emergency room. Vomiting bright red blood—emergency room. Attack lasting over eight hours—emergency room. She had done her research, and was careful to take no medication for pain or nausea so she would mask no symptoms, not flying blind like she was; she didn't want to die, after all.

The vomiting subsided. She rinsed her mouth, spit spit spit into the toilet bowl, flushed it again. Wiped her mouth on the front of the sweater, spit again, wiped her mouth again, used the washrag to bathe her face.

Wally watched from the doorway, head on paws, a look of compassion in her eyes. She did not question Emma, she was just there. Dogs never questioned you, they never got mad, not even when Emma once told Wally to stop wagging her tail did the dog so much as blink. Dogs were so much better than people.

Emma wanted to lean against the wall, but she was afraid to move. If she stayed very very still, she might not throw up for a while. She checked her watch. Only twenty minutes into the attack. Two hours and forty minutes more, at the very least.

Just be very still, she thought, back aching, but her side hurt too much, and she shifted against the wall, and that set the nausea off, and she was once again on her knees throwing up hard and loud. Sometimes she cried when she felt like this, but not today. Today the pain was no more than a six, and she sweated and shook with the chills and leaned against the wall and watched the clock.

It was over in three hours and fifteen minutes, leaving her exhausted but relieved. She slept awhile afterward, dreaming of her mother, then woke, hungry but afraid to eat. She often thought that something she was eating set these attacks off, but as soon as she'd decide she knew what it was, it would be set off again by something else entirely.

She sat on the couch for a while, scratching Wally's ears and looking at the mess of her house.

Her mother had not been the most particular of housekeepers either, and that was something that she and Emma shared. Emma found herself thinking a lot about her mother these days—not so strange. When you were in trouble, you always turned to Mom.

Not there, of course, but somehow always with her, particularly in this small cottage of Great-Aunt Jodina's. The presence was subtle, but nonetheless quite a particular thing, like a scent, like the crisp feeling one has just after a breeze has blown through the window, scattering loose papers and enticing the dog to sit up, nose twitching.

The older she got the more she looked like her mother—bon vivant, curvaceous, dark hair, eyes electrically blue. Her mother had often been asked if she wore colored contacts, when such things became common. Emma had stood with her mom in a grocery store line while the woman ahead of them turned and said to her mother, "Are those your eyes?" as if they might have belonged to someone else.

Her mother had been enough like the other mothers to land in the comfort zones, but different enough to make Emma—and everyone else—pay attention. Everything had to be pretty—

pretty paper towels, pretty tissues, pretty napkins. Yes, the white ones in packs of one-point-twelve million were cheaper, at three cents a thousand, but so long as the budget was not too badly stretched, much better to buy fifty for three dollars and eighty-seven cents because they were thick and heavy and folded long-ways, and because they came in rich colors—deep greens, cobalt blues, the maroon of a marching band. Cloth napkins were even better, as far as Emma was concerned, but her mother had never used them. Her father, of course, had been king of the blue-light specials at Kmart, in the days before the domination of Wal-Mart, and Emma remembered walking way ahead of him in the parking lot once, pretending they were not together as he carried two bundles of toilet paper stacked twenty rolls high and sway-ing over his head like columns of embarrassment. He pretended not to notice how she had distanced herself, but her mother had laughed and called to her across the asphalt, shouting, "Emma, hon? Can you come help us with this *toilet paper?*" Good ole Mom. Now, of course, she was disposed to torture her own daughter Blaine in the same way. You never really appreciated how amusing these things could be until you had a teenager of your own to annoy.

Her mother's passion was her old horse, Empress, a skittish mare, half Arab, half saddlebred, and all nerve. Her mother had bought the show horse, then freed her from the cruel bits and the severe German martingales used to tie her head down. People were afraid to ride this mare without fierce controls, because for the horse, riding meant *pain,* and pain meant run, which meant the only way to stop her was to apply more pain or pray.

But Emma's mother had seen the mare's gentle heart and her will to please, and had brought her home, and never again put anything but a simple snaffle bit in her sensitive, damaged mouth. The mare was never safe to ride anywhere but in the tiny round pen, where Emma's mother would walk her, round and round, cutting across, making a figure eight, the mare always moving with the action and grace that had racked up ribbon after ribbon in horse shows in Kentucky, Florida, and Tennessee, back in the days of cruel bits and martingales and the breakneck speed of the hand gallop. Empress moved so sharply in the oval of the show ring that her rider could have scooped dirt between his leather-gloved fingers, had he felt inclined and safe enough to take his hands from the reins.

Her mother had sent the horse to a trainer once, someone known to work slowly and with kindness, but he'd sent the mare back in two months, bringing her himself in his silver six-horse trailer and battered pickup truck. Emma had been watching, listening. She remembered his heavily gloved hands and the matter-of-fact way he led the horse out of the van; she remembered the mare rolling her eyes and snorting as if she'd never seen the barn before, quieting only at her mother's touch, but still dancing sideways at every shadow and sound.

The trainer had just kind of shrugged at her mother. "The mare's just too old—experience wise, if you know what I mean—for me to make that much difference. I'm wasting your money, and to tell you the truth I'd rather be working a horse where I can make a difference."

"She's a good horse," her mother had said.

"I don't mean that." The trainer had pointed to the grooves over the mare's eyes. "That's always the sign of a kind heart and an old soul, but she's never going to trust me or anybody else enough to get where she doesn't spook six ways to Sunday over every little thing. I've sacked her out; she's better. But if you don't work with her every day, she'll just go back to her old self. You're not going to get the spook and run out of her—not with those bloodlines, and not with the kind of past she's had. Course, you can get another opinion."

But Emma's mother had not wanted another opinion, and she'd seemed content to just ride Empress around that round pen, and gradually the horse had calmed down and learned that riding wasn't so very bad. She'd walk around that pen quietly with her head down, instead of nose to the air like she'd been when Emma's mother had first brought her home. Emma remembered somebody stopping by watching her mom on the horse, and saying what a quiet little mare she was. She remembered how her mama had grinned at Emma over the woman's head and then just smiled and said "thank you very much."

She was a smart horse. She'd had a bad infection once, and Emma's mother had to inject her twice a day with penicillin, a painful shot, and yet Empress had stood quietly, and her mother had been able to administer the shot in the mare's short, stocky neck, with one hand, while holding the halter with the other.

And while the house might be kept half-assed, the barn was always clean and organized, and one thing Emma remembered more than anything was leading the mare into her stall at the end of the day. In her memory it was always fall, and chilly, and getting dark early enough that it was dark by the time Emma brought the horse in. She remembered the red and gold of the leaves, the crisp chill in the air, and the way the barn looked, all lit up, as she walked in the dark through the field. Empress would trot along beside her, anxious for her bin of sweet feed, and the evening pleasure of slowly munching the orchard-grass hay after the lustful gorging on feed, the stall clean and pungent with the smell of cedar wood shavings, a bucket of cold clean water, and the mineral block the horse liked to scrape with her teeth. Emma loved tucking a horse into a stall for the night, and no matter what anybody told her about horses being better off outdoors twenty-four hours a day, she knew that Empress, at least, liked the coming and going, in the barn, out of the barn, and being snug inside a clean, well-bedded stall with plenty of good food and clean water, a bit of apple or carrot, and always a kind loving word.

Her father had sold that little country cottage where she grew up, the three acres with the sagging tobacco barn and the little round pen, and the paddock circled by the black four-plank fencing that had to be patrolled and maintained. She had a strong memory of her mother, in that torn blue flannel shirt she used to wear around the barn, hammering away at some sagging board with a mallet because as usual she'd misplaced the hammer, and the mallet worked better anyhow.

Her mother had depressions. Times when she was listless and sad. She still did the mom things—the laundry was clean, if not folded, the meals were cooked—but only the bare minimum was done, and then her mother would spend hours curled up with a radio, unmoving and dull. It was something that Emma accepted then and now. A brilliant exuberance like her mother's was often balanced, or, more accurately, weighed down, by dark things. It had driven her father nuts, and she had memories of him shouting at her mother, telling her to snap out of it, and her mother telling him to go to hell.

It was the horse who always brought her mother out of the dark periods. Emma learned to facilitate with small steps—just an invitation to come with her to the barn and keep her company while she groomed the horse. But then she'd hand her mother a brush, and the very act of stroking the horse seemed to provide some kind of comfort for her mother's soul. It was hard to explain, but something Emma felt herself. She had not gotten the depression gene, but it was something that ran strongly in her mother's family, from what she gathered from little hints about sour maiden aunts or angry cousins. For that reason, Emma saw depression as a sickness, not a weakness. Nothing shameful, mainly just miserable, something that had to be taken care of so it could pass. She watched Blaine and found that her daughter had the same tendency. One could not be sure—all adolescents had bouts of depression—but Blaine seemed to hit the searing depths, like her grandmother. Depths that made Emma read up on antidepressants. It was a subject of conversation she learned to avoid. She found that the word *depression* meant other things to other people, and that she was rare in her inclination to take it in stride, like a sprained ankle, a tendency to freckle and burn in direct sunlight, an allergy to wool.

Emma had canceled all her dance lessons for the week as soon as the article in the paper came out. She knew it was the worst thing she could do, but she did it anyway. She wasn't ready to face people. But it was a mistake staying in the house all the time. She needed to get out. And she knew where she wanted to go. She gave Wally another pat and wandered through the house, looking for her car keys.

CHAPTER TWELVE

Emma's mother was buried in one of the smaller cemeteries—nothing at all like Lexington Cemetery, with its cultivated gardens, lush walkways, and historical significance.

Emma knew her way on the worn, snaking asphalt drive that wound in figure eights in and around the various graves—some marked with small headstones, family plots made noticeable by large monuments proclaiming their surname as if it were an advertisement. Her mother was buried in one of the newer sections, and when she had first been laid to rest, it had one or two large old trees, and a lot of new saplings. Emma supposed that she would always think of it as one of the newer sections, though the saplings were tall now, and lush, the grass thick and well rooted for not being recently dug up.

The tombstone was a doublewide, the plot next to her mother on reserve for her dad. He had remarried several times since, and Emma looked forward to the day when his latest wife would put him defiantly to rest into a cemetery of her own family choice, hopefully miles and miles away from Kentucky, and her mother's own resting spot. Then Emma would have the headstone removed and a new one put in, this of rose marble, and bearing her mother's name only, and it would be back to back with the small white lamb that marked her son's resting place. She would have liked to have them side by side, but it was only back to back, head to head, that was available. She had been surprised to learn that you can bury more than one person in a grave; you could bury up to three. The knowledge had been given to her with kindness and a practicality regarding the cost of funerals.

She'd brought Neddie a toy. Wrapped up, because like all small children he had loved presents. It was a little thing, a Pez dispenser in the shape of a dinosaur. He'd have loved it, and really, it was not quite a good idea for his age, as he'd have chewed the head off, possibly choking—Ned put everything in his mouth in the universal way of toddlers. But it posed no danger to him now, and she left it in the paws of the lamb that marked his grave. She stroked the head of the lamb, taking small comfort in the rough concrete, running a finger along the carved edges of the stony ears.

She did not feel guilty about being ready to be happy again. Her son's death would stay with her always, like a scar on her cheek, and it was an integral part of her, that regret, that *missing him,* but she was ready now to be happy again.

Except she was never quite sure that she'd followed the rules for a proper show of grief. There were rules about such things, and while the rules might change with the people around you, they were as tangible as the ground on which you stood. And if you violated those rules—it was as if you had cut the ground from beneath the feet of the friends, acquaintances, and even strangers who watched your sorrow so judgmentally. They did not know what to do with their discomfort, but they sure as hell knew who to blame.

People were so odd in their expectations. You were supposed to grieve forever the loss of a parent or child, but to do it in such a way that you never intruded upon their happiness. Make sure to keep the anger out of the way. And please, no self-pity. You are never supposed to get over it, but you are also supposed to almost, but not completely, hide this fact. The thing is, when they look for your grief, sniffing away at your tragedy like dogs in the woods, they want to be rewarded with the smell of something. There had to be something tangible for them to see, something to let them know that it was there, as if it not being there meant that it could come from behind and mount a surprise attack. People had to see something to validate their pity for you, and to separate you from them, so that they were always safe from bad things, because they don't know how you handle it, they simply could simply not.

Her mother, on the other hand, had been expected to be brave, and to pretend that nothing had happened and that her life was still happy thanks to courage, tenaciousness, and the art of medical science. Because her mother had taken that mare out to ride, out of the round pen, on just the kind of October day that Emma liked to remember, and the horse had spooked and bolted and after three years in the round pen, well, hell, her mother just didn't have the legs she used to when she really rode, and down she'd gone, breaking two of the vertebrae in her back.

The strange thing was her walking back to the barn—catching the horse first, leading her along as she limped across the pasture, calling to the house, to Emma, who was annoyed at being interrupted, couldn't her mother see that she was *on the phone,* did she always have to call her like that, and in that tone of voice?

Her mother had looked scary pale. She had gone into the house to lie down and handed the horse over to Emma, warning her to cool the mare down and to rub her with a rag, one of those old cloth diapers, her mother liked those best. Emma had been annoyed, but immediately solicitous because her mother had looked off, sort of, and mother and daughter were very close, close enough for Emma to understand something was very wrong.

Her mother had made it in the front door, getting no farther than the couch, and if she'd looked pale at the barn, she was chalk white by the time Emma made it back to the house.

"You're okay, then," her mother had said, as soon as she'd set foot in the door. "She didn't give you any trouble?"

"No, Mom, not really."

"And she's okay."

"She's fine, Mom. Can I get you something? Some Advil and a Coke? Do you want me to call Dad?"

"Your father?" Her mother had thought about it. They were not close, her parents, something Emma had not noticed at the time, thinking, as everyone does, that her family was the soul of normality. It was mainly Emma and her mother, and the animals—Empress, whatever dogs or cats they'd had at the time. Once, for a brief while, there'd been a bird.

"Mom, you really should let me drive you to a hospital."

"I think you're right."

That sentence had heralded the beginning. That sentence had woken Emma up, and let her know that things with her mother were very, very bad.

Emma had put the seat as far back as she could on the Mazda, and added a blanket on the bucket seat and a pillow, and her mother had cried, suddenly, when she was helping her to the car, slipping against the side door because she couldn't make her leg work or support her weight. Emma had caught her, awkwardly, and sort of rolled her into the front seat, and she had been rended by the tear track in the dirt on her mother's cheek. Jesus, even when they'd had horrible childhood accidents or illnesses, involving vomit, blood, and stitches, her mother had always had her take a bubble bath first, and put on clean clothes.

They had joked on the way to the emergency room. Carrying on mock mother-and-daughter fights—now, now, watch your driving, slow down, and all that, though Emma, unlike her usual habit of "driving like a Frenchman," her mother always called it, kept her speed so slow that she was passed, honked at, and cursed by impatient drivers on that long drive in from the farm.

They'd been rescued at the turnoff onto Old Frankfort Pike from Pisgah, the vet that saw to Empress driving up behind them in his truck with "Woodford All Creatures" stenciled on the side. He'd honked and gotten out and appeared at Emma's elbow, his sunburned face and permanent eye crinkles as welcome as Superman in a cape.

"What's wrong, Emma? Kitty? Did you fall off that damn mare?"

"It wasn't her fault."

"No, it was yours for taking her out of that round pen."

Emma had flushed and been ready to defend her mother— after all, the last thing she needed when she was hurt was to be yelled at—and her memory of how she herself had complained about having her phone call interrupted by her mother's call for help was conveniently, though temporarily, absent.

But her mother had chuckled, and told him not to try and boss her around, and he had said heaven forbid, and Emma had been relieved, so very relieved, because even if she was eighteen, and mature for her age, sometimes you did want the grown-ups to take over.

The vet, Dr. Bender—Martin, her mother always called him—had opened the car door where her mother was sprawled, saying, "Lady, you don't look too comfortable."

Emma remembered very well how she had looked across at him and saw the way his smile had faded, saw the way he frowned when her mother said she couldn't roll sideways, she'd tried and she just couldn't no matter what. Emma had expected things to get more complicated then, had expected him to tell her to follow the truck, or call an ambulance, or even drive his truck, but they'd actually gotten simpler.

"Hop in the back there, Emma, while I move my truck to the

side of the road. I'm going to drive you all into the University Med Center."

"Baptist is closer," Emma's mother had said.

Martin Bender hadn't argued, and he hadn't moved Kitty an inch. He'd just driven them straight to the emergency room, telling them about a cow he'd delivered after coaxing her out of the pond where she'd been stuck, mired in mud and labor pains, all the while folding in precise little questions about how Kitty had fallen, and where she hit, and where it hurt, and the details of how she actually got up and walked, and other things that made Emma think that everything might be okay. Only his tone of voice, his air of something bad, told her something different. Still, she hung on to that one thing, that her mother had walked back to the barn. It was the other thing, her mother saying she could not roll sideways, that kept her hands bunched into fists.

It was a long, slow process. There were a lot of tests. But the end result was a wheelchair, the special kind where patients can move only their arms and their shoulders, and her mother had been ten days home from the hospital when she'd called Emma to her room. It was cold then. January. Christmas nothing more than the memory of a family straining to pretend a joy in the holidays that not a one of them felt.

They had talked for a long time, the two of them, Emma sitting by her mother's bed. Her mother was her old self, like she hadn't been since she'd gotten hurt, and Emma had remembered thinking, *Okay, I can do this. I've still got her, she's still here.* One is understandably selfish about one's own mother.

"Emma, honey, I need your help."

"Of course, Mom, anything. Tea and toast?" Emma made her mother toast broiled in the oven on white bread, a delicate, perfectly buttered treat her mother praised to the skies.

"I need something different from tea and toast. I need you to go to the drugstore for me, and get my prescription refilled. And

I need you to bring me in that bottle of Maker's Mark we have next to the china cabinet in the kitchen."

"You just got your prescription. I saw Dad bring it in last night."

"I know. And I want you to go and get the refill."

Emma had taken a long, slow breath, and her mother had put a hand on her head. "If there was any other way, I wouldn't involve you, honey. I'm not asking you for a decision. I've made that myself."

Emma had known, of course, what was in her mother's mind. She had heard the angry conversations behind bedroom walls, her mother railing at the doctors for refusing to help her do what she wanted to do, at her husband who had found the cache of pain pills she had so carefully saved away. He had taken them from her like you might snatch a cookie from an overindulgent child, and her mother had not even looked at her father since then.

"You can say no, Emma. You can say no, and I won't be mad at you. I'll just find another way. But if you help me, you'll just make it easier for me. I won't stay like this. I won't be brave. For me, this is not a life."

"What about me?" Emma had said.

"Honey, you're eighteen, well, nineteen now, and you have two years left of college, and then you're going to grad school in Denver just like you planned. I've got all that money set away."

"I won't leave you."

"Yes, I know, that's exactly what I'm afraid of. You have to live your life, Emma. And I have to live mine. Now mine is over. And it's been a good one. But this that I have left, this isn't a life for me, much as I love you. I'm in so much pain, honey. And it's only going to get worse. And I've got two arms now and shoulders and a head, but I'll lose ground. That's my future, and it's one I don't want. I don't care what's socially acceptable. Can I make you understand that dying isn't the worst thing that can happen? Can I make you understand that for me, dying is another form of life that is much better than this? Can you respect me and love me enough to let me make up my own mind?"

"You're sure?"

"I'm sure. I'd do the same for you. Martin Bender will take Empress and turn her out with his horses when you head off to Denver."

"You've got it all worked out."

"Can you see this as a choice, and a simple end of the day for me?"

"Sure, Mom."

She'd done it, and she'd never regretted it. She'd gotten the pills and handed her mother the bottle of Maker's Mark. She'd wanted to stay, but her mother had forbidden it. Her mother had kissed her good-bye and told her to feed the horse, leave the door open so the dogs could come in, and head out for her evening class as planned.

"We don't want to let them know you helped me, Emma. That stays between you and me."

"They'll know somebody had to help you."

"I've got that covered too."

"How?"

"Kiss me good-bye, Emma. And know that what you are doing is the kindest, kindest, most respectful thing any mother ever had to ask of a daughter. I hope someday you have a daughter just like you. And know this"—and her mother had tugged on Emma's sleeve, pulling the cotton material out of shape—"I will always watch over you, and I will always be with you. I am going to be with my mother and my father, and I am going to be happy and okay like I can't be in this body I'm in right now. If I had any choice other than to have you help me . . . but there is no one but you, honey. I need you more now than I've ever needed anybody. Don't let me down."

And Emma hadn't. She hadn't let her mother down.

But she hadn't finished school, and she hadn't gone to Denver, and somehow her father had known. Instead, she'd worked low-end jobs, and gotten pregnant with Blaine, and married his father, a son of a bitch she'd stayed married to for seven long stupid years, till she dreamed that she had lunch with her mother, and told her she was getting a divorce and not to try to change her mind or talk her out of it, and her mother had patted her hand and said, *Honey, what took you so long?*

Round the corner, a backhoe and crew worked the ground to open a grave site for someone new to death, and at the genuinely new section across from her mother's grounds, a green awning and chair were set up for another service. For a small cemetery, there was always plenty of activity. Off in the distance, Emma could hear traffic, but here behind the fence and among the trees and tombstones, it was quiet. She left the toy by the lamb on Ned's grave, and moved over to face her mother's tombstone.

"So there you are," Emma said. She sat down cross-legged in the grass, and the ground felt cold against her thighs. But the sun was bright, and it was October in Kentucky, and with any luck the temperature might hit seventy, or more likely, sixty-eight degrees. Or maybe not. The air had that crisp edge to it that meant the first frost might surge, when the temperature dropped on the outgoing tides of darkness and night.

You and I have business, Mama my dear. Because you owe me. You owe me, and you failed me once, but I'm giving you another chance and calling in your debt.

I know I haven't been here in ages. Eighteen months, and no little visits, no flowers on your birthday, no tears or fond memories on Mother's Day. No pats on the tombstones or nostalgic memories. I've made it a point not to even think about you, because when I do, it makes me mad.

You know, when you died, I was here every day. Then maybe a few times a week. Nobody knew how often I came here, nobody but you. And it got funny because every time I sat down to have a good cry, there'd be some damn backhoe and a huge noise of digging or some such mundane and noisy thing to interrupt my peace. I suppose you thought that was funny. I didn't blame you then.

But that was because I was nineteen, Mama, and didn't know any better.

And like all good grieving, mine followed the usual pattern. I came less and less. At first, it was the only place I could find peace, because it was the only physical way to be with you, a place where I could sit with your remains and your commemorative tombstone, which by the way, you might never have gotten if I hadn't guilted Dad into it by telling him I'd like it in place before he actually remarried. Otherwise, you might still be waiting. I sure as hell couldn't have afforded to buy you one. Not then, anyway.

I know it isn't fair to blame you because Ned died. I know you would have interceded if you could. I know that my hours here—praying to God, and begging you to look after him . . . not foolish, I think, and certainly worth a try. It shakes my faith in you, just a little, but I suppose if dead relatives could keep all bad things from happening, no bad things would happen. I'm sure you did what you could. I'm sure the two of you are together now, and that you look out for him. Believe it or not, it gives me peace of heart to know you are together, because I believed you, in that dream, when you came to me and said you'd watch out for me, always. Watching out for me means watching out for my babies.

For the longest time, Mama, I couldn't figure out why Ned dying meant I was so angry at you. It's not that I blamed you for his death. It's just that his death, my grief . . . it stripped away all the bullshit, and the excuses I made for you, and left me with the hard cold THING. You killed yourself. And you made me help you.

And now that I am older and wiser and have children of my own, now I see what a terrible thing that was that you did to me.

I'm not much for suicide, Mama. Those of us who survive those of you who do it never are. We turn a deaf ear to the excuses, because we know how the reality of the act rips the people who loved you right in two. Only, in your case, I can see it. Paralyzed, the prognosis that you would lose more mobility as time went on, constantly in pain, and mar-

ried to a shit like Dad . . . I have to say that yes, I can see it. I could make the same choice—yep, I admit it, in that circumstance only because for me and obviously for you, that isn't life. So it's not like ending life, but it's more like ending a death-life.

One thing for sure, between you and Ned, I am definitely not afraid to die. I see it for the blessing and the relief that it is. And once in a while I catch myself thinking, not just "beautiful day" but that if . . . I mean when I die, it wouldn't be so bad if it was a day like today. Sometimes I envy you here, because all the cares and the worries and the bad things . . . they don't mean anything to a woman in your position, as in six feet under. Nothing can hurt you now.

But you should have never involved me. You should have found a way not to put me in the middle of it. You should at the very least have protected me from the rage of good old Dad, who did not give me the money you so generously left me in your will, the money that would have seen me through school and a whole other life. When you died, that other life went with you, and you left your mark, your suicide mark, on me.

So Mommy darling, I won't say as yet I forgive you, and I won't say I'll be here to visit you like I used to do, because forgiveness, as they say in bridge, isn't my long suit.

I do ask you one thing. And that is that you look after Blaine, and don't let them take her away from me. Keep her safe and keep her with me, and let me take care of her the best way I can, because really, Mom, when it comes right down to it, as good as you were, I'm an even better mother than you were, because not only did you teach me what to do, you also taught me what not to do. So you just keep your eye on her—you watch over her like you said in the dream, and I'll do the rest, because I'm not like you, Mama. I never give in, and I never give up.

Emma did not bother with her seat belt. The cemetery speed limit was about ten miles per hour. She had thought she'd cry this morning, and had brought a box of Kleenex, but the box sat unopened in the seat beside her, and she was as dry-eyed as a stone.

She felt bad about the way she had talked to her mother. In her mind's eye she could see her mother walking that mare who killed her, the horse well-meaning but afraid, while her mother spoke to her in low comforting tones, letting the mare settle and lose her fear. Her mother had always told her that animals suffer when they are afraid. Emma had pushed those memories away since her mother died, all the times with that mare, all the mornings she'd seen her mother grooming the horse, combing through the tangled mane, rubbing the yellow bots off the mare's legs with the pumice stone, right around this time of year. All the times she herself had led the mare in, gentled now, so that her mother felt safe letting Emma bring Empress in from the field, out of the dusk and settling darkness, into the warm and well-lit barn.

The flush of shame made Emma's cheeks go pink. Her mother had needed her help at the end. That was all. Her mother had not given up, she had simply accepted what had happened, and for her it was not a life. She had a right to that decision. She had the right not to stay just to humor her family.

When had Emma let the world's stock of judgmental hypocrites tell her that her mother had been wrong?

Emma, glancing to her left, noticed the person putting a wreath on a grave at the far end of her mother's section, but she followed the code rules of cemetery politeness, so she did not stare, or nod hello. And in truth, she was deep in thought as she drove by, and did not look into her rearview mirror, where she would have been intrigued to see the person put the wreath back in the trunk, cross the lawn to Ned's grave, and pick up the small wrapped gift she'd left in the paws of the small stone lamb.

CHAPTER THIRTEEN

Emma hadn't gone into the studio at all yesterday, and was finding less and less urge to dance. She had closed down her own studio while Ned was sick, thinking she could open back up again later. The opportunity to get out of a three-year lease had come up when the optometrist next door had wanted to expand, and he'd dropped by with an air of apology, mentioning that he wasn't trying to take advantage of her problems with a sick child, but if she was feeling trapped by the lease and wanted to let it go, he'd be glad to take it over. The building owners had agreed—all she had to do was sign, and she was off the hook.

Emma supposed he'd noticed that the clientele had dwindled along with the economy. In truth, she had not seriously considered shutting the place down until he'd stopped by, a nice man, slender, with thinning blond hair, wire-rim glasses, and a sweet smile. He'd fixed her sunglasses once for free, like they'd been Ray-Bans instead of Wal-Mart specials.

So she'd let the lease go, and had joined a new studio over in Homburg Place, an easy drive from her little cottage. Instead of carrying the mixed burdens and blessings of self-ownership, her own studio, and doing everything her way, she worked at a studio co-op owned by the dance teachers themselves. You paid a reasonable monthly fee, and whatever you made from your students was yours to keep. Plus, you had the practice area whenever you needed it, a private locker, and the company, good and bad, of other professionals—real professionals who were in the business for the long haul, not people you'd coaxed in off the streets.

Her teaching load was moderate right now, but the students she had were committed regulars, and without the overhead of the studio weighing down the finances, and without having to pay rent or mortgage, or car payments, she was doing okay. She'd done very well in the competitions before Ned had died, managing to put some prize money in savings, in fact felt she'd hit a creative turning point. When her son became ill, she'd been unable to compete, and had sadly, grinding her teeth, but trying to be fair, wished her dance partner well when he'd moved on to work with someone else. The only competitions she'd done since were the pro-ams, where she danced with her students. She enjoyed those enough that not competing did not seem the blow she'd thought it would be. She was oddly content, which bothered her. She'd danced all her life, achieved her lifelong dream of her own studio, and had been doing well in professional competitions (her specialty the mambo). Letting all of that slide away seemed like a betrayal of everything she'd worked toward all of her life. But she didn't get the pleasure out of it that she used to; she was happy to teach, dance with her advanced students, and enjoy the dance nights and the occasional workshops she took herself. She had always assumed that she was on a straight uphill climb where she would rise further and further in her field, and now she was leveling out, even dipping backward. But she was tired of worrying about bills, and the studio, and how to lure in enough clientele to keep all of her teachers happy, and making enough money to stay that way, and should she expand, and how could she let people know she was not high pressure like the competition without *being* high pressure like the competition, and should she sell dance shoes, and if so, should she also sell costumes, and how much price break should she give on the package deals . . . and the million and one other things she had worried about for years now. For absolute years. She was tired of it all, and what had once been a joy had been grinding her down to fine dust. It seemed she had lost her ambition. Maybe she should do what she'd planned to do all those many years ago and go to vet school.

Right now, she was happy to do as little as possible. Enough teaching to live on, that's all she wanted. It made her feel lazy, but in truth, she felt that maybe she deserved a rest. She had worked so hard for so many years, two jobs, or hours and hours at just one, practicing and keeping her body in shape to dance, and God, since Ned had gotten sick she'd gained a good thirty pounds, and what was she doing right now but drinking a Coca-Cola and sucking on a Tootsie Roll Pop like every other fat American.

She marveled at the woman she used to be, the woman who took care of Blaine, worked the PTA chili suppers, was once actually the cookie chairman of Brownie Troop 113; the woman who kept the house in fairly good shape, cooked dinner most weeknights, taught at other people's dance studios until she opened her own, and sometimes took on a temporary job when the dancing money did not come in fast enough to keep her and Blaine in good funds. Living with Clayton had spoiled her; two incomes instead of one.

The slam of a car door brought her head up, and she went into the living room just as her daughter's voice drifted in through the open windows. Blaine was in a good mood. She could always tell by the way her daughter walked up the front steps, across the porch, and through the front door how good or bad her day had been. More often than not it was bad, and Emma worried late at night and couldn't sleep. There is no such thing as a happy teenager, but Emma wondered how much of Blaine's unhappiness was due to losing her little brother, losing her pseudo stepfather, moving one more time to a new school and having to make a whole new set of friends, a difficult math teacher . . . any of the one hundred and one things that can go wrong for any teenager, and Blaine's load was heavier than most.

Nobody has a perfect life, she told her daughter, and she had to remind herself of the same thing. It's a funny thing, when you have a child, how reason gets sucked away. You look at that baby and feel yourself changed, and you know that there is nothing you won't do to keep your child's life safe and happy. And you vow that nothing bad will ever happen to one of your children; you will be that much more diligent, that much more careful; watchful, wise, caring . . . in short, perfect. The kind of stupid things all new parents think, in the same category with *Nobody touches the baby until they've washed their hands with antiseptic, My child will never eat candy, My child will watch no television and only play with educational toys, and will only be fed homegrown organic foods with no additives and preservatives.* And then somehow there you are, turning on cartoons the minute they walk in the door, tossing a frozen pizza into the oven, and burrowing through the basket of clean but never folded clothes to find them something clean to wear to school.

"Hey, sweetie!"

"Hey." Semi-surly, and just a flicker of eye contact.

"How was school?"

"Ummm." Blaine went to her bedroom and shut the door.

The thump of Blaine's stereo muffled the noise of a tractor that had been thrumming through the air as Emmet Michaels, who owned the farm behind them, worked his fields for the last cutting of hay. Emma preferred the tractor. She looked at the phone extension in the living room and saw that the red light flickered. Her daughter was already plugged in.

She went into the kitchen. Staying near the refrigerator would be the most likely place for the next sighting of her daughter, and by then maybe Blaine would have a few words to say. Emma did not expect conversation until Blaine had been home for at least an hour—what she called after-school detox. She remembered what hell high school could be, especially a new high school. It was the idiots who told teenagers that they were going through the best years of their lives who caused all the trouble.

Emma was making biscuits. She wore her favorite "Mom Cat" apron, and, as usual when she cooked, was unintentionally spreading flour all over the kitchen. It had not gone unnoticed, how Marcus had appreciated Aunt Jodina's homemade biscuits, and Emma was baking them for him. She was feeling a contented domesticity that would have panicked her in her twenties. It was different, cooking for Marcus and Blaine, cooking for the three of them. Different than it had been cooking for Blaine's father, a chore, and for Clayton, less of a chore but definitely not a pleasure. Of course, in those days, she'd been slacking if she wasn't doing at least two or three things at once. Now, she had the pleasure of doing one thing at a time, guiltlessly. It wasn't the world that had changed, it was Emma.

Blaine appeared in the doorway. Emma gave her a floury hug and was rewarded with a tense little body and a cringing squint. Daughterly love.

"I'm making biscuits," Emma said to her daughter's back.

Blaine opened the refrigerator. "That's nice."

Emma felt a curious role reversal. As if she were a three-year-old telling her very uninterested mother about the picture she had colored and awaiting her dollop of praise. *Motherhood sucks.*

Still, she pinched off a chunk of the dough she was kneading and offered it offhandedly to her daughter, who took it with an actual smile. A child's love for raw dough in any form was one of the few things that did not change as they grew into hellions.

"So how was your day?" her daughter asked, though her nose was still in the fridge. Blaine slouched sideways, and Emma did not recognize the jeans she had on. For one, they were too big and too long, which probably meant they were borrowed from that kid Twyla. She wondered what Blaine had handed over for the privilege of the jeans that someone had written "FART" on in blue ink. *Fart? This kid couldn't even come up with an original offensive slogan? No imagination at all—except for devising ways to set their house on fire.*

Emma knew that the more she openly disliked Twyla, the more Blaine would like her. She wasn't totally stupid. She just wasn't totally controlled. It was hard to keep her mouth shut, especially when she had so much so say.

"Hot Pockets in the freezer if you're hungry," Emma said.

"The meatball ones?" The freezer door opened, closed. "Did you get that lotion I asked you for?"

"Next week, honey—that stuff is six dollars for a tiny little tube. Maybe it's cheaper at Wal-Mart."

"I *hate* Wal-Mart. And meanwhile, I asked you for that, like, months ago, and my face is zit city, thanks to you."

"Yes, I just read in *USA Today* that mothers are the surprising cause of acne."

Blaine rolled her eyes.

Emma looked at her daughter over one shoulder. "Try to save up a little appetite, honey, because I've got a roast going in the oven, and I'm making a pie."

"Is Marcus coming over? Good."

Good?

Emma looked up in time to see her daughter's back, the part of her she saw the most often, as she headed into the living room to turn on the television.

She was pleased, but not entirely surprised. It was as if Marcus was the piece of the puzzle she and Blaine had always been missing. His ease around Blaine was inexplicable; he had no children of his own. But then, he had no preconceived notions of children either, and clearly, as far as he was concerned, Blaine was the definition of *wonderful daughter.* He gave her the kind of unconditional acceptance one might expect from a grandparent, who felt nothing but pleasure in your presence in the world. They talked together easily over the little dinners the three of them had eaten together in the kitchen, and during last weekend's pizzas in front of the TV. Watching movies at home wasn't loserlike if Marcus was there, like it would be with just Blaine and her mother. Blaine actually had fun when the three of them went bowling. Bowling with her own mom—her definition of hell, was what she'd said, but Marcus had just grinned at her, and they'd had a really good time. Blaine was fascinated by his work, and the dinner-table conversations between the two of them sometimes sent Emma running out of the room.

"Did he say anything about . . . you know?" Blaine was back again, watching her from the doorway.

"You know? What do you know about *you know?"*

"Mom, don't be like that. I know he's looking at Ned's organs, and running tests and things."

Emma let the dough go and turned and looked at her daughter. "You've been eavesdropping?"

"No, Mom, he told me about it. The other night, when we were watching Glenn Close boil the rabbit in *Fatal Attraction."*

"I hate that scene."

"You were asleep, Mom, snoring away."

"Oh, God, was I snoring?"

"No, no, I'm just kidding, you were all curled up really pretty."

Emma knew when her daughter was lying, but she also knew when to be grateful. "I can't believe Marcus discussed that with you."

"Oh, God, you've got that look."

"What look?"

"The mush face you make whenever anything comes up about Neddy."

"Go. Eat. Your Hot Pocket."

"God, Mom. I'd think you'd want to know."

But Emma wasn't listening. She was back down in the clinic basement, approaching the stainless steel table where her child's liver and kidneys were in jars, little tiny baby organs because he'd been only two and a half, stored away like he was produce in some big canning factory in Hell's Kitchen.

Emma had to be ready for whatever it was that Franklin would say. She had to be ready for finding out and for not finding out. How did you get ready for that sort of thing?

Leave it to her precious child to take the joy out of the afternoon.

CHAPTER FOURTEEN

The sound of someone trying his office door woke Franklin. The someone knocked, but did not wait to be invited in. His sister, Lucca, stood in the doorway and frowned at him.

"Did you spend the night here?" she asked. She was only half kidding.

Franklin nodded. He remembered watching the sun rise as he sat behind his desk, and that was the last thing he remembered, before now.

"What time is it?" he asked.

"Quarter to eight," Lucca said.

So he'd slept then, a couple of hours anyway. He was hungry, but other than that he felt pretty good.

"What are you working on?" she asked. She knew full well what he was not working on. She managed the office, after all. "Marcus, are you doing some checking or extra work for somebody who won't go through channels? Because I hate to see you get taken advantage of."

"What you mean is, you hate not to know what's going on."

She shifted her weight to one hip. She was giving him the same look Blaine gave him when she thought he and Emma had stayed out too late. It occurred to Franklin that there were certain disadvantages to working with a nosy little sister.

He waved a hand. "I'm starved. I'm going to go to IHOP and have a steak omelet and pancakes. You want to come?"

"Some of us have work to do."

She sounded prissy, and it made him grin.

"I'm the boss. I'll let you off work for breakfast. Come on, Lucca, get the stick out of your butt and come have breakfast with me."

"I already ate breakfast."

"Then eat again."

"Marcus, what is going on with you?"

"What makes you think something is going on?"

"Because you are so weird lately. You're . . . you're erratic. You go home at five."

"You always told me I worked too much. Now you're complaining?"

"You're not home at night when I call. And you don't return my calls."

"I don't remember you leaving any messages. Or were you just checking up on me?"

"And all of a sudden, you have time to go out and get food?"

"I was here all night, Lucca. I think the office can live without me for forty-five minutes." He gave her an evil grin, because he was just parroting back the phrases she'd been drumming into his head since they'd worked together.

"So what were you here all night working on?"

"Nothing I want to share, at present."

Her chin came up. "Fine, then, I have work to do."

"Lucca?"

She paused.

"I've met someone."

"You've . . . like a woman?"

"Very much like a woman."

"Oh. That's wonderful, Marcus." His sister's voice was flat and joyless.

"What's the problem, Lucca? You've been telling me for years I need to find someone nice and settle down."

"Settle down? It's a little early for that line of thought, isn't it, Marcus?"

"What, I should wait until I'm fifty?"

"I mean early in the relationship. I mean . . . you're not going to marry her or anything, are you?"

He'd been thinking about it. "Why not?"

"How long have the two of you been dating? You need at least a year, two even—"

He shook his head at his sister. "What am I, seventeen? We're not kids here, Lucca. And I seem to remember you telling me that you knew that Bill was *it* by the third date."

"And Bill and I got divorced."

"After eighteen years of marriage, which, from the outside looking in, were pretty happy years. Look, I can't help it if your marriage failed. There aren't any guarantees, Lucca. I've listened to you, I've listened to my own friends. Their relationships have to pass this test, and that test, and watch for this red flag with this man and that tendency with that woman."

"You can't tell this soon, Marcus."

"I think I can. But don't worry. I haven't asked her, and she'd probably say no."

He waited for her to reassure him that any woman would say yes, but she didn't, she just gave him a tired, superior look, one that reminded him of their mother, and not in a good way.

"Is there anything else?" he asked.

"So now you're the big boss?"

"No, now I'm hungry, and I'm going to breakfast."

"You never go to restaurants."

"I'm going now. And I'm expecting some faxes this morning. If they come through while I'm out, put them right on my desk, if you would, please. No copies for the files."

"That's a violation of office procedure."

"These results don't fall under the purview of the office, Lucca. It's private and personal."

"It's got something to do with this woman, doesn't it?"

"Why are you being like this? You remember my friend Ernesto? You remember what happened when he finally got married after being single for eleven years? Remember how his family reacted, and what they said?"

Lucca's face went dark red. "This isn't like that," she said. And left, slamming the door.

But it was like that, he thought. Ernesto had been single eleven years after a horrible divorce. He'd become the single friend and fixture everyone loved, relied upon, and felt just a bit sorry for. And then he'd met a woman, Cilla. Strange name, nice woman. Not bad looking, and very much in love with Ernesto. And all those friends and relatives who'd encouraged Ernesto to "find someone" suddenly found fault after fault with Cilla, and Ernesto, fool of a man, had decided not to marry her after all. She'd moved away rather quickly, and six weeks later Ernesto followed her. He'd called Franklin just before he left. Said that he'd been sitting alone in his apartment, and thinking of all his friends, and the things they'd said about Cilla, and the things they actually put up with and overlooked in their own relationships. How there they were that night at home with their families, secure in the knowledge that if they called him to come over once in a while, he'd be available, and how right at the moment he never wanted to speak to any of them ever again, except Marcus, who actually liked Cilla. He said he was going after her, actually moving to her new city to show her he meant business, and he was investing in a ring even though there was a good chance she'd say no, because when she left she told him, kindly but firmly, that she never wanted to hear from him ever again, and what did Marcus think? And Franklin had said, Don't go into debt, but make sure the ring's impressive. And Ernesto had laughed and said, Thank God for you, Marcus. For a guy who's been single all his life, you give pretty good advice.

People always thought you gave good advice when you told them what they wanted to hear. Two weeks later he'd had an early-morning call from Ernesto to say that Cilla had relented and they'd put on their best blue jeans the previous afternoon and gone down to the courthouse and gotten married. Nobody ever heard from him anymore, except for Franklin, who got the occasional card at odd times of the year. Ernesto and Cilla were now living happily or unhappily ever after, however it may have worked out.

Franklin looked at his watch. Too early to call Emma, she'd be driving Blaine to school. He'd call her when he got back from IHOP. And he smiled to himself, thinking about how Ernesto and Cilla had just wandered down to the courthouse and gotten married and gone on with their lives, which might not sound romantic to some people, but sounded pretty close to perfect to him.

Franklin, being Franklin, was unable to eat alone in a restaurant without a briefcase of work. He set the case on the table, top up, so people could not look at him. He usually felt self-conscious in public, and worried that people felt sorry for him because he was by himself, but today it didn't matter. He realized that he was not the kind of man people should feel sorry for. But he did have the briefcase open so he could go over some of his notes. He was trying not to be quite such a workaholic these days. He was more interested in seeing Emma and Blaine (his girls, as he liked to think of them) at the end of the day, and though his job still interested him, it no longer consumed him. This was what his sister had noticed.

Feeling pious, Franklin scraped the scoop of butter off his short stack of pancakes onto a napkin. The waitress set a blue plastic pitcher down on the table beside his orange juice.

"Hot syrup," she said, and winked.

Definitely flirting. Franklin smiled at her, friendly but discouraging. He slathered syrup on the pancakes, thinking that ever since he'd met Emma, women were noticing him more and more. Before Emma, he couldn't get a second look; now they were falling in his lap. Maybe it was because he was happy and more confident. He just felt good these days. Women probably found that attractive. Or maybe they were intrigued because he didn't notice them anymore, not like he used to, wistfully and covertly. But to Franklin, any woman who was not Emma, was . . . not Emma.

He cut the pancakes into bite-sized pieces—bite-sized for a man with a big bite. That way he could eat with his right hand and hold the paperwork with his left, without interrupting the flow of food.

Being the state pathologist gave him easy access to pretty much whatever he wanted. Being an MD put him in the brotherhood. Medical doctors were the last holdout—governing themselves like gentlemen, which meant pretty much not governing themselves at all, and always careful not to step on each other's toes. It had its good and bad angles.

Clayton Roubideaux had wisely stored his son's remains with a private lab, which had been happy to comply with Franklin's requests for tissue samples. Roubideaux had carefully given Franklin all possible permissions, and had tied it all up in precisely legal documentation, and Franklin had not told the man that he could have gotten everything he wanted with no permission from the family. It would only have upset him.

Franklin himself was not one of those pathologists who *kept things*. Squirrels, is what Franklin called them in the privacy of his thoughts. He disapproved of the squirrels. He himself was a stickler for family permissions and medical releases, and he had a weary contempt for his colleagues' insistence on collecting tissues, samples, and out-and-out body parts. Oh, yes, they'd argue up one side and down the other about medical science, and the advancement thereof, but in Franklin's opinion, the end did not justify the means, and even if it did, most of the time very little use ever came of these samples. Until the Human Genome Project, which had started a government-sanctioned and -funded genetic gold rush. Until the eighties, when it became legal to use the genetic material of Joe Public and use it without his permission to patent certain genes. Franklin had colleagues who had literally made millions selling the patents to pharmaceutical companies, and the patient had never been notified or compensated. It was *bio-prospecting* and *bio-plundering,* and there were *bio-pirates* trolling the seas of modern medical research.

His colleagues could refer to their "sources" as "carriers of genetic information" or "subjects" or "data sets" or even "gold mines"; but they were still people, whether you reduced them down to the molecular level, or viewed them as a whole, *les corps humain.* Terms like *extracted, harvested, mined,* or *procured* were tossed around by doctors who sounded more like the guys in the agriculture or engineering department than the medical college.

Franklin was well aware how much cadaver tissue found its way into commercial lanes. Doctors, researchers, hospitals, pathologists, funeral directors—everybody was in the game. He knew of obstetricians who harvested eggs and sold them for research on birth control. Knew of incidence after incidence where family members donated organs or tissues for altruistic research, completely unaware that these tissues found their way into cosmetics, and that somebody somewhere was making an enormous profit.

And the police were no better. Putting together their DNA databases "for the good of everybody" to identify criminals. Cops were snatching genetic material left behind on coffee cups, or cigarette butts, and bringing them in as evidence, without the consent or knowledge of the subject. Franklin was just waiting for the mess to make it up to the Supreme Court. Do people own their genetic material? Do they own their genetic material if they're suspected of a crime, or only if they don't want to donate their kidneys?

DNA typing was considered gospel these days. Which wasn't exactly true. The results were only as good as the technician who provided them, and Franklin had seen enough screwups to empty a state prison.

Years ago being a pathologist was the kind of job you didn't like to admit having, because you'd get the "look," the logic being that no normal man spends his time in pathology. The fact that his job was in fashion now, and considered trendy and cool, made him believe that eventually everything must go in and out of public popularity and that a room full of monkeys would eventually write the Great American Novel. Your average Joe was so into forensics these days, Franklin was beginning to think there were great numbers of people with regular jobs who could perform an autopsy, with the right tools and a little professional supervision. Like learning to tune up your own car.

Franklin was not against knowledge. Knowledge was power. Knowledge would help him protect Emma and Blaine, would let him puzzle out what had actually happened to Emma's dead son, and would let him build an arsenal with which to annihilate the attentions of the Commonwealth Attorney's Office, Child Protective Services, and the accusing finger of Dr. Theodore Tundridge.

He took a bite of steak and egg. The omelet was about the size of a deflated football, and it tasted wonderful.

Tundridge had been very cooperative. Franklin had made it clear that he was not asking for Ned Marsden's medical records for any official investigation. Of course, Franklin had sort of buried this request by asking for the records of all children who had died of liver failure or complications in the last ten years.

Tundridge, in the spirit of one researcher to another researcher not in direct competition for funds or fame, had been happy to comply, assuming that Franklin had been compiling some kind of mortality trends or records. Franklin had not said one way or another, but had agreed to credit Tundridge for his work should there be any publications involved.

This sort of cooperation was generous in an age when most researchers guarded their results and patented their work. Tundridge really did come across as a man who was genuinely concerned about liver function in children, and he had been rather excited by Franklin's interest, no doubt envisioning the gateway to lucrative government grants.

Still. A doctor who had provided bad medical care to a patient would not be so willing to fork over the information, even in the good-old-boy, dog-eat-dog world of medical research. Which meant that Tundridge did not think he had anything to hide.

It begged the question of his little basement laboratory, and the tissues and body parts he'd preserved in formalin with only the vaguest consent from his patients. Tundridge, if Franklin read him correctly, was dedicated to his work, and arrogant enough to think he had the right to do whatever he deemed reasonable to get results.

Dangerous thinking, and utterly common.

And he'd missed the cause of death.

Ned Marsden had died of aflatoxicosis—poisoning due to the ingestion of aflatoxins, presumably in contaminated food. Aflatoxins were the metabolites of the fungus *Aspergillus flavus,* resulting in mycotoxins produced by fungi. Toxic mold, in other words.

Aflatoxins were not uncommon—found in corn, beans, nuts. A problem for farmers, who had to take care that their livestock feed did not get contaminated and moldy and therefore become toxic to their animals. There were various tests one could perform with black lights, or by sending samples off to labs. Pretty simple really, and most farmers could test on their own. The problem was the sample. Stored corn, for instance—you get a sample from one spot, and it comes up clean, only to find that dead center is a literal hive of toxicity.

There were lesions on little Ned's tiny liver, and from his medical records and blood work, done over a period of six months, it looked like the child had been exposed several times. Emma had given him the food diaries she'd kept, but he had yet to go through them. He'd do that this afternoon. Thank God she'd kept them. Either advertently or inadvertently, the child had been exposed to toxins, which had gradually weakened his liver and overwhelmed his immune system—he was such a little guy, after all. The last exposure had swamped the boat and taken him under.

Franklin thought about how he would give this news to Emma, and to Blaine, because he knew, just from the time he had spent with his two girls, that although there was a great deal of tension between them, there was a great deal of love too. They were closer than they realized. And they had both loved Ned very much, and suffered over his illness and his death. Blaine already knew too much to be left out of the information flow. She would know something was up, and possibly imagine worse things from secret whispered conversations than she would from actually facing the facts.

He had a high opinion of Blaine. He had to remind himself sometimes that he'd never been a parent, because he had a great deal of confidence when dealing with her. There had been a definite rapport after that first dinner. Blaine was highly intelligent and deep in her heart very kind, but she masked it sometimes just like Franklin did. He knew it was crucial to let her keep that mask up, and always assumed the best regarding her behavior. And in truth, though Blaine was very hard on Emma, she was almost always very good to him. He loved taking her bowling, the way she concentrated and never got mad when she wasn't good at something. He loved her very offbeat sense of humor, and he loved the way she had let him right into the family, so that when the three of them were together, he never felt like an outsider. To a man who had been an outsider all of his life, it was a pretty amazing feeling.

Emma had asked him, several days ago, if he was looking to have children of his own someday. He had answered immediately and honestly without even stopping to think. He had told her that any man who had two females in his life like Emma and Blaine would hardly need anything more. It had taken her aback, his honesty, and the way he'd made it clear how he was feeling about the two of them, but she had recovered quickly, and laughed at him, and said, "What about Wally?" And he'd squeezed her hand and said, "Wally, too. But we might have to get a cat."

He hadn't seen Blaine eavesdropping, so either she had been, because he knew she did sometimes, or Emma had told her what he'd said, because after that night she had started dropping hints about getting a kitten. He thought he might like to surprise her with one. Put it in a little basket with a bow and bring it home to her. He could just see the smile on her face. It gave him such a feeling, to know that he could put a smile on that little girl's face, he, Franklin, who had never been married and never been a father.

He wouldn't be putting a smile on her face tonight. But in the long run, it was for the best, and he'd make sure to use the knowledge to protect them. The thought of anyone else taking the smile off the face of either Emma or Blaine stirred a slow but enveloping anger, and an urge to protect that he had never known he had.

CHAPTER FIFTEEN

I had just lit a small cigarillo when I stood on Emma Marsden's porch and rang the bell. Nothing happened. I didn't hear it ring either, and decided it probably wasn't working, so I knocked. There was a turquoise Nova in the driveway, kind of junky and banged-up. It had a vanity license plate that read "LPN." The promised Amaryllis Burton from the Tundridge Children's Clinic, I presumed.

The front door was opened with a kind of slow deliberation that left me tapping my foot, and it wasn't Emma Marsden at the door. The woman who stood behind the glass gave me a toothy smile that was sharklike. She looked past me into the driveway, and the smile went one-sided.

"So you're the lady detective."

I can think of almost no greeting more likely to piss me off. If I blew smoke in her face, it could easily pass as an accident.

"I guess you better come in," she said, as I walked past her and into the house. "You'll have to excuse me for answering the door, but Emma isn't feeling all that well."

There was a smugness behind the words. An implication that she and Emma were very close and that like any intimate of the family, she had the run of the house, whereas I was merely a guest, and one who was as welcome as Christmas decorations the day after Halloween.

Emma herself was curled up on the couch, with a large golden retriever taking up three-quarters of the cushion space, head on her feet, kind of holding her down. She tried to shove the dog off her feet, which looked about as easy as moving a hippo with a nudge, and I shook my head.

"Don't get up, Emma. I have it on good authority that you're sick."

She did look sick. Pale and exhausted, but whether it was illness or general stress was hard to tell.

"Don't be silly, I'm fine. I just put on a pot of coffee, it should be ready. Let me get you a cup."

I sat in a blond cherry rocking chair right across from her, and she pulled her feet out from under the dog, who had barked once when I came through the door, but now just wagged a tail.

I got back up just for a second to pet the dog, who grinned widely and licked the back of my wrist, then began to snuffle my hand more closely.

I pulled away and sat back down. "She smells my cat."

I wondered why people always feel the need to explain what animals find interesting. Maynard would inspect me closely over this dog smell when I got home, and if Joel was there, I'd probably explain the dog smell to him. If he wasn't there, I would no doubt explain it to Maynard himself, who would already know.

"Everybody want coffee?" Amaryllis said, and headed without permission back to what I presumed was the kitchen.

Emma was already on her feet. "No, Amaryllis, I'll get it."

But she was ignored, and she shrugged and rolled her eyes and sat back down.

"You okay over there?" I asked.

She waved a hand. "No biggie. Just sick last night, and it

always wipes me out the next day. I don't know what it is. I think I have an ulcer or something."

She looked like she had an ulcer or something.

She smoothed the loose white shirt over her jeans. She had no makeup on, and her hair was pinned on top of her head with some kind of comb. She was barefooted, and her toenails were painted a sort of khaki beige, an interesting color, and she wore a silver toe ring. I liked the way it looked. It made me want to go out and get a toe ring of my own. I was always last to get in on these sorts of trends.

"Where's the cream?" Amaryllis said, her voice high-pitched, and raised to be heard all over the house. There was a loud sound of cabinets slamming.

Emma grimaced, and I got the feeling she did not like the other woman wandering through her kitchen.

"Excuse me," she said, and headed toward the noises.

I looked at the dog, who looked back at me.

Amaryllis appeared back in the living room, looking a bit startled to see me in the rocking chair, which let me know that was where she had been sitting. She turned to glare at the dog.

"Down."

The dog panted but smiled at her; definitely friendly.

"Down." Amaryllis Burton shrugged and looked back at me. "If one is going to keep pets, they should be disciplined, don't you think?"

I wondered if she was asking me. I decided not to have an opinion. She coughed a little, so I put the cigarillo out in an ashtray that was thick with ashes and two cigar butts. I wondered who'd been smoking with Emma.

Amaryllis sat on the edge of the couch not occupied by the dog, which I found odd, since there was a chair free. I committed the social breach of staring at Amaryllis Burton, since she was staring at me. It felt a little childish, and I could hear myself explaining, *But she did it first.*

She had an oddly self-aware quality, and faint little baby-blond hair that was long and wispy around her square and solid face. There was a thickness about her that had nothing to do with the extra forty pounds she carried.

Note to self, Lena. You are really a bitch.

Her eyes were ever so slightly crossed, either from a physical deformity or a personal habit of self-focus. Her nose seemed prone to run; no doubt she had allergies. She wore a beige ribbed sweater, short-sleeved and stretched just a bit shapeless, as if it were a personal favorite she wore more than she ought. It gave her a sort of bland look, a fashion statement that said "vanilla yogurt," fat-free with aspartame and lots of nasty unnatural toxic additives.

Her hair was long, and she wore it in a thick braid that hung to her waist, and she had bangs neatly cut across her forehead. I tend not to trust women with bangs.

Her arms were covered in fine blond hair and there was a large mole on her left elbow. Much bigger than the ones on her neck and face.

"So you're the detective," she said, squinting her eyes and letting her voice go ever so baby soft.

I was only vaguely aware that there was music playing, turned way down. It sounded like Etta James, but it was hard to tell, because the volume was so low.

I could not put my finger on exactly what it was about Amaryllis Burton that irritated me so much, but the look she gave me, the smile suspiciously sweet, said she sensed my animosity and returned it in full. I got the sudden impression that she was jealous—that Emma Marsden was *her* friend and *her* personal project, and I was poaching on claimed territory.

This sort of person annoys the ever-living shit out of me.

"Has Emma told you everything? Because someone like you, someone who has never had a child to love or given birth, you can't really come along and understand, if you know what I mean."

"No," I said. "I don't know what you mean."

My answer puzzled her.

Emma walked in holding a bright, hand-painted tray that read "SALSA!" and made me think she threw fun parties. There were coffee cups on the tray, and a little pewter pitcher with cream, and a sugar bowl, red enamel.

"Well, this is very fancy," Amaryllis said. I couldn't tell from her tone of voice whether or not she approved.

I took the coffee and loaded it down with cream, grateful that it wasn't the powdered stuff that I hate. Amaryllis took a cup and gave her shark smile.

"Usually I drink tea. No, no sugar, I don't take refined sugar, so bad for you."

"Smoke?" I asked, opening my little packet of Al Capone rum-dipped slims.

Her eyes went wide. "I have allergies," she told me.

"No doubt," I said, but I did put the cigarillos away.

I saw that Emma was trying not to grin. She set the tray down on an antique table that looked like it cost thousands, though she was as casual about it as most people were about plastic. If she thought it odd that Amaryllis was perched uneasily in her place by the dog, she didn't show it. She was gracious in a way that reminded me of my older sister, who used to entertain in her modest little starter home as if she was in one of the drawing rooms of the Biltmore. Like my sister, Emma had the knack of making people feel at home and genuinely welcome. If she served beer in bottles, nobody would mind, whereas if I did it, my ex-husband made comments.

Emma sat down in a ladder-backed chair with an embroidered cushion that looked scuffed and worn enough to be an actual antique. Wally immediately jumped down from the couch and settled at her feet, jogging Amaryllis's arm with her tail and sloshing coffee into the woman's lap.

"Well, really now, Wally," Amaryllis said, with a small hostile laugh.

Emma handed her a napkin. "Sorry, Amaryllis. She's a very bad dog."

"She's not so bad," Amaryllis said, then glanced over at me, as if she had suddenly remembered her earlier comments on badly disciplined pets.

I decided not to smile or be friendly. This woman and I were already off on the wrong foot anyway.

Amaryllis looked sadly at Emma. "I've been trying to explain to the lady detective here what it's like to lose a child."

Emma frowned. "I'm sorry, I should have introduced you. Lena, this is Amaryllis Burton, from the clinic. Amaryllis, this is Lena Padget. Like I told you on the phone, Lena asked if you could talk to us a little about the clinic, and the staff, just so we get an idea what we're up against."

"I appreciate your time," I said.

Amaryllis Burton put her coffee cup on the floor, still full of coffee, and placed her hands in her lap. "It's okay. I worked a double shift yesterday, just so I could take some time today."

I raised an eyebrow. We were meeting at three o'clock on her suggestion, as I understood it, but maybe Emma had set the time.

"Amaryllis, I'm sorry," Emma said. "We could have met after work. I didn't even think."

"Oh, no, that's okay. I want to help, Emma." Amaryllis looked across at me. "When you've been through the kind of things that Emma and I have been through, well . . . you learn how important it is to be a good friend." She looked over at Emma and smiled. "Sometimes it's the only way to survive. There's nothing I wouldn't do for Emma."

It was odd, watching this exchange. Emma just smiled, grateful and a little uncomfortable, and seemed to be totally oblivious to the notion I had that Amaryllis Burton disliked her with studied intensity. Which didn't make sense, on the surface, but on the other hand, maybe Amaryllis was loyal to Dr. Tundridge and had something of an agenda.

"You worked a double shift yesterday?" I said. Because I hadn't seen her at the clinic, and I wondered what hours she'd worked.

"Seven to seven. Makes for a long day. I usually do ten to three."

"I see." I hadn't noticed her. Maybe she was tucked away in a back office. "What exactly do you do, there at the clinic?"

"Me?" She pressed a hand to her bosom.

"She does just about everything," Emma said. "Answers the phones, puts together the gift baskets, counsels patients—"

"I'm an LPN," Amaryllis Burton said stiffly.

"I didn't know that," Emma said. "I didn't realize you were part of the nursing staff."

"I got away from the clinical side of nursing when I had my son," Amaryllis said. She looked at me. "I had had miscarriages. So when my son was born, I knew just how precious he was, and I didn't want to work then. I wanted to be a stay-at-home mom. I suppose you think that's boring."

I didn't answer, and she didn't notice.

"My son died of liver disease, just like Emma's little Ned. Dr. Tundridge treated him. It just devastated me . . . well, it's nothing someone like you could understand. But this sort of thing, this kind of deep, deep tragedy, it changes a woman. A mother. And I wanted . . . I just went into a deep, deep decline—"

I blinked, but stayed quiet, wondering if she'd actually said "decline." Kind of like the old southern relatives of mine who "took to their beds."

"It took me a long time to come out of it. A long time." She closed her eyes, and we observed a moment of silence. "But then, slowly, very slowly, I started to get back into things. I knew I would never be the same again, that there would always be a . . . a shadow. You should have known me then. Before the tragedy. I was such a happy person. Always laughing, always kind of singing, and doing creative things. But after my son died, and I came out of those dark, dark days—it's something I can't really describe to someone like you."

I literally bit my tongue.

"I realized, then, that I have a purpose. I started working at the clinic. Volunteering at first, but then Ted said to tell the accountants to put me on the payroll for heaven's sake, I was doing more work than anybody there. I started up with the gift baskets. I don't know if you're aware, but Ted . . . Dr. Tundridge, I mean, has a charity clinic for people without health insurance."

"People like me," Emma said.

Amaryllis gave her a quick look.

"Just kidding," Emma said. "But I always get the gift baskets."

Amaryllis shook a finger at her. "That's because you're one of *my* friends, you know that."

Emma nodded and looked over at me. "They give them out every couple of months. Amaryllis decorates the baskets, and puts in all kinds of stuff, like homemade jams and jellies and my personal favorite, homemade peanut butter. Cookies sometimes, and those bourbon balls she makes . . . to die for. I'm surprised you got Dr. Tundridge to go for it."

"It was a project I took to his wife, actually, Syd. She's great, Emma, have you ever met her?"

"No, I've never seen her."

Amaryllis looked back over at me, one hand on her knee. "Syd and I have become very close, working on the baskets like we do. She's got four children to look after, and so she usually leaves most of the details to me, but she likes being in on the planning and everything. Sometimes I think she feels a little left out of things, you know, because she's a stay-at-home mom. So doing the baskets is a way for her to be involved, and it's a special thing for our patients, and it's something she can talk about at the staff meetings and parties. Sometimes she calls me just to keep up on what's going on at the clinic, because Ted, you know, when he gets home . . . I guess he just doesn't want to talk about work. Ted always tells me he likes to leave the office at the office, although he stays on call, which is unusual these days. So many doctors now just leave a message to call nine-one-one."

"You like working for him?"

She pressed her hands against her thighs and glanced over at Emma, who was watching her. "To tell you the truth, I'm having my doubts, after finding out what happened between him and Emma. I'll be the first person to tell you what a good mother she is. Believe me, I've been a pediatric nurse, and I know the difference. I have known of cases . . . I can understand where Ted is coming from, but he is so wrong about Emma. I'm hoping we can work something out here, which is why I'm willing to do anything I can, even if it costs me my job. Especially after finding out about what was going on down in the path lab, down in the basement."

"What do you know about that?" I asked.

"Well, I mean, we all knew about the lab, but most of the time it's locked up, only Dr. . . . only Ted goes down there. It's mainly for storage, I thought. I had no idea he kept things that were sort of against people's will. It's really pretty horrifying. If that happened to my son. Like it did to Emma. I think I'd have just died on the spot. Emma, I don't know where you get your strength."

Emma stayed quiet. She wasn't smiling.

"What else do you do at the clinic? Besides the gift baskets?"

"I work in reception. I take the patients into their rooms, and put the charts in the slot—you know, we have this system, little colored arrows beside the door to let the doctor and the nursing staff know what's up. Like green means the patient is ready for the doctor, yellow means the nursing staff goes in. I keep the toy area stocked and organized, and file charts, stock and order supplies."

"You don't miss the nursing end of the business?"

"No."

But the question dampened her down, and I thought it was at least the second lie she had told me, the first being that she had worked a double shift yesterday.

Wally leaped to her feet and barked, and the front door opened. The sound of a school bus lumbering by penetrated the living room. Emma Marsden's teenage daughter walked in, saw the three of us, and gave a panicky look to her mother.

"Hi, sweetie," Emma said, rising and giving her daughter a hug. The girl endured it but did not return it.

"Everything okay?" the child said softly. She looked young and very beautiful in that child-woman way of teenage girls, who could be any age between thirteen and twenty-three.

"Everything's fine," Emma said. "This is my daughter, Blaine. Blaine, this is Lena Padget."

The girl smiled at me and walked across the room to shake my hand firmly. "Oh, right. Mom told me about you. We really appreciate everything you're doing for us."

She had a lot of presence, this little girl, and I felt approved of.

"And you know Amaryllis."

Blaine's back went stiff, but she forced a smile and nodded at Amaryllis.

"Oh, Blaine, come and give me a hug." Amaryllis opened her arms, and the girl leaned over and endured the embrace. Amaryllis smiled at me over Blaine's shoulder. "Blaine and I are old friends. Makes up for not having a daughter of my own."

"Thank you," Blaine said. She glanced at her mother. "Umm . . . when you get a chance, I need to talk to you."

"In a little bit," Emma said.

Blaine nodded. "Can I get you all something to drink or anything?"

"We've got coffee, but thank you, Blaine," Emma said, and she was smiling at her daughter.

Blaine nodded, let the backpack slide halfway down her

shoulders, and disappeared down the hall, Wally right behind her. She talked to the dog softly in a high-pitched animal voice until the door of her room closed and she shut us all away.

I stood up. Offered Amaryllis Burton a hand to shake, which she hesitated over but finally took. Her fingers were damp, and her hands were very, very soft, like a person who has just applied lotion.

"You've been a lot of help," I said, which was true.

CHAPTER SIXTEEN

It fascinated me that a woman as savvy as Emma Marsden didn't get how much Amaryllis Burton hated her. It was a jealousy thing. At least that was part of it.

The Amaryllis angle made perfect sense to me, as I am comfortable thinking the worst of everyone. The women met when Emma lost a child. And lost the father of the child as her romantic partner. And was left with a shaky income, a house unfashionable, and a teenage daughter. A woman like Amaryllis could identify with this sort of thing. She'd lost her own child, and could rehash all her old tragedy with Emma, who would no doubt provide a sympathetic audience and a fresh ear. And she herself could do the same for Emma, and they could be woebegone together. And Amaryllis, who did have a husband, and a job she seemed to enjoy, a job that gave her contact with other mothers in similar situations, could sigh over her tragedy from time to time and also feel superior to Emma.

Except, of course, that Emma got better. And Emma, completely unaware that her house was considered only so-so by the Amaryllis-type women of the world, was perfectly happy with her home, was even proud of it, even loved it. Emma got tired of being sad all the time. She cut her hours back at her job and wiped out the overhead, meaning she kept more money in the long run and worked less. Emma Marsden was the kind of woman who was hard to keep down. She had so much joie de vivre that it spilled over onto the rest of us, a quality that was likely attractive and repellent to a woman like Amaryllis Burton.

It is my job to hold uncharitable viewpoints, and I am good at it. Jealousy between women is a dangerous thing.

Of all the people on the staff at the Tundridge Children's Clinic, I was most interested in Amaryllis Burton. I was going to spend some time with her, on my computer. I'd have to use the one at home, because Rick was not speaking to me at the moment. He was furious that I had not let him come to the clinic. It was best to let him sulk.

By the time Joel got home from work that night, I had completely wrecked the living room.

My computer, which usually sits in the spare bedroom upstairs, was in the middle of the floor in front of the fireplace. The phone line was draped across the floor, and hooked up so I could surf the Net, although without a high-speed hookup it was more like snail the Net. After using the computers in Rick's office, I hated the slow-drip agony of the one I had at home. Eventually I had brought the printer downstairs too, along with an open ream of paper and the coffee cup full of pens. I had made about twelve trips up and down the stairs in the last six hours, and now most of the stuff I used in the spare bedroom was littered on the living room floor.

"Hey," Joel said, when he walked through the door.

"Hey." I was sitting cross-legged in front of the computer, using the telephone book as a mouse pad, and I lifted my face so Joel could kiss me.

"Did you move your office down here?" he asked.

"Just for the day. It's so depressing up there, with all the boxes and junk."

"You look frustrated."

"My eyes are crossing. This Internet connection is so slow, it's driving me nuts."

"Not using Rick's office?"

"He's not speaking to me right now."

Joel raised a brown paper package. "Would you like a glass of wine?"

"I'd love one. Are you cooking, or am I?"

"Do you want to cook?"

"Actually, I refuse. I'm working here."

"Then I guess I will."

He went upstairs, came back quickly in his sweatpants and sweatshirt, and went into the kitchen. He was gone awhile, then he returned to the living room and handed me a glass of red wine.

I took the glass and arched my back. Too many hours without a chair.

"Lena, why don't you get a new computer, get cable access for the Internet, and make that room upstairs into a decent office?"

"I will, Joel, just right now I can't afford it."

He sat in his favorite chair and flipped the switch on the stereo. Somebody or other on classical guitar. Tolerable.

"What is that look?" I asked him.

"Just that if you had kept that insurance money from when your sister died, you'd be able to afford a really good office and a new computer. It seems like a waste."

"I think revenge is a very good way to spend your money. I've never had any regrets."

"Lena, if there were grudge Olympics, you'd bring home the gold every four years."

"I just bailed him out of jail and let nature take its course."

"You knew those people were after him."

"That's right, I did. That's why I bailed him out of jail. He killed my sister. I wanted retribution."

I tilted my head to one side. I could not tell what Joel was thinking. I can never tell what he is thinking. And he never tells me when I ask.

"Are you saying I was wrong, Joel?"

"It's not up to me to judge you."

"Just sitting over there with tight lips and that look is judging."

He finally did meet my eyes. "I won't say I wouldn't have done the same in your place."

"The thing is, you wouldn't." I got up, found the half-smoked cigar I'd left in the ashtray, and lit it back up. "You're not vengeful. I am. *Vive la différence.*"

"It's not a good thing, Lena."

"Vengeance? Let me tell you something, Joel. It is a good thing. Revenge is one of the most underrated pleasures in the world." I puffed on the cigar, tapped ash into the ashtray.

"If you don't forgive him, Lena, you will carry this around for the rest of your life."

"I don't ever want to forgive Jeff Hayes, and you know why?"

"Because you want revenge."

"No. I got revenge. But if I forgive Jeff Hayes for what he did, it feels like I'm saying it was okay."

"Forgiving isn't saying it's okay."

"It is to me. I'm past anger and all the bitterness. I don't think about it that much, and when I do, I sidestep it. If forgiveness is divine, I'm not divine. And it's kind of arrogant, isn't it? Who am I to judge and then forgive? Leave that to the divine being. The thing I do know is that if I forgive Jeff Hayes, it will crush me. It'll kill the strong part of me that keeps my head above water and won't let me drown."

"I'm sorry I brought it up."

"I forgive you."

He finally grinned. "What are you working on, impossible woman?"

"Amaryllis Burton."

"Who?"

"She is a supposed friend of my client, Emma Marsden, and also just so happens to be on the staff at the Tundridge Children's Clinic. She is turning out to be a very interesting person."

"How so?"

"She trained and worked for many years as an LPN, but she only does low-end reception work at the doctor's office. She had a little boy who died when he was eight—and he was a patient of Dr. Tundridge, for whom she now works. It took me a while to track this down, but evidently, at the time of the child's death, she lived in Sevierville, Tennessee."

"Why bring her son to Lexington for treatment?"

"Because of Dr. Tundridge. He specializes in pediatric liver disease. They ran an obituary in the Lexington paper when her little boy died, and they mentioned she was from Sevierville. So I checked out the archives of the *Mountain Home Press*—there was a fee, and I put it on your credit card, I hope that's okay."

He nodded.

"It covered the boy's death there, too. It also mentioned that Amaryllis had two other children, previously, and both died of SIDS."

Joel narrowed his eyes. "Interesting."

"It also listed her as being a nurse at the county hospital up until a year before her son's death."

"So what are you thinking?"

"Just that it's odd. That she no longer gets a job as a nurse, when that's what she trained for, that's what she's got experience in. A nursing position would bring in a lot more money than the one she's got."

"Maybe her license was suspended."

"May well be, Joel. I went through a list of all the nurses who had active licenses and couldn't find her listed, in Kentucky or Tennessee. I called County Hospital, down in Tennessee, where she worked, and told them I was looking for references, and that she'd given me their name. First they swore up and down that she had never worked there. Then when I pushed them, they said she had been an employee, but one of the computers had crashed, and they'd lost some permanent employee records, and they could give me no references one way or the other."

Joel made a little noise.

"Yeah, I know."

Joel rubbed his forehead. "The medical profession is a thicket of people who watch each other's backs. Sounds to me like she was fired, and they don't want to say why. Which could be anything from stealing drugs, to insubordination, to killing off patients."

"Don't you think she'd be in jail for that?"

"Not necessarily. Medicine attracts a lot of dedicated, intelligent people, Lena. But it attracts other kinds, too. Angels of Death, in cop jargon. I can name three cases right off hand— Dr. Michael Swango. He liked to poison people—and not just patients, he went after his coworkers. They called him 'Double-O Swango' because so many of his patients died."

"I don't get that."

"License to kill. Medical black thumb. He got a big kick out of informing the families when a child died. He liked accident scenes."

"How long did it take to catch up with him?"

"He practiced medicine for twenty years."

"*What?*"

"Everywhere he went, patients died and colleagues got sick. When things started closing in on him, he just left and took another position. Sometimes he lied, sometimes he faked his employment history, maybe changed his name. But a lot of the time he didn't even have to bother. Once he left, the hospital administration was just relieved he'd gone. They didn't want a lot of lawsuits, from him or their patients, so they closed the book and let someone else deal with him."

"Now Amaryllis Burton is looking even more creepy."

Joel tilted his head to one side. "No criminal charges on her record?"

"None that I could find, but I don't mind you checking into it."

"Chances are there won't be charges. And you'd have to twist a lot of arms to get any official inkling of what was going on. You could talk to people who worked with her in the past—if they're willing to talk. That's your best bet."

"So you're saying it's a power thing?" I took a sip of wine.

"It's a mix. Some of them like to put patients in harm's way and then stage a rescue. They love the attention and the excitement. The code with everybody running in and them playing hero."

"Not unlike Munchausen by proxy."

"I thought you didn't believe in it."

"I don't. At least, not in Emma Marsden's case. But Amaryllis—evidently she had a baby who died from SIDS. Something she did not mention."

"The motives are complex, Lena—each one of these cases is unique. There are the heroes, the mercy killers. There was an oral surgeon who was molesting his female patients when they were under anesthetic, and he accidentally overdosed them. There is a surprisingly big category of experimenters. They go into medicine because they are curious, and medicine is the only way to have access. A lot of their patients die for the good of science and mankind, and these guys often have government grants.

"For some of them it's literal bloodlust. Swango admitted that he'd come out of the ER with a big erection when he had to inform parents of the death of a child."

"This is the guy who was in practice for twenty years?"

"What do you expect from an organization that polices itself? Some of these killers consider themselves the moral arbitrators of society, and they kill or punish people they disapprove of. Then there's guys like Dr. Harold Shipman. He killed patients who questioned him, killed some for their money and then forged their wills, making himself beneficiary. Whenever he got upset about his unhappy childhood, he killed a patient instead of killing himself."

I rubbed the back of my neck. "I don't understand how they get away with this under everybody's nose. This kind of genuine sociopathic behavior is recognizable. There are plenty of experienced professionals in hospitals who should be able to spot these guys, and not all of them are going to put the medical brotherhood above tracking down a cold-blooded killer."

Joel frowned. "Have you ever heard of the doubling theory? It's often used to explain the Nazi doctors, and it could apply to any medical person. Basically it's a psychological mechanism that divides the self into two functioning wholes."

"You mean disassociation? An identity disorder?"

"No, because it is a conscious choice. It's really a survival mechanism that goes too far. Everybody has their at-home personality, their work personality, their hang-out-with-friends personality. These guys have their compassionate medical guy, and they have their killer. And the compassionate guy makes up for the killer guy. Some of these personalities will kill under certain very precise circumstances. Others do it at will for pleasure. And others are conflicted, guilty, unresolved. Always struggling."

I realized the cigar had gone out, and I set it down in the ashtray. "And doctors already have to have a sort of medical self to deal with the death of their patients, and the corpses they train on. Like a paradox. The healer and the killer, in separate realities. Is there like a percentage of doctors this happens to?"

"No, because it isn't a coping or survival mechanism. It's a mechanism used by someone who already has the capacity for evil."

"You know, Joel, all this points to the doctor as much as or more than it does Amaryllis Burton. The experimenter—the guy with the path lab who keeps all the patients' organs. Keeps them and feels entitled to do it. And there's a certain type of person— have you run into this? Where they accuse other people of what *they're* doing?"

"But what's the crime here, Lena? Do you think that Tundridge killed Emma Marsden's child? Or was it more a matter that she caused trouble, and so he punished her by accusing her of Munchausen by proxy?"

"I don't know yet. I think it comes down to who made the videotape."

A timer buzzed from the kitchen. "Come on," Joel said. "Let's eat."

"Do you know anything about the videotape, Joel?"

"I know they're working on it."

"And?"

He hesitated. "It was mailed to the station from the post office that happens to be the closest to the Tundridge Clinic."

"Aha."

"It's not proof, Lena."

"No, but it's interestingly suspicious."

CHAPTER SEVENTEEN

Office gossip is always revealing.

Second only to the angry ex-employee, and infinitely more objective, is the cleaning crew who regularly works in an office. I left early the next morning to cash in on some magic beans.

Six AM was the absolute latest you would catch Michael Borneo in his office, and it was ten after when I arrived at the large complex off Alumni Drive. Office Pro had a ground-floor suite and a private entrance, and if Michael was still driving the Chevy Illumina van, he was still there.

I knocked on the outside door and waited. The door opened immediately—clearly I had caught the man on his way out.

I could tell from his face that he recognized me but could not remember my name.

"Michael, it's Lena Padget. How are you?"

"Fine," he said. He shook my hand, concentrating, trying to place me. "Oh, wait, you're the one who helped Lee Ann."

"That's right. How is she?"

"She's great, great. We got married right after all that business. Six kids between us and happy as clams."

"That's good to hear, Michael. Can I come in?"

"Of course you can. I'll even make you a fresh pot of coffee."

"I appreciate it. I know you were on your way home and you've had a long workday, -night, whatever you call it. But I need to talk with you a bit."

He grinned at me over his shoulder while he locked us into the office. "Lee Ann always warned me you'd be back someday calling in favors. Like the Godfather."

"I like to think of it as magic beans."

"Magic beans?"

"Like Jack and the Beanstalk."

"Is that supposed to make sense to me?" He was flirting, and I just smiled. "Go on into the office, door's open. Sit down. You take sugar or cream?"

"Just cream, and lots of it."

"Yes, ma'am."

Borneo's office was small, very neat—a metal desk he'd likely bought used, some filing cabinets. The walls were freshly painted white, and I looked at the pictures. He and his children, he and Lee Ann, Lee Ann and her children, all of them together. Michael had just gone into business when he met Lee Ann. She answered his ad for office help, newly separated and back in the workforce after six years at home with her kids. They had fallen in love.

But Lee Ann unfortunately had a complication in her life. Somewhere along the line she had picked up a stalker.

A stalker is like a computer virus. You can get one from a million different sources, and once you have one, he or she can cause endless trouble and be nearly impossible to get rid of. The ex-husband is always the first place you look, but he turned out to be an okay guy. Michael's ex-wife had disappeared with her guitar teacher three years earlier, and I checked her out without ever letting her know we were looking. Michael didn't want her getting any ideas about coming back to complicate his already complicated life.

The stalker, as it turned out, worked at the Kroger store right around the corner from Lee Ann's house. The usual loser, with a low-end job, who bagged groceries, loaded them into cars, and showed a tendency to engage the women customers in long, annoying conversations. He told a lot of them that he had a side-line business as a birthday clown, and asked them to consider hiring him to work their children's birthday parties. He had a record of peeping and indecent exposure, and we sent him to jail for eighteen months. After that I lost track.

Michael brought me a white ceramic mug of coffee. He clearly had not put enough cream in, but I didn't complain. My mama raised me right. If coffee is hot enough, you can drink it almost any way it's prepared.

Michael sat behind the desk and grinned at me. He was semi-irresistible. Dark curly hair, brown eyes, athletic build. "How you been?"

"I've been good, Michael. How are Lee Ann and the kids?"

"Perfect. Business is good. I'm going to gross over a million this year for the first time."

I put my cup down on the floor. "Michael, that's wonderful."

"I'm sorry, I know I'm bragging, but I can't believe how well this turned out. You know, when I met you, I didn't have a dime."

Nevertheless, Michael and Lee Ann had paid me in cash, not favors. They'd drawn up a payment plan, and about halfway through had paid off the debt in one big chunk.

"I'm glad you're doing well. Have a staff now, to do all the dirty work?"

He shook his head. "It's all about overhead, as in having as little as possible. I still do most of the cleaning myself at night, when the offices are closed, so I'm free during the day to coach tee ball and soccer."

I glanced over my shoulder at the trophies and the team pic-tures on the walls. "I never would have guessed." I turned back around. "Ever hear from your old friend again when he got out of prison?"

"Not a peep, Lena. Whatever you did, it worked."

I nodded. In truth, Lee Ann and Michael were lucky. No doubt the stalker had found someone else. These guys never stop for anything but prison or a new obsession.

"Michael, I saw one of your business cards on the office manager's desk at the Tundridge Children's Clinic. Any chance they're one of your clients?"

"Oh, yeah. Mr. French. They're one of the newer accounts. I've been doing them about six months."

"Do you have an ethical problem with talking to me about them?"

He grinned at me like I was kidding, then thought for a minute. "Is it for a good cause?"

"I think so."

"Ask me anything you want."

"Tell me about the lab."

"Frankenstein's gym? Okay, let's see. Mr. French runs the place, talks affected, is married with one kid. Hyper particular, but pays on time and is reasonable to deal with. The path lab has to stay well lit—they go ballistic if even one of the fluorescent lights go out, and for these guys I replace the lights before they go out, causes less trouble and I can use the ones that still have some juice around here."

I smiled at Michael. He was frugal, as a man with six children might well be. Maybe I could pick up some tips.

"You ever stopped to look at what's in there?"

"It's horrible, Lena. Hearts, lungs, livers. Little ones, from children. They give me the shivers. The doctor works late—sometimes I've passed him on his way out, and I usually get there around two AM. A lot of changeover in the staff there, too, except for Mr. French. The little nameplates on the desks are always changing."

"What about Amaryllis Burton? Are you familiar with that name?"

"Oh, the weirdo. Yeah."

I nodded at him. "Keep talking."

"She's been there since I have, but then I haven't been there all that long. She has a desk she uses that's stuck in the supply room, but it's not like it's really her desk. Her nameplate was printed on a computer, you know, just white paper cut to size and stuck in the slot, like she made it herself. And other people put stuff on the desk, and she's always moving it off and on top of the shelf of paper towels and toilet paper and supplies like that. She always has this jar of homemade peanut butter on her desk."

"Huh."

"Yeah. But the weird thing is the flowers she has."

"What do you mean?"

"They're cemetery arrangements. My dad was a florist, and there are certain types of urns and flowers you use for grave sites—some of the urns have little hooks so they can attach to the top of the gravestone. And people use a lot of plastic and silk in the winter, lots of gladiolas and carnations. A lot of them are brown and dead or plastic, and they look like they've been left outside for a long time. I mean, it looks like she takes them off graves."

"That is definitely strange."

"No doubt. And I opened one of her desk drawers one day— I don't want you to think I make a habit of that. It's just I needed a pen, didn't have one, and her desk was the office catchall. So I opened the middle drawer, and there were all these little bitty presents. Still wrapped up, but again, like they'd been left in the rain or something. And bits and pieces of balloons that said Happy Birthday, like you get in the floral section of the grocery store. And that with the flowers made me think about the way people always put stuff on graves. You know, some people do that, especially with kids that die. Take a balloon out to the cemetery on their birthday. So maybe she had a kid die and keeps that stuff. Except there's a whole lot of it. And why not take it home?"

"What you're saying is, she has a collection?"

"Yeah, that's what I'm saying. I got intrigued and I went through her whole desk. The bottom drawer is full of mason jars of homemade peanut butter. And in another one, in a bag, she's pilfering medical supplies. Syringes, that tube thing they wrap around your arm when they take blood. Bandages."

"Anything else?"

"The doctor's wife comes in late sometimes to work on taxes. She's actually pretty nice."

"Anything you pick up about her?"

"She's crazy about Pecan Sandies dipped in milk."

It made me wonder what the house crew that Joel hired had picked up about me.

Borneo leaned back in his chair.

"I will tell you one thing. That clinic has a lot of money. You would not believe what they spend on equipment."

"And you would know that because?"

"Invoices in the trash."

"Ah." I gave Michael a smile that I hoped looked more friendly than wicked. "I have a favor to ask."

I met Michael at his office that night. His van was the only other car in the lot. Reynolds Road was quiet at two AM. I had taken a nap from nine until a little after midnight, long enough to get myself deeply asleep. Getting up was agony. My stomach was still dormant, and I had not even been able to choke down a cup of coffee.

Borneo's office was lit from every window, and he opened the door before I could knock.

He glanced at his watch, then grinned at me. "Almost on time. I like punctuality in my employees."

I saluted.

"Come on back, and let me get you outfitted."

We'd decided earlier that I would wear the company over-alls. We even had a short written agreement about me working for him on a temporary basis. The structure of legitimacy seemed to make him feel better about the appalling ethics of letting me into the clinic to "assist." It was done all the time, but not by straight-up guys like Borneo. He didn't even owe me any favors, like the majority of ex-clients, but I have gotten so good at calling in markers that Borneo was happy but conflicted about helping me out. In truth, the path lab had been getting under his skin for months, and getting the background on the Marsden case provided enough motivation to prod him across ethical lines.

There was a bounce in his step.

"Are you always this perky at two AM?" I asked.

He looked at me over his shoulder. "It's my workday, Lena."

He opened a rolling closet that reminded me of the coat closet we'd had in elementary school. White work overalls of various sizes wrapped in dry cleaning bags hung like robots from the rack. He frowned, slid some hangers until he came to the very end.

"Try this one. It'll be too long, but I don't have any smaller ones. I'll get you a cup of coffee to go while you change. Do you take cream?"

"If it's that gummy powder stuff, I'll take it black."

"Black it is."

I shut the door and shed my jeans. I'd come prepared in a white T-shirt, with a white sweatshirt over it. Michael was a stickler about the company logo and the uniform, particularly since he wanted to make it clear he and his employees were legitimate and not burglars. Alarms and security guards were an occupational hazard.

The overall was lightweight, well worn, and entirely comfortable. I tightened the straps as high as they would go and bent over to roll up the hem of the pants, which were a good six inches too long.

"Ready?"

I opened the door. Michael handed me a Styrofoam cup that felt too hot to drink, and put a white company ball cap on my head. He immediately bent down and rerolled the hem of my pants. I suppose attention to detail was what made him good at his job, but it occurred to me that one night working with him was going to be enough.

The parking spaces in the front of the clinic were empty. We drove to the back lot and entered through a side door. No keys here, but an electronic locking system and a pass card. Michael seemed distracted, his mind on the job, and I sipped at the strong and terrible coffee and winced. My mind was waking up.

Michael propped the door open to bring in his cleaning gear, the heaviest piece being some kind of floor buffer, and I slipped into the ladies' room off the hallway and poured the coffee into the toilet. When I came out, Michael was locking the door behind him and turning on all the lights.

"It's safer that way," he told me. "Anybody who wants to rob the place knows when I'm here and when I'm gone. They stay out of my way and I stay out of theirs."

He handed me a huge black garbage bag. "The first thing I want you to do—"

"Michael?"

He frowned at me.

"Show me where the desk is where you found the trophy items—the cemetery flowers and all that. Afterwards I want to go down to the path lab. I'll try not to disturb you while you work."

"Oh, right. Sure, this way."

He looked at me warily. We had set very rigid parameters. He didn't mind if I looked in the storeroom desk and cabinets for the trophies or wandered through the lab. Desk drawers and file cabinets used by the regular staff were off-limits. I could take pictures, but nothing else.

"But I will take the bag." I held out my hand. "Just in case someone sees me through a window or something. Then it will look like I'm on the job. But don't expect me to actually clean anything, okay?"

He grinned. "Okay."

He pointed me to a room in the center of the hallway. Some of the doors were locked—this one wasn't. There were no windows, and the walls were lined with shelves and storage cabinets. I stood in the doorway, taking in the details. None of the furniture matched, and the room had the air of a catchall for things that weren't needed anywhere else. One cabinet held mostly office supplies: staplers, rubber bands, a stray computer keyboard, stacks of used but empty file folders. There were no medical supplies here.

A pinkish beige metal desk had been shoved into a corner next to a stack of boxes. Computer parts were piled on top of the desk. Someone had arranged them into the smallest footprint possible. A faux brass name plaque sat on the corner facing the doorway. AMARYLLIS BURTON had been printed out on copy paper that had clearly been cut to fit. It made me think of a child playing office. The chair behind the desk looked like a castoff from the waiting room—metal arms and a plastic aqua seat cushion. One of the legs was broken off at the bottom, and the chair sloped sadly to the right.

The desk drawers were locked. A new development. Michael had said they were open before, and full of random clutter. Amaryllis had taken her "office" one step further.

The file cabinets had pens, paper clips, a magnifying glass (for some odd reason), stacks of paper towels, rolls of toilet paper, and one flathead screwdriver with a broken plastic handle. No doubt Michael Borneo had plenty of tools and keys, but there was no point asking him for help getting into the desk. He might object to opening drawers that were locked. It was always best not to ask a question unless you wanted an answer.

The desk lock was easily picked, but the screwdriver slipped and I broke the latch to the center drawer. It gave me a moment of guilt. I was more careful with the other drawers.

The center drawer held a clump of string, balled up with little tacks. Some project or other that hadn't worked out. Pens, paper clips, pencils. Rubber bands, and way at the back, a little cache of order forms preprinted with the clinic's address and phone and account numbers. The deep drawers on the right held mason jars of peanut butter. All of the jars were dated and labeled. Some of them had little stickers of flowers in the corner, and some did not. That interested me. I took two jars, one with a flower label and one without, and tucked them into my overalls. I took pictures of the drawers' contents, and the nameplate on the desk. The bottom-left drawer was stuck, and hard to open, mainly because it was stuffed. Dried flowers, flaking and crumbling, plastic flowers, water-stained and worn, heavy foil balloons that said *HAPPY BIRTHDAY.* Small bedraggled stuffed animals. A plastic Pez dinosaur that looked newer than the rest. Silk flowers with wire and clips made for attaching to the top of gravestones. A weird collection. I took pictures of those too.

I relocked the desk, except for the center drawer, which was broken, and put everything back the way I had found it. I could hear a vacuum from the other side of the building. Michael was hard at work. I wandered down the hallway, past office doors, until I came to one labeled DR. TUNDRIDGE. I tried the handle. The door was unlocked. No surprise. Michael likely went through and unlocked all the doors so that he could go in and out freely while he cleaned. So long as he kept the outside doors locked, there was no problem.

The light was on. I went inside.

The office had a heavy feel to it, and there were stacks of

papers and books on the desk, the floor, and the buttery-soft
brown-leather couch. Clearly, Tundridge spent a lot of time
working here. The shelves were crammed with books, some in
neat rows, some stacked and shoved in tight. There was a large
flat-screen computer on his desk, next to a laptop, and another
table held yet another computer, as well as a printer and a fax
machine.

I wandered carefully, studying the papers on the desk but not
touching. Formulas, chemistry notations that made no sense to
me. Nothing in the fax machine. I looked at the desk a long
moment, wondering if all of the drawers were locked. I glanced
at the file cabinets, the notepad beneath a huge chemical reference book. I was in clear violation of my agreement with Michael
Borneo. I backed out of the office and into the hall.

Tundridge's office was right next to a stairwell. Lights on,
like everywhere else. The basement or the pathology lab or both.
I slipped through the fire door and headed down two flights of
steps. Opened the bottom fire door and stepped into complete
darkness.

Light switches are never placed for the convenience of short
people, and it took me some time to find one. There were three
switches, and I flipped them all. The blaze and hum of fluorescent light made me blink.

It was hard to take everything in all at once, though the
white tile floors and whitewashed cinder block walls made me
remember immediately how Emma had talked about the way her
worn shoes had looked against the floor. The lab was sanitized
with the sort of aggressive medical cleanliness that smells harsh
and makes your eyes ache. I smelled bleach. The black tables
were a visual relief beneath the brightness of the lights, a track of
fluorescent tubes that ran along the ceiling.

The tables were narrow and long and built in. Some of them
were bare. Many of them held microscopes, laptop stations,
screens and monitors. It was the white metal shelves that drew

me. The jars of formalin, the disturbing shapes. I went closer slowly, curious, my stomach tight with butterflies.

There were pieces of small children in the jars. The first one I saw held an ear. One tiny ear. Next to it was a slender cylinder that held a ropy mass of some kind of internal organ I could not identify. There was a heart, and next to it what were clearly a set of small and immature lungs. Everything was in miniature, a pediatric chamber of horrors.

It was the floating arm that stopped me. Up until now, every jar had been labeled with a series of numbers and letters, like a code, and a last name next to the age of the child. This one had a strip of yellowed masking tape slapped across the front, and someone had written *BABY ELMO* in capitals. It was my first experience with being offended by someone's off sense of humor. Some things were sacrosanct. Some things were not funny.

The arm was small, infant-sized, and the little fist rested against the top of the lid, as if it wanted out.

Whose child did that little arm belong to? How long had it been in the jar? Did some family actually consent to that arm being put in a jar and kept on a shelf, or had they signed a generalized blanket consent form with no inkling that their child's tiny fist would be labeled Baby Elmo for a stranger's fleeting amusement? The impersonal clinical coding seemed infinitely kinder—benevolent in comparison.

The echo of footsteps made my stomach jump. I looked over my shoulder, expecting Michael, but did not recognize the face I saw behind the wire mesh window.

I began patrolling the lab tables with my trash bag open, and glanced up, trying to seem bored, to stare at the man who walked in. Tundridge was about five six and stocky, his thin dandruffy brown hair cut short. He had green eyes, a narrow worried face, and an air of anxious distraction. He was not what I expected. Not tall or commanding or evil. Just a stocky, average man who looked preoccupied.

I tilted my head, gave him a quick nod, and went back to the patrol, looking for trash cans to empty.

"Excuse me?"

The voice was curt but not particularly unfriendly.

"Garbage cans are through there." He pointed to a metal door at the back of the room that I hadn't even noticed. Even if he hadn't had a name tag over a creased white coat, I would have known he was Dr. Tundridge. He picked up a printout from one of the machines and turned his back, heading up the stairs. I wondered when he'd arrived and why Michael hadn't warned me. No time, I supposed, and of course Michael hadn't known I was down here.

I spent another twenty minutes in the lab. I did my job, looking at everything I could look at. Some of the things I saw floating in jars still come to me at unexpected moments. I did not like to think of Emma Marsden standing in this lab all alone.

EMMA

Chapter Eighteen

They left late, Blaine and Emma, late enough that Emma was going to have to write Blaine a note to get into school. Blaine punched one radio station after another, till Emma reached out and turned the radio off. The night before, with Marcus there between them, Emma thought Blaine had taken the news about the details of her half-brother's death surprisingly well. But this morning, enduring the attitude and the atmosphere, and seeing the quick and ready tears when Blaine had dropped one of her old elephant bowls and broken it into three big pieces, she thought maybe not. Blaine was usually at her best around Marcus. Something about having him there lightened the atmosphere in the house and put a cheerful buffer between mother and daughter. It was hard not to be pleased by a man who seemed to adore both of them and had no mission but to please. And there was none of the tension, the odd-man-out feeling around Blaine, not with Marcus. Emily did not realize how strained things had been with Clayton until Marcus came into their lives.

Sad to admit, but her daughter was a hell of a lot easier to get along with when Marcus was around. But they only had to get through a fifteen-minute drive to school.

"We've got the whole weekend," Emma said. "You want to rent a movie tonight? Order pizza? Or do you have plans?"

Blaine was looking out the window, and she shrugged, and did not answer for a while.

"Can I have somebody sleep over tonight?"

"Ummm . . ." Emma was tired and the house was a wreck, and she didn't want anybody who wasn't Marcus around. On the other hand, Blaine needed friends, peers, not just parents all the time.

"*Never mind,*" Blaine said. "I'll just have a loser night with my loser mom."

"That's a charming way to get what you want. You can have somebody sleep over if you want, Blaine, you don't have to spend the evening with your loser mom. And Marcus will be here. He's not a loser."

"How about Twyla? It would be fun to go bowling, all four of us. Or she and I could stay home, and you and Marcus could go out."

"God," Emma said.

"What? What's wrong with Twyla? Or do you feel like you need to pick my friends for me, like you control everything else in my life?"

"You know what, Blaine? You can have anybody *but* Twyla. Last time she was here she kept trying to start a fire in the fireplace."

"Yeah, where else would you start one?"

"How about you *don't* start one, which is what I told her at least three times. It being hot outside, with the air-conditioning on. And not to mention the chimney being seventy years old with cracks in the mortar. She could have set the whole house on fire."

"Yes, I know, *Mother,* you've brought it up a million times. I get it. You hate Twyla."

"If a *guest* can't respect the *rules,* she isn't welcome to come back." Emma glanced at her daughter. The sulky look, as usual.

"You're just spoiled, Blaine, you know that? The first time something doesn't go your way, you throw a temper tantrum."

Emma flicked the turn signal on and moved onto Melton Road. It was a pretty stretch of highway, on the back roads so the traffic was minimal, and it wound alongside a lake on the left, and woods on the right. She heard the road noise first, then looked and saw that Blaine had opened the passenger-side door on the Jeep and was poised over the side of the car.

"What the hell do you think you're doing?"

Emma grabbed her daughter by the hair and yanked her back into the car, and Blaine screamed and hit her, hard, on the arm. The car veered to the right and into the oncoming lane, but there was no traffic, and Emma got the car back into its own lane before a car came toward them from around the bend.

"Pull over, Mom, right now, pull over, I want out, let me out, let me out of the car."

Blaine's voice hit the upper registers of hysteria, and Emma drove with her left hand, keeping her right hand wound tight in her daughter's hair. Blaine hit her over and over and over, until she pulled the Jeep to the side of the road, the two of them screaming at each other.

It made Emma sick. Sick at heart. Sick to her stomach. Her arm hurt where Blaine had punched her.

Emma let her daughter go. Blaine jumped out of the Jeep, tripping on her way out, then scrambling to her feet, and running, then disappearing, into the woods. Emma sat in the car, chest heaving, tears running down her cheeks, watching the woods, wondering what in the hell had just happened. She waited a long time, door hanging open, cars whizzing by her on the left, but Blaine did not come back. And Emma did not know what to do.

CHAPTER NINETEEN

Blaine's feet hurt, and she could feel blisters bubbling up on her left heel. She would pick today to wear the platforms and skirt. The sun was out, but it was cold and she wished she'd worn a jacket.

Blaine looked down the road. She had a long walk ahead of her, a long walk to nowhere. A rusty orange pickup truck went by, slowing, the driver honking. Blaine kept walking, and did not even give the guys in the truck a look, reaching inside for what Mom called the "inner bitch." The truck kept slowing and Blaine felt her heart beat fast, but then another car came behind the truck, and the driver picked up speed and moved on.

It was really stupid, being on the side of the road like this. Her mother had put her in a terrible position. Blaine had stayed in the woods and waited awhile, and then she had looked out just in time to see her mother drive away. And part of her had crumpled. Her mother just leaving her like that. What kind of a mother leaves her daughter by the side of the road?

But it was a relief not to have to go to school. The girls all hated her. They'd all been good friends since kindergarten, and they didn't need any new people in the clique, especially not ones as pretty and smart as Blaine Marsden. The boys liked her too much. They followed her to class and honked at her in the parking lot, and girls she didn't even know came up and got in her face because some boy they liked was looking at Blaine. She couldn't go to the cafeteria—none of the girls would sit with her, and the boys wouldn't leave her alone.

She hated it here. She hated school, she hated the other kids, and she hated her math teacher, who could not speak English, made no sense at all, and ignored all of her questions. Blaine needed to keep her grade point average high to qualify for the kind of scholarships that would get her through college, and right now she was carrying a low D in Algebra I. She needed a tutor, but saw no point in asking Mom for a tutor when she had that worried look every time they went to Kroger. Her friend Brandon was good at math, and he'd promised to help her. Not that she'd ever see him again. She was on her own now, and never going home.

So where was she going to go? She could call Great-Aunt Jodina, but what would she say? I beat up Mom, come and get me? She couldn't bear it if Aunt Jodina stopped loving her. Plus she lived all the way up in Harlan, and it would take a long time for her to get down here.

Franklin had given her his home and office numbers, in case she needed him. Blaine had been touched, but there was no way she'd call him. It was just too awkward.

And Blaine realized that she didn't have any money. She'd jumped out of the Jeep without her purse or her backpack. *Shit.* Her mother had driven her nuts that morning, asking over and over, *Do you have lunch money, Do you have lunch money,* and had finally shouted, "I'm putting ten dollars in your purse for lunches this week."

That ten bucks was still in the Jeep.

Blaine sucked her bottom lip. At her old school, there would have been friends she could have called. At this dumb school they confiscated the cell phones, so nobody had theirs on. Twyla couldn't drive anyway.

At least Twyla had been nice to her. True, Twyla was a lot more out there than her mother knew. For one, she was pregnant again, and trying to decide what to do about it. Two, she was cutting school to hang out with Brian and Art, who were Mormon rednecks, looking for trouble and wives, which was a combination found only in weird places like her own high school. And Twyla was doubly attractive to both boys, being both trouble and open to marriage. She sure wasn't looking to go to college like Blaine was, although Blaine hadn't given up on the girl. She was smart enough, if she could just focus, although asking Twyla to focus on anything other than getting a fake ID so that she could sing country music at karaoke bars and get discovered was like trying to get Wally to stop barking when the doorbell rang. Impossible and noisy, both of them convinced you were interfering with their sacred role in life.

It was true that things happened when Twyla was over. The girl could not leave the fireplace alone, she had to light the kindling, like it was some kind of compulsion, and she was more likely than not to forget to open the flue, so the room would fill with smoke. But Twyla was no better at starting fires than she was at anything else, so at least they went out pretty fast.

The problem was, there was nobody else to hang out with. And whose fault was that? Who had moved her every two years, who had made her go to the stupid high school in Kentucky where she didn't have any friends except guys who wanted to *do* her? And then when she wanted to hang out with the one kid who was halfway interesting and acceptable as a friend, her mom says no, she can't come over, pick somebody else. *There wasn't anybody else.*

Anger or despair, which way did her mother want her to go? Her real dad did not care enough to even call her or send her a birthday card, he forgot her at Christmas, and Mom had kicked

Clayton out the door. At least Clayton had tried. Her mother shouldn't have let him move in unless she was going to keep him.

Blaine felt light-years away from her peers. Their biggest worries were which college to select; hers was whether she could even go to community college. Grades and financial aid would make or break her.

And now it was over between her and Mom. She might never see her mother again.

And the dumb thing was that school was finally getting better. Brandon was helping her with math during lunch, and Twyla sat with them, begging off half of Blaine's lunch every day, and with the three of them there in the cafeteria, bent over the books and laughing at stupid stuff, Blaine had felt normal, finally, like she blended.

Back at her last school she had been popular, she'd had lots of friends and was on the actual short list for homecoming princess. And she'd traded this for a hick high school with no computer lab and a foreign language program that was a joke.

Since Ned got sick, everything was always awful. Blaine was just trying to break out of that, and it was clear her mother wasn't going to let her. She and her mom had been okay before Clayton came along. Blaine knew her mother needed adults in her life—she needed a boyfriend. And it wasn't like her mother ever let them spend the night, or be there all the time. Not unless Blaine liked them. Blaine had nixed more than one, but she was more careful about that now, and sometimes, though she would never say it out loud, she wished her mother wouldn't give her quite so much power. But it was mostly a comfort. She had too many friends whose lives were ruled by the parent's boyfriend or the girlfriend of the hour, who came in and changed everything and shoved the kids out of the way.

She'd always admired her mother for staying independent. It meant money troubles, but she'd never handed the power over to some guy in exchange for a wallet.

But then her mother was pregnant and throwing up with really bad morning sickness. And she and Blaine had sat together and had a really adult talk about abortion. Blaine had been on the fence about it, as had her mother, but they'd decided to have the child because Mom did not get pregnant easily, and because she loved Clayton and he really, really wanted a baby. Her mom had told Blaine before she told Clayton, and they'd made the decision to have the baby without his help or input. And her mother had warned her, always be prepared to take complete responsibility for any child you have, Blaine, because you'll be the one responsible no matter what any man says. Some are good fathers, some aren't, so be ready to take it all on yourself.

But the dance studio had been making good money, and Mom could teach pregnant for a long time, and so they'd gotten kind of excited about it and bought a lot of baby stuff. Clayton had moved in, and for a while they'd been the kind of two-parent family Blaine occasionally envied. She, who did not have a father who cared for her, was not one to underestimate their value.

Then Ned had gotten sick. He'd cried and screamed and turned red in the face, and thrown up so much it was scary. But Mom had been calm the whole time, calling doctors and taking him to the hospital. Sometimes he got better, then he'd get sick again, but Blaine never thought . . . she never thought he could die. Not these days, with all the advances in medical science. It had happened so fast too. Sick, screaming, off to the hospital. And then Mom coming home in the middle of the night, opening the door to Blaine's room, and in the light from the hallway Blaine could see her mother's eyes, dead eyes, with deep pockets of black beneath, and she knew that something awful had happened. It never made much sense, the details about liver enzymes, and his system shutting down and organ failure. She just couldn't believe it. This kind of stuff didn't happen in other families. It happened only in hers.

Everything was a mess, and nothing would get better, it

couldn't. And there was no point in saying hang on till you get out of high school and go to college, because she had two more years of high school, and what college would give her scholarship money if she couldn't even pass Algebra I?

And then, all she did was ask if Twyla could spend the night. A small little request, for God's sake. She didn't want to go home to that *sadness,* those quiet dreary weekends where her mother walked around like a robot and other kids hung out with their friends, and the only thing Mom said to her was *Clean up your room, Have you done your homework?* and *What do you want for dinner?*

Blaine felt her eye swelling. It was going to be a shiner. Her own mother had given her a black eye. So now she had an abusive mother. Maybe it had something to do with the drinking.

Blaine had been worried about her mom for months now. Hearing her get up in the night, hearing her throwing up so violently, seeing her face go white like it did, and watching her hold her side. It was Amaryllis Burton who had told her what was going on. She had been over to the house with one of those baskets from the clinic, and her mom had been sick the night before and was sound asleep, and Blaine had refused to wake her mother up. But she had been very polite to Amaryllis, although she didn't much like her. She was Mom's friend and clearly disappointed that her mother wasn't available, and kind of hinting that Blaine should wake her up anyway. But Blaine had stuck to her guns, though she had invited the woman to sit down in the living room and offered to make coffee or hot tea or get her a soda. Amaryllis had given her that sickly sweet smile and made some remark about how grown-up Blaine could be, the kind of remark that sounded polite to other adults, but that Blaine knew was meant to put her down and make fun of her.

Amaryllis had said that perhaps they should have a talk. That Blaine should know that her mother was drinking, and not to think too badly of her, because her mother had been through hell, though it was a shame she could not put Blaine before this weakness.

Blaine hadn't believed her. She didn't like Amaryllis, and the way she was so obviously jealous of her mom. Mom was pretty, she wasn't fat, she was *built,* and she was funny and smart and a great dancer, and she would never embarrass Blaine in front of her friends by showing off her double-jointed arm like her grandmother used to do to her. Blaine was kind of proud of her, too. Mom, at least, had lots of friends—girlfriends as well as men friends, and boyfriends, because her mother at least was fun.

Blaine had tried to talk to her mom about it, but her mother just denied it right to Blaine's face about even being sick at all. That was a lie—her mother was sick all the time, Blaine heard her in the night. She knew she should get up and help her, but she was scared, because what if Mom had what Ned had? What if she died too? Blaine stayed in bed and pretended not to hear, which was what her mother seemed to want.

It was over between her and Mom anyway—for real this time. Her mother had gone too far; she herself had gone too far. Blaine couldn't go home if she wanted to, and she didn't want to. It was a cold empty feeling, knowing for a fact that her mother did not love her, that her mother was an alcohol addict with no concern about raising her daughter. And here she herself was saying no to all those drugs, most of them anyway, most of the time, and was that good enough? Oh, *hell* no. Nothing was good enough for *her* mother.

Today was one of those days when Blaine envied those kids with parents from the perfect households, where the money never ran out or got short, where both parents were home every night for dinner, where all the siblings stayed together and none of them died a long horrible death that nobody knew the cause of, where you didn't have to get used to new fathers. Blaine wasn't like her friends who never wanted their parents to remarry until they moved out, for no better reason than they didn't want to share the bathroom and get bumped down the line when it came to who got the first shower. She was more mature than that, she was kinder, she wanted her mother to be happy. Not that her mother appreciated her. Nope. But she remembered those years with her father, remembered how mean he was, remembered how she had missed him, but not near as much as she'd expected, and never ever wanted her mom and him to get back together. Most of the time, she liked the single-parent home. She liked it just being her and Mom, and she felt she'd been through life experiences that her friends had no idea how to handle. But money was too tight too often, and Blaine did not like having to sweat the deposits for the school field trips, and see that tight look on her mother's face when she made out the checks. If her mother was a better budgeter, these things wouldn't happen. If her father actually paid his child support, their life would be easier. Blaine never understood why all the newspaper articles and information made it seem like there were all kinds of agencies and help for single mothers to collect child support, when she knew better. It was like all that mythical grant money for college. She worried constantly, about financing her education. She wanted a top-notch private East Coast university, Harvard or Yale or maybe even Brown, and the odds were against her mother coming up with that kind of tuition, and her father made too much money for her to qualify for anything, even though he wouldn't dream of using any of that money to put her through school. Nope, college grants were just as mythical as child support. It always gave Blaine a sick feeling, thinking about her dad not paying. She knew lots of kids of divorced parents, and the dads paid child support, plus bought the kids stuff. She thought that maybe she was just the kind of daughter that a dad didn't want to pay child support for. In her head, she knew that was crap, but sometimes she couldn't help thinking it.

It had been better when Clayton was there, but Blaine always knew he wouldn't last. A man who didn't marry you when you were pregnant was a guy who wasn't going to stick. That was something Blaine knew at the age of twelve.

Blaine set her jaw. She missed her little brother, and thought about him all the time. She didn't think anybody knew that, how much she missed him. Sometimes late at night she'd think she smelled his milky, baby powder smell, and it was crazy but it didn't scare her. It happened mostly right after he died, and it hadn't happened for a long time now, and that made Blaine sad. She never minded watching him, or playing with him while Mom cooked dinner, or changing his diapers or giving him a bath. She liked reading to him, and doing puppet shows with the stuffed animals. He had this amazing belly laugh, and he would topple over, and he would always run right to her when she came home, calling "Bain, Bain." She'd taught him to say "Kick butt" for his first sentence, and Mom had laughed her ass off, but Clayton had given her the pursed lip.

Blaine kept her heart in cold storage. It was safer that way. Safer not to think of the bewildered look on her mother's face, about how she had cried. Blaine had no idea why she'd gone off like that, but she'd wanted to kill her mother, she really had. The rage had washed over her with a violence that literally made her almost throw up.

There was a Texaco station down the road, a long way down the road if you were in platform shoes that were already rubbing blisters. But Blaine set her jaw and kept walking. She'd just get whoever was behind the counter to let her use the phone. She hoped it was a woman, and not some man who would stare at her. Please God let it be some nice older woman. She could decide who to call while she walked. But she already knew, in the back of her mind, she would call her mother. In Blaine's life, there really was nobody else.

By the time Blaine limped into the Texaco station, her left foot was so sore she could barely put her weight on it. The woman behind the counter, taking money from an old man who had a wad of tobacco stuffed in his cheek, looked approachable. She had gray hair and brown eyes, and wore a sweatshirt that read "I Love My Grandchildren."

She caught sight of Blaine standing shyly just inside the door. "Well, honey, you must be freezing to come out on a day like this without no jacket or coat."

Blaine smiled and said, "Yes, ma'am." She felt the shyness hit her. She tensed as the older man turned to look at her, but he just nodded at her in a friendly way, and didn't *look* at her or make her feel uncomfortable.

"Morning, little missy."

"Good morning, sir."

Blaine waited till the man gathered up his pouch of Red Man and shuffled toward the door. His back was bent; he wore heavy work shoes and a thick and muddy corduroy jacket, and looked like he spent most of his days working outside. He nodded at Blaine as he went by, but didn't stare, then settled himself in an old chair near the door. He smelled like dust and tobacco.

The woman smiled at Blaine in kind of a worried way. It was a school day, and Blaine knew the woman would be wondering why she wasn't in class.

"I'm sorry," Blaine said. "Is there any way I can use your phone? I need to call my mom."

The woman motioned for her to come around the counter. "Why don't you hop up on that stool there, and you can use the phone while I ring the register? I got two people coming in to pay for gas."

So Blaine went behind the counter and climbed up on the wooden stool, and used the black phone that sat on a ledge near the back wall to call home.

She got the answering machine, and her stomach dropped. Was her mother there and not picking up? Or maybe she was looking for her, for Blaine, driving up and down the road? Except she hadn't seen Blaine walking to the Texaco station. So where was she?

The woman's back was turned, she was ringing up people at the register. Blaine felt she should just slide off the stool and leave, but then what?

"Did you get your mama?" the woman asked.

"She's not there," Blaine said.

"How about your dad?"

"He's—" Blaine didn't have to explain, though, because the woman waved a hand the minute she heard the hesitation in Blaine's voice.

"Why don't you try her again in a few minutes? Meanwhile, I think you could use a hot chocolate to warm you up. And don't you worry about paying, because I work here so I get them free."

Blaine had friends who worked part-time in gas stations, and she knew the woman didn't get the hot chocolate free, and she wondered if her grandmother who had died before she was born would have been like this. It would be so nice to have a grand-mother like that. Of course, she did have Great-Aunt Jodina, and Great-Aunt Jodina was like her grandmother, so that was good.

The woman brought her hot chocolate, a package of Dolly Madison White Gem Donuts, and a big Band-Aid for her blis-tered heel. Blaine ate the doughnuts and got powdered sugar all over her shirt, and she looked like her mother looked when she was baking something and getting flour all over everything. The lady helped her with her shoe buckle, which was awkward to reach when perched up on a wooden stool, and Blaine put the Band-Aid over her heel and put her shoe back on, the lady buck-ling it really loose, so that it would stay on but not rub so much.

Blaine tried her mother three more times, but she wasn't home, and she wasn't at the dance studio.

"Does your mom have a friend you could call?" the lady asked.

Blaine thought of Amaryllis Burton. For one, she could get

ahold of her, because she would be at work, at the Tundridge Children's Clinic. Amaryllis would know the name of that detective who had come to the house, and the detective might very well know where her mother was. It was worth a try.

"Do you have a phone book?" Blaine asked.

The lady rummaged under the counter, then brought up a tattered Yellow Book that had coffee rings on the top. "I've got this."

Blaine thumbed through, found the number of the Tundridge Children's Clinic, and asked for Amaryllis Burton. She waited on hold while the phone made regular beeps until Amaryllis came on.

"Blaine Marsden? Well, hello there, young lady. How can I help you today?"

Amaryllis sounded friendly and fake, like somebody was listening to her talk.

"I was wondering if you knew where my mom is?"

"No, honey, I don't. Why? What's the matter?"

Blaine didn't say anything. She wasn't sure exactly what to say.

"Aren't you in school?" Amaryllis asked.

"I need my mom to come and pick me up. I was wondering if she might be with that detective—the lady who was at the house, remember?"

"Of course I remember. Blaine, honey, I'll come pick you up."

"Oh, no."

"Where are you?"

"I'm at the Texaco station on Melton Road."

"All the way out in Athens, ha?"

"See, it's such a long way for you, and you're at work and everything."

"What's the number there, in case I have trouble finding it?"

Blaine put her hand over the mouthpiece. "Can you tell me the number here, ma'am?"

The woman wrote it down for her on a piece of paper and smiled, happy that Blaine had found someone to come and pick her up.

"Okay," Amaryllis said. "You just sit tight and I'll be there as soon as I can."

"Thank you so much," Blaine said. The woman was being incredibly nice, and Blaine felt bad that she had misjudged her.

The woman in the grocery was named Mrs. Webb, and she showed Blaine pictures of her grandchildren. There were three of them, all little and cute. Blaine felt conspicuous sitting up on the stool, but it was nice to be warm, and off her feet. It was a relief to have a ride coming, although it seemed to be taking Amaryllis Burton a long time to get there. Not much chance of getting to school by lunchtime. Maybe it would be better just to go home, since she didn't have a written excuse for being tardy. She would spend the afternoon studying her algebra and get her homework assignments from Twyla.

Blaine recognized the car as soon as Amaryllis drove into the Texaco station—a turquoise Nova with a crumpled front bumper.

She jumped down from the stool. "That's my ride. Thank you so so much for being so nice to me."

The lady gave Blaine a hug. "I enjoyed the company, honey. I've got loads of sons and grandsons, but the only girls we get are the ones who marry into the family. It was a pleasure to pretend you were my little granddaughter, even if it was just for one morning."

"Thank you," Blaine said. Perfect strangers were nicer to her than her own family sometimes.

Amaryllis was waiting for her in the car, and she reached across the seat and opened the door from the inside.

"Thank you so much for coming to get me," Blaine said. She slid into the front seat. The woman had been running the heater and it was nice and warm, a little too warm, but she had been cold all morning so it felt good.

The interior was a surprise. Wadded tissues on the floor, a lot of cardboard boxes on the backseat, magazines with the covers torn off, and candy wrappers and fast food bags. Every time Amaryllis had been at the house, she had looked around like she was judging them by their housekeeping and they were coming up short, so Blaine would have expected the woman's car to be vacuumed and free of the trash that was all over the place.

"I'm so sorry that you had to leave work to come and pick me up," Blaine said. "Was it hard to get away?"

"Oh, no, I had to stop off at my house and pick up a few things. To tell you the truth, I was only supposed to work the morning anyway. I'm taking some time off."

"Are you going on vacation?" Blaine asked politely. "Oh, you missed that turn. You have to go left to get to my house."

"I know that, honey."

But she did not turn the car around.

Blaine waited, hands knotted in her lap. Maybe Amaryllis knew another way to go. Or, more likely, she just thought she did, and she'd go another mile or two before she realized she would have to turn around. Blaine took a deep breath. She would just be patient. Amaryllis Burton would figure it out sooner or later.

"The thing is, Blaine, I called your mom right after we hung up."

"You did? Why?" Blaine felt the oddest sense of panic, rising in her stomach and to her chest.

"What happened between the two of you anyway?"

Blaine didn't answer.

"I guess you had a pretty big fight."

Blaine nodded. "What did she say?"

"Blaine, nothing she said made a whole lot of sense."

"What do you mean?"

"I mean, honey, that when I talked to her she was home, and she'd evidently been drinking. A lot. And she was kind of incoherent, I'm sorry to say."

Blaine felt the tears spilling down her cheeks, and she rubbed them away. She did not want to cry in front of this woman.

"I don't think it's such a good idea for you to go home right now. My brother and I have a little getaway house, down in Tennessee. I go there a lot on weekends and for vacations. I'm starting a little business down there, and that's where I was heading today when you called. I was thinking it might be good for you to come on down and stay with me, just a night, and give you and your mother a time-out."

"But what about school? What did my mother say?"

Amaryllis gave her a pitying look. "She said a lot of things, honey. Things I know she wouldn't have said if she hadn't been drinking. Things I know she didn't really mean. Let me put it this way. Your mom thinks it would be a good idea for the two of you to have a little break."

Blaine turned her face to the window. It was hard to cry and be quiet about it.

Chapter Twenty

Blaine had been cold all night. Racked with chills. Someone had come into the room during the night and covered her up with a blanket. Normally, she was a pretty light sleeper, but last night she had slept really hard. It was creepy to think of Amaryllis coming into her room and looking at her when she was asleep. Blaine listened for noises in the house. She had the feeling she was alone, but she needed to be sure. There was no lock on the door. Amaryllis had come in and covered her up with the blanket.

She wasn't sick anymore, just exhausted. But last night she had started vomiting, suddenly, right around midnight, her stomach heaving so hard she'd just about stood up with it. The pain in her stomach had been so sharp, she could not talk or call for help. The chills had been terrible. Freezing, freezing, freezing. And she had been all alone, and so far away from her mother.

Sick just the way Ned had been sick. Sick like her mother, except her mom brought it on herself now with the drinking. How she could stand it, Blaine did not know. How she could make herself that ill and still drink. People were right, it had to be a sickness.

But the thing was, Blaine never found empty bottles of alcohol in the garbage. Never saw her mother buy anything but wine, and not enough of that to make her as sick as she got. Blaine had been through the liquor supply after she'd talked to Amaryllis the first time. She knew where everything was kept; she'd tasted everything she wanted to try ages ago, with her mother's blessing. Mom took the mystery out of these things. She remembered one of the Mormon guys telling her that a friend of his could get them some beer. If I want beer, I'll ask my mom, she'd told him. He'd looked at her like her mother was the Antichrist. Her mother hated the boy. One time he'd asked her mom if he could marry Blaine, and Mom had said no, without hesitation or explanation, her words like the blow of an ax. The look she'd given the kid had embarrassed Blaine, and secretly pleased her. It was reassuring to know her mother would not let her do anything stupid, like get married too early to a Mormon boy who really knew how to surround a girl with his attention until she was so tangled she didn't know which way was up.

There was a bathroom off the bedroom, which was nice. Private. Blaine looked at her face in the mirror. White, her freckles standing out a mile. Ned had had freckles too. He'd looked like Blaine. He'd looked like a brother. Funny, she hadn't realized how alike they looked. Now that she felt like crap, with no makeup on and the night from hell behind her, she could see the resemblance. Face stripped of everything except the aftermath of misery, honed down to the outline of their features, they looked amazingly alike.

Maybe she had what he had. Maybe she was going to die. Last night when she'd been throwing up so hard, when she had continued to throw up long after everything was out of her stomach, long after her system was out of yellow bile and she spewed nothing but soapy white froth, she knew something was bad wrong. She knew her system was reacting, lashing out in survival fury, her body rocked by something really, really bad.

She needed her mom. She needed her now, before she got sick again. Only it looked like she really had gone too far this time, and her mother didn't want her back home. Amaryllis had told her to wait, when Blaine had brought it up again, kind of panicking when they were halfway to Tennessee, deciding she wanted to go home no matter what. And Amaryllis told her that her mother was still furious, didn't want her to come home, and was making arrangements either to put her in juvenile detention or in Charter Ridge. Amaryllis said her mother wasn't sure she could afford Charter Ridge, and it took Blaine's breath away thinking her mother had already been looking into it. Was that where she was when Blaine had called? Amaryllis said just wait, give her time to cool down. She'd been drinking, clearly, and wasn't thinking straight. But wasn't her mother worried about all the schoolwork she was missing? She'd been out of school for two days now. She was falling behind. She was losing more ground in Algebra I, and now she'd never pass. The unit test was coming up at the end of the week. Better to miss that, actually, and make it up later. After she'd had a chance to study.

She could call Twyla, and get all her assignments. Provided Twyla was actually going to school. But she didn't have her books.

There was a phone in the living room, and Blaine turned the knob of her door. It made a loud noise, and she held her breath, she was not quite sure why. The house had that empty feeling to it. She did not think that Amaryllis was there.

She heard a voice and stopped, then realized it was coming from outside. A man, right across the tiny lane. The house was one of eight on a small horseshoe drive, so close you could hear the neighbors open and close their front doors. The driveways here were weird, kind of like half drives, like little aprons in front of each house. Most of them were rentals. Somewhere, just out of her sight, someone was practicing jumps on a skateboard—she could hear it slamming against wood, then hitting the concrete on one of the driveways.

Amaryllis was not in the kitchen, or the bedroom. Blaine went to the phone in the living room and dialed home. Nothing but a busy signal, so no long distance. She could call collect, but what if her mother would not accept the call? Blaine dialed ten-ten-two-twenty, appreciative, for one swift second, for the commercials that she had always found annoying. At least she remembered the number.

She realized her arm was sore, and she saw that the inside of her left elbow was deeply bruised. She didn't remember doing that.

The phone rang. Six times, and then the answering machine picked up. Blaine felt her throat go tight and her nose start to run as the tears ran down her cheeks. Just this once, couldn't her mother be home?

She listened to the sound of her own voice, sounding tinny and weird, "Hey, you've got the Marsdens. Leave a message . . . ," and then, like a miracle, her mother's voice. "Blaine, if that's you, I love you. Come home. Wherever you are, it's okay, I'll come and get you."

"Mom?"

Then a beep, and Blaine realized that her mother had added this message onto the one already there. Her mother wasn't there, on the other end of the line, but she wanted Blaine to come home. She sounded so much like the same old mom, with that little catch in her voice at the end because she was obviously going to cry, and nothing at all like this new mom who drank herself sick, wanted to put her daughter in jail, and didn't seem to care how much school Blaine had missed.

"Mom, it's me, I'm . . ." Blaine realized the machine had shut off. And that she did not know exactly where she was.

Blaine hung up the phone. She could go outside and get the name of the road off a street sign, and maybe the address would be on the mailbox or painted on the curb. She didn't know the name of Amaryllis Burton's subdivision. She could still hear whoever it was out there practicing jumps on the skateboard. She could ask the skater.

The front door was locked and dead-bolted. Blaine went out on the front porch, looking for people. She didn't see anyone, but she could still hear the skateboard, coming from the left side of the house. She went down the front steps and onto the road.

The skater was right next door, male, sixteen or seventeen. Skinny and tall, wearing jeans with holes and boxer shorts over the top. His hair was tucked behind his ears; reddish brown hair, thin and silky, sticking-out ears. His Adam's apple was knobby and huge, and the toes had been cut out of his Skechers. He rode the board up the jump, then off, then nudged it with a toe, sending it spinning, catching it in his hand as he landed, lithe as a tiger.

He looked bored. Skaters always looked bored.

She just stood there, but he didn't say anything, just looked back, not unfriendly.

"I'm not local," she said. It was her usual introduction. She and her mother always moved so much, it applied to way too many situations.

"Me either."

"No?"

"From Tucson. Visiting my mom." He inclined his head toward the house behind him, the house exactly like the one she'd come out of, exactly like the one on either side. Across the street the houses were different. Same brick, same trim, but one story instead of two.

"You're not in school?" she asked. Another stupid dropout?

"Suspended."

She nodded.

"I live with my dad," he said. "Don't much like the new husband. But my father had to go to Toronto on business, and didn't want me running loose while he was out of town."

Blaine nodded. "What'd you do to get suspended?"

"Explosives in my locker."

She raised an eyebrow.

"It was just a few firecrackers. But, you know. Suddenly I'm a terrorist. An enemy of the state. A threat to homeland security."

Blaine rolled her eyes. "Bad break."

He shrugged. "It's a chance to get out of town. See my little brother. He lives with Mom. I don't get along with the new guy, that's why I'm with my dad. My mom's new husband is a prick. You know him?"

"No. I'm . . ." She looked over her shoulder. How exactly did she explain this one? "Look, I know it sounds retarded, but see, I had this big fight with my mom."

He nodded.

"And so now I'm kind of staying with a family friend, just a little while."

"What about school?" he asked.

"I'm flunking algebra. The thing is, it's kind of awkward at this lady's house. It's like . . . her own kid died years ago, and she doesn't want me to leave. But I want to go home, you know? If things are cool with my mom."

"Why don't you call her?"

"I tried. I left her a message. Then I realized, I don't exactly know how to tell her where to find me. What city is this, anyway? I feel like I'm in suburbia from nowhere."

He laughed. "Good instincts. This is Sevierville, as in Pigeon Forge, and Gatlinburg, Tennessee."

She shrugged. "Okay, Smoky Mountains and all that. Look, could you, like, call a friend of mine? Her name is Twyla. Ask her to get the down-low on this and see what's up at home and all? And tell her where I am?"

"Sure."

"It's in Kentucky. Where I'm from. So it's long-distance from here."

He nodded. "Sure, I'll do it. Just give me the number. By the time they get the phone bill, I'll be long gone. I've already talked to all my friends in Tucson."

Blaine heard a car on the pavement behind her, heard the slam of a car door. "I don't have a pen," she said, voice going breathless and panicky.

But he did, and he wrote her number down on his forearm. "I'll take care of it," he said, quickly and softly.

"Blaine?" Amaryllis, in her softest baby voice, only she sounded mad. Well, Blaine was mad too.

"Got to go," Blaine said, and turned away.

Amaryllis had opened the trunk. She did not put the car in the garage. "Blaine, can you come and help me carry these boxes? Goodness, never mind, your feet must be cold, what are you doing out here barefooted?"

Blaine put her hands in her pockets and walked carefully, avoiding rocks. Amaryllis was wearing that same stupid brown sweater, the one that had been worn so much the shape had stretched right out of it, but instead of the skirt she had on a tentlike denim jumper. That and dirty white tennies. And her long, long fake blond hair, clean and shiny, all pride and joy in a ponytail. Her bangs needed cutting. They came to her eyebrows now. The woman should wear makeup. Her eyes were so bland, so nothing in the pale round face.

"Who's your little friend? Not much of a gentleman, I guess. He could have offered to carry something in."

Blaine didn't try to explain that boys just didn't do things like that anymore.

Blaine expected grocery bags in the trunk, but no, just taped-up brown boxes. Small. She picked up two, and followed Amaryllis up the front porch steps and into the kitchen. She didn't like the kitchen here. The light wasn't right. It was dark and depressing, and there were thick cotton curtains over the windows, frilled curtains, curtains that her mother would have dismissed with a roll of the eyes and a mutter of "frou-frou" before she installed plantation shutters, like she had in their kitchen. Okay, crooked, but Blaine wasn't going to point that out.

Blaine poked at the boxes on the kitchen table. A round glass table with fabric-covered chairs. Ick. One of the boxes read "Scottie's Medical Supplies."

"I think if a boy really likes a girl, he acts like a gentleman. I guess that boy didn't really like you all that much. Although your mother always tells me how popular you are. With the boys. Guess this is one you missed."

Blaine smiled politely, but she was hurt. She was not a slut, and she did not care if that boy liked her. This Amaryllis said things in a nice voice, but she was always digging. Why was it her mother never saw that? It was as if having lost a child like they had lost Ned meant this woman was okay no matter what she did.

"Look, I need to go home. I know it's a lot to ask, but could you drive me back? I really need to go back to school and work things out with my mom."

Amaryllis gave her a look over her shoulder and headed to the sink, opened a drawer, and took out a pair of scissors. "You know I have about a million things to do myself, Miss Blaine. I have a little business I'm trying to get established down here so I don't have to stay at my job, which is pretty unhappy for me these days because I've been helping your mother, taking her side against Dr. Tundridge. I'm using my vacation time to get this done. It will take me four and a half hours just to drive you back to Lexington, and then another four and a half to drive back here."

"Maybe you shouldn't have brought me down here."

"Maybe I should have left you by the side of the road."

Blaine blinked. It was one thing for her mother to say things like that. This woman was weird and mean.

"Fine," Blaine said. "I'll find my own way."

She was to the door and out on the front porch when Amaryllis caught up with her, puffing away like she'd run a hundred miles.

Outside, a good wind was kicking up, and the sky had gone dirty blue. The air was snappish, and it was oddly warm.

"Blaine, don't be silly. I talked to your mother last night. She's driving down to get you this afternoon."

Blaine felt her knees give just a little. *Mom. Finally. Thank God.*

"Come on back in, it's going to storm."

Amaryllis watched her, eyes very round and unblinking. And Blaine stood in the doorway, hand on the screen, thinking how good it would feel to walk away and get out of this house because Amaryllis was really starting to creep her out. But Mom was coming. If her mom had already left, she'd be there before dinnertime. No more gaggy peanut butter sandwiches.

If she walked away her mother would never find her. All she wanted was to go home. Blaine looked back up at the dark kitchen, the living room, overfurnished and cluttered. And followed Amaryllis back into the house.

CHAPTER TWENTY-ONE

It was surreal, sitting on the worn fabric of Amaryllis's couch, in god-awful Sevierville, Pigeon Forge, Gatlinburg, Tennessee, listening to the woman's brother snore, trying to avoid looking at his large feet and his big toe thrusting through a hole in dingy athletic socks. Amaryllis had been talking about her brother all afternoon, saying he had called and was coming to stay, because they shared the house and he used it when he was in the area.

She talked about him like he was this very savvy-cool entrepreneur. Actually, he was tired looking, with slicked-back hair that was either oily or wet with rain, a potbelly that stuck up over the waistband of his cheap navy blue cotton trousers, and hair growing out of his ears. So totally unattractive and masculinity-gross that Blaine said an actual thank-you to God that hers was a single-mother household. Thank God her mother had never brought anything like this back to the house.

He had seemed startled to see Blaine sitting on the couch watching reruns of *Roseanne* in the middle of the day; seeing him had taken her equally aback. She had heard him first, the grinding metal noise of a semi truck, only it was just the cab, being parked on the street beside the house, because no way was there room in the actual driveway or out front. The cab was purple. Like bubble gum.

He had taken his shoes off when he entered the front door, and Blaine connected that with the pile of shoes on a mat by the entranceway and concluded that this was one of those "shoes off" households she and her mother always made fun of. No doubt she had already offended Amaryllis by wearing her shoes around inside, and while she normally went barefooted at home, or sock-footed in the winter, she now kept her shoes on at all times. It made her feel better. Like she was ready to go.

Blaine got up and looked out the window. She did not care if she woke Stanley up. He had introduced himself as "Stanley the Manly," and she had smiled really hard, unable to even force out a laugh.

No sign of her mother. She made a point of not looking at Stanley. Just being in the room with him brought on more intimacy than she liked.

She had eaten two of the peanut-butter–stuffed celery sticks that Amaryllis had brought her on a plastic plate. Blaine felt like a snob, but her mother never used plastic plates, and if you stayed at their house, her mother cooked or took you out and did not just give you peanut butter all the time—even though the peanut butter was homemade. Amaryllis always gave out jars of the homemade peanut butter like it was a kidney she was donating, and always with that aura of the overworked, perfectionist housewifey. But looking around this place, that was a joke. Dust, dirt on the carpet. Dishes with dried-up food stacked in the sink. It smelled. It smelled like garbage. Blaine felt a bit of nausea back in her throat, and she took slow, steady breaths. Please God she was not going to be sick again, not like last night. It was just a wave of stress nausea, she got that sometimes.

She looked out the window again. It was getting dark. Lunchtime had passed to dinnertime, and where was her mom?

She should have been here by now. *Please come, please come, please come.*

It had been raining hard, since before Stanley the Manly had driven up. She'd overheard him talking in the kitchen to Amaryllis. He didn't sound happy she was there—Blaine wasn't any happier about it.

It made Blaine uncomfortable, knowing he was just sitting there waiting for her to leave. She should be home by now, in the cozy little house Great-Aunt Jodina had given them so they would always be safe and have a place to live. She thought of her room, and the new furniture she and her mom had bought, the mahogany desk they'd found. She shut her eyes hard, trying not to cry. She should have called Aunt Jodina for help, or even Franklin. Why had she ever called Amaryllis Burton?

Blaine wanted to go home, to hear her mother in the kitchen chopping away at cloves of garlic, slicing onions, and playing her old-lady jazz music on the CD. She wanted to zone out in front of the TV with eight hundred cable channels instead of the ridiculous four Amaryllis and Stanley got with that stupid antenna on top of a television that was so old it was in a faux walnut veneer console cabinet. She wanted to go home to her mother's weird but wonderful kitchen, where her mom would be pulling out the iron skillet and sloshing it slick with olive oil, and probably making some pasta and singing to herself, and asking Blaine how her day was. Just the two of them. Normal. Ned was gone, and they'd always miss him, but it was okay, just her and Mom, and better than okay when Franklin was there.

She liked Franklin a lot. She knew he was crazy about her mother. They actually smoked cigars together and watched old movies in their sweatpants. What a cool relationship. And the best part was that it was the three of them hanging out, not a couple with a kid in the way. Sometimes Blaine and Franklin got on so well that her mother left them to whatever they were doing—usually killer backgammon or chess. Franklin was a fantastic chess player, and Blaine was still learning. And Mom would cook while they played, and it was just kind of easygoing and nice, and then Blaine could go out later with Twyla or something and not worry about leaving her mother alone. And Franklin liked to take the two of them places. *His girls,* he would say, clearly so happy to have two girls to call his own.

Had her mother told Franklin what had happened between them? Had she told him about how Blaine had gone berserk and "attacked" her in the Jeep? Maybe Franklin hated her now. Maybe he'd take her mother's side against her and never like her again.

Blaine pictured the two of them, Mom and Franklin, driving up in front of the house to pick her up. Maybe the rain was slowing them down. She heard a car outside and got up to look out the window again. Some car she didn't know, that didn't slow down. She was standing on tiptoe, trying to see farther down the street, when the pain hit again, sudden and hard, stabbing just under the rib cage on her right side. Any minute now she was going to throw up.

She wanted to run to the bathroom in her bedroom, but the pain was so bad she could hardly stand up, so she moved carefully, carefully and slowly. Stanley didn't even wake up. Amaryllis was in the kitchen, back turned, when she headed past the doorway and down the hall, but she was aware, on some level she was *sure,* that Amaryllis watched her while she held her side and bent double, and Blaine expected, even dreaded, some kind of concern, a question, a *Do you feel all right?* But there was nothing but silence, and Blaine was in too much pain to turn around and look.

She left the bathroom door open because she knew that Amaryllis would probably be in to see about her any minute. As expected, the vomiting was violent, so deep and so violent that Blaine felt she should be vomiting blood. There went the peanut butter, the celery, and that was all she had in her stomach. Bile next, then the white milky froth.

She knew that she was really bad off. She knew she needed help. She threw up, again and again, as if a vomit switch had been thrown and her body could not stop no matter that there was nothing left in her stomach. And the pain up under the ribs was so bad, she could not call for help. She had no breath for it. She could not speak.

The chills came, like they had the night before, and now she was seriously scared. It was like her body was going into shock or something. She curled up on the floor, head next to the toilet. If she didn't move, maybe she would stop throwing up. But no, that didn't work, and she was back up on her knees, until she could not get back up again, and she just vomited, sideways out of her mouth, on the floor.

Where was her mother? Why didn't she come? Why didn't one of the adults out there come back and put her in a car and take her to an emergency room somewhere? She had always hated going to the doctor, had cringed when people even spoke about surgery, and had thought after dark thought about the things Ned had suffered in the name of medical science. She didn't like remembering all the red marks and bruises on his little puffy arms when he came back from the hospital. But right now she would give anything to see a brightly lit emergency room, and she would tell a doctor to do whatever kind of surgery he wanted, just make the pain go away, make the vomiting stop, get her a blanket.

Footsteps, finally, and someone in her room. A heavy tread, then Stanley's face in the doorway. Help, she wanted to say, but it hurt too much to talk to him, and he looked at her with a certain amount of pity, but also a certain amount of shocked revulsion. What, she wanted to say, have you never seen barf? But she could not talk, she could barely breathe, with the pain that radiated beneath her ribs.

More footsteps, soft sliding ones, and Amaryllis was there right behind Stanley. Blaine closed her eyes, then heard the bathroom door close and realized that Amaryllis had shut it. They were just leaving her there, in a pile of spew. Her throat went very tight, and she could not stop herself from crying. None of this made any sense. Why would nobody help?

She shut her eyes tight. She could hear them.

. . . needs a hospital, Amaryllis . . .

. . . no, no, it's the drug . . . the Antabuse. She has a drinking problem, this kid, and she's violent, and she attacked her mother and refuses to go to school. Poor poor Emma Marsden, she was just at her wit's end. And couldn't afford the Charter Ridge thing again . . .

Again? She'd never been to Charter Ridge. And she didn't have a drinking problem, her mother did. Did her mother really say those things about her? Had she really betrayed her that way? It made no sense.

And Stanley was getting angry. Going on about how Amaryllis let people take advantage of her good nature, and they weren't running a halfway house for teenage delinquents, and Emma Marsden was taking advantage, and for his peace of mind he was pushing on to Orlando, he could make it by early tomorrow morning and pick up a load down there.

The voices faded. The bedroom door shut. And Blaine, who was a very smart young woman, figured it out, sick as she was. No, she did not have a drinking problem, and neither did her mother. Amaryllis was lying. Lying about Mom—after all, there were no other signs. The only sign had been her mom getting sick—sick just like Blaine was sick right this minute. Mom was not a drunk, and Blaine was not a drunk, and Amaryllis . . . Amaryllis was an evil bitch and up to no good, but what exactly she was up to was hard to figure.

But the worst thought was that if Amaryllis lied about all those other things, had she lied about her mom being on the way to get her?

Blaine remembered the wind kicking up before the storm, the way the breeze had felt, so warm and so inviting, and something inside her had wanted to just take off then and there, and oh, God, why hadn't she gone? In her mind she saw that open front door, and knew how far away it was, for a girl who did not even have the strength to sit up when she spewed. She closed her eyes tight because she knew one other thing too. She knew that her mother had no idea where she was.

CHARLIE

CHAPTER TWENTY-TWO

Charlie had been with Child Protective Services for seven years, though back when he and Janine had first located in Kentucky, Child Protective Services had been the enemy. Charlie was still career army then—a sergeant major. He'd been offered OCI three times, and his wife had gone doe-eyed at the notion of him going to Officer Candidate School and leaving for work every day in the color and confabulation of the management uniform. Neither one of them cared so much whether or not the family moved up in the social pecking order that rules military life, and Charlie had never seriously considered it. He was a rescuer, and a molder of young men, and his calling was to nursemaid teenage boys throbbing with the hormone dumps, inexplicable rages, and confusion that came with the territory. He knew when to take them seriously, when to ignore them, and he knew how to earn their respect. Better still, he knew how to motivate them, inspire them, and, most particularly, how to scare them utterly shitless.

And all that wonderful knowledge, all that experience, all that ability to be objective, to reassure the parents of his charges and to bask in their gratitude when he worked wonders with the kids

who had baffled, enraged, and grieved them since puberty . . .
yeah, all that shit had gone right out the window when it came
to his own sons, most particularly the oldest, most particularly
Kirby.

The trouble began with the transfer to Kentucky. Oh,
Kirby had shown the usual teenage flickers before then, but it
was the move that shifted everything into high gear. No
teenager wants to leave his friends and his school, but army
brats know the drill, and this transfer was going to be a good
one. The army was going to reward Charlie and thus Charlie's
family with a few years in a recruiting assignment—a nine-to-
five, and crucial to a military that was converting to an all-
volunteer army. They needed someone who could find the right
kind of recruit, and then inspire said recruit to commit to a job
that wasn't just a buck ninety-five an hour, and wasn't just the
chance to become a servant to the whims of the U.S. government, it was the opportunity to become an indentured servant
with benefits. Lots of benefits.

They'd moved from Denver, Colorado, to Lexington, Kentucky,
settling into an apartment complex near Tates Creek High School
and Tates Creek Middle School. The rent was cheap. Kirby was
enrolled as a sophomore at the high school, which shared a parking lot and campus space with the middle school, where Mitchell
was placed in the seventh grade and where his wife Janine got a
job teaching geometry to advanced ninth-grade students. It had
seemed perfect.

The cost of living in Lexington was high, housing in particular, but the economy was humming. It was horse farm
country, which put land prices at a premium, kind of like Los
Angeles, although this town was nothing like California. It was
pretty here. The horse farms that circled the town would take
your breath away, and the people weren't as conservative and
Bible Belt as they were farther south in Tennessee. Everything
was pretty, nothing junky, just miles and miles of rolling hills

ankle-deep in green grass, four-plank wood fences painted tarry black, houses that just made you shake your head, and horse barns that would have been impressive on *Lifestyles of the Rich and Famous.*

So they'd signed a lease, unconcerned and in fact smugly pleased that their home was enmeshed with project housing. Charlie wasn't a snob, and he and Janine believed in helping people when they needed it. Charlie figured the projects would be nothing to a man whose family was used to base housing, and who worked with teenage boys and now girls every day of his career. For a man who'd handled himself pretty well during Desert Storm, it was no big deal to imagine a life where he was happy to help the single moms who might need some man-work done around the place; and the gang kids, he'd be happy to kick their butts. Charlie and Janine had never lived near project housing, and Janine's best friend, Natasha, who had grown up in the projects, told Charlie he was being an ass.

But he and Janine blithely ignored Natasha and her sour attitude and figured they'd buy or rent a house later on, after they'd had time to get acclimated to the city. They'd have time to find a place they liked and more importantly could afford in the Tates Creek School District, where the housing prices weren't so bad. They could have gone on and bought a house, they'd found one they liked on Boston Road, but Charlie had been swept up in the beauty of the farmland around Lexington and was toying with the idea of living in the country. Janine was dead set against it—said it would be hard on the boys at their age. Said they had enough trouble in the move-every-minute world of the military dependent and no point making it harder. So they'd rented and decided to wait and see. They were going to be more particular this time. Charlie was getting close enough to retirement that they were thinking about digging in someplace and staying put. Teenagers were difficult enough without moving them every six months. They'd seen a lot of that. A lot of their friends with families on the move—people with highly developed coping skills and tight family camaraderie, and all of it going to hell when the kids hit the age of the enemy.

In retrospect, Charlie often wondered if they'd been able to settle somewhere a couple of critical years earlier, maybe Kirby wouldn't have hit the wall like he did. Not that Charlie had been in a position to have made such a thing possible. It was just one of those guilt-inducing parent thoughts that he countered with the example of other parent-veterans he'd talked to—many of whom never moved once, but still went through a lot of shit with their kids, so who knew? The hardest thing he'd learned was that he *didn't* know.

He'd eaten a lot of crow. The man who had been understanding on the outside but sneering on the inside when he saw the shit storms some of these moms and dads took from their kids—he'd become one of those bewildered dads. He'd joined that club of Parents Without a Clue—the club he and Janine had joked about since before they'd even had children. They sure as hell weren't going to put up with any crap. They were going to be loving, but firm. They weren't going to be weak. Their kids weren't going to walk on the other side of the mall because they were embarrassed to be seen with Mom and Dad. Their kids wouldn't slink down in the car and will themselves invisible. And they'd know better than to mouth off—in public or private.

Just listing the kind of stuff he and Janine used to think had often helped them keep a sense of humor, helped relieve the tension and make them laugh, but it also made them cry. Ignorance is bliss, Janine said. Sometimes he could hear the echo of his own voice, when he'd said something stupid like "Any parent who thinks disrespect from their child, and the way they act, isn't their fault for being a weak or a stupid example is just kidding themselves." He'd eaten those words every day for six years. They didn't taste any better now than they had the first time.

Now the boys were out of the house and into the dorms. Both Kirby and Mitchell had survived, and Charlie and Janine had made it through with their marriage intact and better than ever. Now they were on their own. The phrase "Sergeant Dad" had acquired an almost affectionate ring. The boys came home to hang out maybe one weekend out of six, not counting finals week, and once in a great while some problem might be approached in that side-angled subtle way young men have of skirting around an issue that could make or break them, something worrisome enough to mention in an offhand way to Dad.

The boys' mother had it even better. Janine, hell, Janine was a goddess as far as Kirby and Mitchell were concerned, and anybody who said the empty nest was a tragic place was either greedy for some sympathy to go along with the good life, female, or maybe just mentally ill.

Mitchell was a freshman at the University of Central Florida now, and continually wondering if he could cut an architecture degree while he kept up an A average, and he had trouble making friends. He'd posed the architecture question to Charlie during the spring of his senior year at Creek—which had gone much better than Kirby's senior year, mainly because Mitchell had been in the band. Put your kid in the band, that's what Charlie told anybody who would listen. Mitchell had played on the drum line, which was what Kirby should have done, but at the time Kirby was just trying to stay alive, and band was the least of their worries.

Charlie's first reaction to Mitchell's question was to say, "Hell, boy, if you want to cut it, then put your nose to the dirt and make it happen, don't sit around whining about 'what if.'" Luckily, that wasn't what he'd actually said. Reactions like that typified the kind of mistake he'd made with Kirby, and his oldest son had come so close to going over the edge that Charlie had been motivated by sheer parental terror into squelching those first reactions. It was almost a habit, these days, being careful with his opinions, and it had the unexpected benefit of keeping things cool with Janine. He didn't make quite so many dumb-guy mistakes.

Charlie was wise enough now to know that his answer to Mitchell's worry should have been, (1) he thought Mitchell was wise to take that kind of academic commitment seriously; (2) that he'd support Mitchell no matter what decision he made; and (3) that he had enough confidence in Mitchell that he had no doubts about his son's ability to not only survive but to excel in the architecture program. All of that would be topped off with a suggestion that maybe more information would be useful, and couched in a very gentle sort of wondering way.

That's how he reacted now with the kids he worked with in his job with the Kentucky Department of Child Protective Services, but at the time he'd just said, "Hey, go for it, what you got to lose?"

The only kind of person ignorant enough to give such an answer was the kind who'd never paid college tuition for his kids and then been rewarded with the grade report from hell. And that only if the kid was inclined to share this bit of information. Universities were clear on one issue—parents were there to fund the universities and their children's education, to enjoy significant responsibilities and zero rights. It was, by God, one time in your life when there was absolutely no hint of discrimination. White, black, male, female, Muslim or Baptist, skinny or fat—a parent was a parent was a checkbook. In high school, you complained that your kid thought you had *ATM* stamped on your forehead, but in college they wanted you to take out loans.

This kid Twyla, who he was on his way to meet with, was a particular frustration. No doubt she had some kind of disorder that made it hard.

It helped to like the kid, though, and he just couldn't stand this little twit Twyla. She wasn't stupid, she was just hell-bent on acting like it. And truth to tell, he just wasn't as good with the girl-child as with the boy-child. Girls were mystifying. Harder to scare, but easier to get under their skin, and then when you did, they made you feel so damn guilty about it— sometimes it just wasn't worth the effort. Girls were better motivated by showing them how to help themselves, or help someone else. By showing them how to get some kind of control over their lives, since, being female, they usually had so little, or so they thought. Helping them find the power was what he liked to do. The power to know what you want, and then go about getting it. Part Two was always harder than Part One, except with kids like Twyla. The problem with her was that what she wanted was just plain silly, plain unrealistic, plain dangerous. She wanted to be the center of attention, no matter what and no matter where, and no matter what anybody said about self-esteem, or upbringing, none of that mattered. She had to be the center. If she had to light a damn fire to get there, she'd do it, and in fact made a habit of doing it, which had landed her in his lap—that and her inability to attend school on any kind of a regular basis.

And he just didn't like her. In fact, he found her the most irritating person on earth. He reminded himself, as he did whenever he had a kid like this, that his own son, Kirby, hadn't been overly likable when he'd gotten into his bit of trouble.

Back then Kirby had been in the habit of wearing a worn top hat, which looked especially silly on a boy no more than five feet one inch tall, a skinny boy at that. A skinny boy in glasses, who oozed intelligence in such a way that he was irresistible to the neighborhood school bus bully—a kid called Reef who had locked on to Kirby like a heat-seeking missile.

Reef was an oversized coward, a six-foot-four, slope-shouldered idiot weighing in at roughly three hundred twenty-five pounds.

Kirby, not one to wait for the fates, had lifted a small pistol from the collection at the house next door—a particular frustration to Charlie, who was strict about keeping firearms out of the hands of children—and gone looking for Reef at the Y.

School shootings and violence surprised Charlie as much as they did other people, just not the same way. He couldn't figure out why it didn't happen more often, considering the weapons people left sitting around.

Kirby confronted Reef in the YMCA lobby, pausing right by the door (for a quick getaway—the boy wasn't stupid). Sure enough, as soon as Reef caught sight of him, he started in. Only this time Kirby pulled out his little handgun and fired and missed three times. Reef had dropped to the ground and gone quiet, one of the few intelligent moments of his life, and the bullets had bounced harmlessly off the glass door, the pistol being of such negligible caliber as not to even penetrate the glass. All of this was witnessed by two women at the desk, one an employee, and the other newly arrived for an aerobics class.

Kirby, surviving in the netherworld of high school, was making sure the right people knew better than to mess with him. He hadn't been worried about that other world—the world of police, social services, the Kentucky State court system, and that fast train to trouble.

Cathy Reardon, on her way to a supervisory position at Child Protective Services, hated kids with guns in their hands and was a no-tolerance brick wall, deaf to any plea. Charlie could see her point. She looked at Kirby and saw the gun in his hand. He looked at Kirby and saw his son.

Kirby had been lucky, sentenced to community service at Cardinal Hill Rehabilitation Facility (where he would assist a brain-damaged victim of a gunshot wound, as it turned out), a strict eight PM curfew that could be checked up on by CPS any time they wanted to drop around, family counseling, and a parent training class for Charlie and Janine that galled like a knife in the gut but made the system happy.

Charlie wanted to be the kind of guy who saw it from both sides, the gun and the child. So far, that kind of even-handed emotion was impossible with Twyla, so as usual, he faked it.

He took her to Sonic. They sat outside at a picnic table on a measly strip of grass and gravel between the two caverns of over-hangs where cars parked. Customers leaned out of their car win-dows and punched the speaker buttons, ordering from their own neon plasticine menus. Twyla loved Sonic. Charlie let her order whatever she wanted. Some kids you had to encourage to order because they were shy about it; others, like Twyla, blazed through the overhead menu like it was Christmas morning.

She ordered chicken strips, a grilled cheese sandwich, jalapeño cheese poppers, and fries. A jumbo drink that was blue and packed with shaved ice. Charlie had taken Twyla for food before, and he told the waitress to please bring out forty pack-ets of catsup exactly, and he would give her a big tip. Charlie did not have an exact figure in mind for what would constitute a big tip at Sonic, but it had to be worth avoiding the aggrava-tion of Twyla's constant recalls for more catsup please, more catsup.

Charlie was less than adept with the chitchat when it came to females. With Twyla that wasn't a problem. She came to every meeting between them with an agenda, and as soon as she had squeezed catsup into a formidable hill of sweet red, she took a bite out of her grilled cheese sandwich, opened the box that held the chicken strips, and canted her head sideways, meeting his eyes.

"How's things at school these days, Twyla?" he asked. So she'd know his agenda right up front.

Twyla chewed, considering. He waited. She didn't have much patience for cat-and-mouse. One of the few things that made her tolerable—except if she decided to outright lie, which was always extremely likely, then she'd stick to her story in the face of ninety-mile-an-hour headwinds and not blink an eye. A good liar, Charlie had discovered, always believes his own version of the truth. The memory of making it up is the first to fade.

"Who told you?" she asked. Sliding a french fry through the mound of catsup.

"I never reveal a source."

The truth was, nobody had told him. Her mother hadn't called, nor had her real father from upstate New York, or her stepfather, from right down the road. No school counselor had called his office. No one had made a fuss. She'd been written off, this child had, and he supposed she knew it. Supposed that was the real source of the trouble. Someone to give a damn. Funny how some kids would not walk straight no matter what—good parents who cared, a school administration on its toes and ready to intervene. But that was the exception and not the rule. Most were like Twyla. Most were like grass in the desert, no chance in a hostile, uncaring environment. His job was to be the touchstone, and then the one who showed them that they could create their own caring environment. That they could discipline themselves and have a good life, if they so chose. Many of them did. Charlie was weary of complaints from his colleagues. If they hadn't come into the job with ridiculous delusions, they wouldn't be so weary. Nobody could save the world, and those who tried were guilty of arrogance and foolish time management. The opportunities to help were frequent, and eminently doable. Whether or not Twyla was one of the opportunities remained to be seen. Charlie well knew that what he tried to teach her now, about herself and about life, might well not sink in for years. If ever. On the other hand, it could sink in today or next week. Many of his clients got over all the acting-out and nonsense. The problem was getting them to that point of reference before they did permanent damage.

"I've got a friend who's in trouble."

"You're in enough trouble yourself, my girl. Better pay attention to that."

She frowned at him and flipped the long blond hair back over her shoulder. She was a little bit chubby, but it did not seem to concern her, as it did 98 percent of the other girls her age. She had a focused self-confidence that Charlie felt he ought to admire, but instead it just made him think of the single-mindedness of a sociopath.

Not that Twyla was one.

"I'm serious, Charlie."

"Mr. Russell."

"Mr. Russell. You know, lots of kids call their social workers by their first names."

"You can call me Mr. Russell."

She glanced over her shoulder, distancing herself. He had just caught on to that little habit. As if when she glanced away, he no longer existed.

"I said I have a friend who is in serious trouble. Like she's been kidnapped, sort of. She's stuck with some weird old lady who won't let her go home."

Charlie took a sip of coffee. He ignored the hush puppies he'd ordered. He knew that Twyla would eventually eat those too.

"Where's her mama and her daddy?"

"Daddy? God knows. Her mother doesn't know where she is. She ran away."

"Do we need to go to the police about this?" Charlie was prepared to call her bluff. He also knew that Twyla might well go through the motions of a police report if she were planning to stick to one of her stories.

"She made me promise not to."

"Twyla, this whole thing sounds like a—"

She looked up at him. He'd been about to say "load of crap," and he stopped himself.

"Twyla, the person I'm worried about right now is you. I'm

worried about why you're not going to school and dropping out your junior year. I'm worried about you flunking Algebra I after we worked so hard to get you some tutoring and you brought your grade up to a C. I'm worried about you not going to chorus class after we got things taken care of so you could go on the field trip over Thanksgiving."

"Let's cut to the chase, Mr. Russell. If I go back to school and stop skipping, will you help my friend?"

"Maybe. If I can. But not until you have six weeks of attendance without missing a day. Not even one sick day."

"Mr. Russell, she's—she can't wait six weeks. How about I promise you six months, not one day missed, and you help her now."

"First you have to talk to me a little about why you've been skipping."

She shrugged.

"Come on, Twyla. You always have a reason for everything you do. And if we don't work on it, then your promise to me, no matter how much you mean it right this minute, will be impossible for you to keep. So what's going on with you right now?"

She looked at the catsup. "I've been thinking about going to live with my dad again."

"Now, Twyla, you told me before you don't like that school up in Syracuse. You said the kids up there weren't friendly, and you didn't have any friends, like you do here, where you grew up."

"I might need to get away."

"From what?"

"From a boy. I ummm . . . I told him I was pregnant. With his kid. And I'm not. And he wants to marry me. And it's kind of getting out of hand. He's Mormon, see, and he wants to keep this baby and settle down."

"Is there a baby, Twyla?"

She shrugged. "Not this time. I did get pregnant once before, just so you know. And I thought I was. I missed my monthly bill."

It still amazed Charlie that such a young girl could talk so frankly about such things and not bat an eye. In his experience, most girls did not discuss these issues with most males. But Twyla, as he had discovered early on, was not most girls.

"Anyhow, I told him I'm pregnant, and now he's pressuring me and calling and waiting for me in the hallway at school. I'm scared I might just marry him to make him leave me alone."

Charlie nodded. In actuality, he did not understand, but one of his first and hardest lessons in social work had been how the female of the species succumbs to pressure.

"How old is this boy?" Charlie asked.

"Eighteen."

"You sure?"

"Yeah. He just turned."

Charlie smiled. "Bingo, then. You're fifteen. He's eighteen. I can make him go away."

Twyla frowned at him. "I don't want him in jail."

"I think a well-placed call to parents in this case will likely do the trick."

"He's Mormon."

"Even better."

"Okay, about my friend."

"Six months, Twyla. A written agreement between you and me, and I expect you to sign it."

"Never hold up in court," she told him.

"It doesn't have to. It just has to hold up between you and me."

She nodded. "Okay."

"What's your friend's name?"

"No names. Not yet. See, she ran away from home."

He wanted to roll his eyes, he really did. "Why?"

"She had a dumb fight with her mom. So she didn't go back home. She went and stayed with her mom's friend."

Charlie raised an eyebrow. "Not a bad move, having a short time-out, unless this friend happens to be male."

"No, a woman. Only now, this woman, she won't let Blaine go home. She's, like, keeping her prisoner. She won't let her out of the house, she won't let her near the phone."

Charlie raised an eyebrow. "Oh, really now? So how did you find out about it?"

"See, she talked to some kid in the neighborhood who was walking by. And gave him my name and number and told him what was up."

Charlie fingered the Styrofoam edge of the coffee cup. Possible, actually. The helping hand of other kids on the street, or off, was a presence in this generation. They trusted each other, and in truth, the trust was often very well placed. Which was a comforting piece of knowledge when one considered the future of the world.

"What about the mother? Is she okay?"

Twyla shrugged. "She just doesn't like me, so it's hard for me to be objective. She thinks I'm a bad influence."

Score one point for the mother, Charlie thought.

"Blaine says she and her mother mixed it up a little."

"What does that mean?"

"Blaine says she kind of got physical with her mom, but you have to understand, it is so totally—well, the thing is, they've had some hard times. But even if Blaine thought she had a good reason. I mean, there's no excuse for beating up on your own mom."

Charlie looked at Twyla and smiled, for real. "There's an opinion we both share."

She smiled up at him, showing a chipped front tooth. Their first moment of rapport. Even though Charlie was fully aware that Twyla was manipulating him, telling him what he wanted to hear to get him to help. He didn't care how his clients got on the right pathway, so long as they got on it.

"Twyla, I admire you for one thing."

"What?"

"That you've agreed to not skip school for six months if I'll help your buddy Blaine. It's selfless."

"Selfish?"

"Self*less*. You're putting her interests before your own."

"Not really, Charlie, since you always tell me it's in my own best interest to go to school."

He gave her a sideways look but let the "Charlie" slide. She was on the right track with him, and she knew it. And no reason she shouldn't.

"Has her mother reported her missing to the police?"

Twyla shrugged. "I doubt it. She's got her own problems. You've read about Emma Marsden, and that Munchausen's thing?"

Charlie felt a headache coming on. "That's your friend's mother? Tell me what you know."

He listened and took notes. Somewhere in the back of his mind, he knew he would have to be very careful with this. Twyla was more than capable of making the whole thing up. He believed her, though. He believed her because she had stopped eating.

One of the biggest problems, to Charlie's way of thinking, was that the kid, this girl-child, Blaine, was across the state line and somewhere in Gatlinburg, Tennessee. He took the problem home to Janine.

They sat out on the back porch, Charlie watching over the steaks, Janine hopping up every few minutes to check on whatever she felt needed checking on in the kitchen. He wished she'd just sit still; knew it was impossible.

"They have a lot of pancake houses there?"

"Like raisins in a cookie," she said. "Why? Who's down there? Something going on I should know about? With the boys?"

"Ah, no, hon, the boys are fine. This is about one of my kids. Twyla."

Janine rolled her eyes. "Twyla? The one who called last night and demanded to see you?"

"She's got a friend in trouble."

"That's no surprise."

"Yeah, I know."

"She probably made the whole thing up."

"Always that possibility, but this time I think not. I did a little research. Her friend in trouble is a girl named Blaine Marsden. Fifteen years old. Her mother is Emma Marsden, the one in the papers?"

"The Munchausen Mama?"

"Yeah. Looks like this kid ran away from home."

"Can't say I blame her. Whatever happened with that case? Didn't they put the mother in jail?"

"No. It's still grinding away in the system. Our office launched an investigation, but only on the say-so of the doctor. The word is, there's not a shred of actual evidence the mother did anything at all. But they are proceeding to take the daughter and put her in foster care. They tried to cut her a deal, according to the paperwork. Said if she'd admit to it, and take parenting classes . . . but she said, hell no, she wasn't guilty, and she would fight them."

"You're telling me they're going to take the child out of her home with no evidence just because this doctor said so?"

"That's what I'm telling you. One of Cathy Reardon's cases."

"*Cathy Reardon?* That piece of work who tried to put Kirby in jail when he took that gun to the Y?"

"Um-hmm."

"Okay, I just changed sides. I'm with the mother."

"So am I. The report says the doctor was suspicious because she was—quote—very proactive in her son's medical care."

"Charlie, you know that's a description of any good mother. You think for yourself, you don't just do like they tell you. Nobody knows your child like you do."

"I'm not arguing with you."

"You can't sit there and tell me they'd take a child away based on that and that alone."

"I can sit here and tell you that with this doctor it's already happened two times."

"I thought Munchausen by proxy was rare."

"It is."

"Then I think the person to be looking at is this doctor."

"He's not my problem. Blaine Marsden is my problem. If I help her out, then Twyla will go to school six months without skipping."

"And I've got a bridge I'd like to sell you."

"It's worth a chance. It's not like I can turn my back on this. And maybe Twyla will help herself if she can do it to help out a buddy. A lot of kids get motivated that way. It's one of the things going right with this generation."

"Charlie, this sounds like something you need to talk to the police about. Somebody in Juvie."

"Juvie? Janine, you know if I do that, this mother and kid won't stand a chance. Cathy Reardon is a runaway train for trouble, and I want to know more about what's going on before I make things worse."

Charlie stood up, opened the grill. He turned the steaks, flipping the raw red meat to hiss against the hot metal, sprinkling the exposed sides, nicely seared, with seasoning salt and lemon pepper.

Janine tapped her fingernails on the arm of the lawn chair. "And besides which, this is the perfect opportunity for you to finally get back at Cathy Reardon."

"That too." He looked at her over his shoulder. "You think I'm wrong?"

"Hell, no, sweetheart, I'd just like to be in on the kill."

"You can live vicariously through me."

She blew him a kiss. "You think you might be going down there, to Pigeon Forge and Gatlinburg?"

"May go on down there day after tomorrow."

"Can I come along? We could go after school lets out, and I can get some early Christmas shopping in at the outlet malls. We can eat some pancakes while we're there."

"Revenge. Pancakes. Child rescue. And shopping."

"Just another day in the life."

Charlie laughed. Janine always made him laugh.

CHAPTER TWENTY-THREE

Charlie hadn't slept much the night before, and was in the office before six. Getting up early was no problem for Charlie, not after all his years in the military. He had gotten worried about that little girl, Blaine Marsden, the kid who really wasn't any of his business.

He'd spent most of the time he'd planned to sleep going over the ethics in his mind. He'd had to do some thinking before he went slogging through Cathy Reardon's case.

He'd never forget how anxious she'd been to throw his son to the wolves, and how the power she held in her hands seemed to eat her up from the inside out. She had the God syndrome, no question about it. And the God syndrome in social work was a disease Charlie himself did not want to catch. So he'd gotten up finally, and flipped through the textbooks, and the statements on ethics, to remind himself exactly what job he was supposed to be doing.

Before he was on the job himself, like most people on the outside looking in, Charlie had been horrified by cases that came to light in the media—caseworkers neglecting their charges or, on the opposite end, playing God and wreaking havoc on families that were already in trouble.

237

Now *he* was a social worker. And he was still shocked—shocked that it didn't happen more often, considering the workload and the legal bureaucracy most caseworkers had to deal with. Seeing the uncaring parents, the crap households . . . how often he busted ass to get some young girl with kids, no husband, and no income into a government-subsidized education program, CNA training at the Red Cross, or some such, only to find she'd stopped going to classes because she didn't want to get up that early in the morning. Those kinds of cases made you crazy.

Everything he needed to know to make his decision was right there in the preamble to the National Association of Social Workers Code of Ethics. It was his job, his *primary mission,* to "enhance human well-being and help meet the basic human needs of all people, with particular attention to the needs and empowerment of people who are vulnerable, oppressed, and living in poverty." He was to "focus on individual well-being in a social context and the well-being of society." The mission of social work was rooted in the following core values—*service, social justice, dignity and worth of the person, importance of human relationships, integrity, and competence.*

It tickled him, more than a little, that the son Cathy Reardon had been so determined to put in juvenile detention three years ago was the son who had taught him how he could hack into the department computer.

Charlie sat behind his desk and organized his work space. Large cup of black coffee. An ashtray, which would disappear at eight o'clock when the official clock began to tick, and a big fat cigar, which would be smoked by the time the workday began. As for the cigar smoke, he would deny it, as always. Though he was sorry, of course, that it made Cathy Reardon break out in a rash.

His first task was to gather the information. He was a slow reader, always had been, always had to read each and every word, sometimes twice if the material was the least bit technical. He made his own private copy of the Marsden files, then scanned the database for names and made copies of files that had those names, which is how he came to cross-reference three other Munchausen by proxy accusations from Dr. Theodore Tundridge.

The Munchausen's cases, few and far between though they were, always bothered Charlie. Only one had come through the department that he remembered. Charlie had been suspicious because it had cropped up right after a television movie on Munchausen's. Too much coincidence, was Charlie's opinion. The jump-on-the-bandwagon effect. But some of his colleagues disagreed, preferring to think it was more a matter of getting the information out so that the syndrome was recognized and reported, like a disease that had gone unnoticed.

He'd trained enough boys in the marine corps to know there were parents who could do such a thing. Some of their kids had wound up under his command in boot camp. But Janine had a point when she said that this sort of charge was invariably made against women.

What bothered Charlie the most was lack of due process. A doctor like Theodore Tundridge had to do nothing more than point his finger, and a child could be removed from the care of its mother, with the full cooperation of Child Protective Services. Usually some kind of compromise was made. If the mother agreed to admit that she was guilty and to take prescribed parenting classes, she could keep her child.

This did not sit well with Charlie. He was personally familiar with having to feign humility in parenting in order to satisfy the agenda of Child Protective Services. What about the woman who was not guilty? She had the choice between losing her child and being ground down by a system that considered her guilty until proven innocent, or saying she was guilty for the sake of expediency, taking the classes, and keeping the child. A lot of women would do that, guilty or not.

What kind of woman wouldn't? An Emma Marsden wouldn't. The whole thing was ludicrous anyway. Her daughter was fifteen, not five, and from all accounts perfectly healthy. What exactly was it that the department had on Emma Marsden, anyway?

It took him three hours of painstaking reading, and he forgot to put out his cigar, and had to slam it into a drawer when Cathy Reardon peered over into his cubicle. He pretended not to see her and kept his eyes on the reports she would have been incensed to know he was reading pretty much under her narrow, pointed nose. He took notes.

Tundridge had certain criteria for identifying his Munchausen's mothers. He'd made three accusations in the last five years, which, considering the number of accusations brought by other doctors, was a hell of a lot. It could, of course, be argued that as a pediatrician specializing in very sick children, he would therefore have a higher level of exposure to this sort of thing.

The profile Tundridge had put together, according to Charlie's notes, included "(1) A child with a medical problem that did not respond to treatment." That one was interesting. It could certainly be the doctor's fault. That one made Charlie uncomfortable.

"(2) A parent who seemed medically knowledgeable."

So any nurses or CNAs or doctors themselves were high on the list?

"(3) A highly attentive parent who either appears unusually calm in the face of crisis with her child, or becomes hysterical."

That one pretty much covered everybody.

Also under suspicion was a mother who encouraged more tests and was very supportive of the doctor, as well as a parent who was combative and disagreed with the medical tests ordered.

Charlie felt the pit of his stomach go cold. So far, he and Janine were scoring high on risk factors. The red flags were broad enough to include almost anyone. Were they prosecuting mothers on this nonsense?

Other red flags included "A mother with a different social standing from her spouse." What did that mean?

"A mother who had at some time in her life committed a crime." How would the doctor know that?

"A mother who had had a dysfunctional upbringing," which was a category that included everyone or no one, depending upon your personal outlook.

"A SIDS death in the family"—okay, maybe and maybe not. It was a terrible thing that often happened through no fault of the parent.

"A tendency toward attention-seeking."

In whose judgment? Charlie wondered. Did that mean a mother who didn't take the doctor's word as law? A mother who got a second opinion, or made trouble if the child didn't get good care . . . in short, almost any good mother?

Where was the hard evidence? Charlie wondered. They didn't seem to have any on Emma Marsden. What they did have, curiously, was a videotape of her having sex in the parking lot of a restaurant. This happened on the anniversary of her child's birth, seven months after the child's death, and it happened with the father of the child, to whom it was unclear whether or not she had actually been married. According to the notes, she had said they were married when in actuality they were not, which was considered suspicious by Child Protective Services. Evidently, in the view of the department, Emma Marsden was a slut, and sluts were highly suspect.

Her other child, Blaine, was perfectly healthy, but the notes made by Reardon said that often only one child is victimized, and the rest are left alone.

The medical records were interesting. Evidently, the boy, age twenty-nine months, had been taken to Tundridge with manifestations of severe liver distress on three occasions, the third one resulting in death. The boy would be brought in violently ill, his liver enzymes spiking. The enzymes would drop, the boy would get better, and then it would happen all over again. Tundridge had run tests for hepatitis, congenital gallbladder disease, various toxins and poisonings including pesticides, and household detergents. He had been unable to find anything other than a severely diseased liver.

It interested Charlie, more than anything else, that Dr. Tundridge had not made the Munchausen's accusation until fourteen months *after* the child had died. What had triggered it? Maybe Reardon had her dates wrong.

He checked the other cases.

One other involved a child who had died, and was made six months after the death of the child. The third had involved a patient who was being treated at the time.

Charlie rubbed his forehead. Not enough information, and he was beginning to worry that he was in over his head on this. He didn't have enough to do anything on an official level, and he had too much to let it go. He for sure didn't like the profiling. And he'd seen a lot of people get railroaded. He was afraid that Emma Marsden might be guilty of nothing more than having sex in the parking lot of a public restaurant on her dead son's birthday. Which surely wasn't everybody's idea of a properly grieving mother, but on the other hand was nobody's business.

Charlie wondered who the hell had been on the other side of that video camera. Awfully convenient for somebody. The video ought to have no influence in the case. Ought not—but Charlie was well aware that it would.

LENA

CHAPTER TWENTY-FOUR

Emma Marsden wasn't alone when I pulled into her driveway. There was a car I didn't recognize parked right behind the Jeep Wrangler that Emma drove. I heard Wally barking when I rang the bell, and I recognized the man who answered the door.

I had seen him in court several times—the state medical examiner, Marcus Franklin. My knees went shaky. Something bad had happened.

"I'm Lena Padget. I work for Emma. She called me?"

He seemed more like a host than a professional when he shook my hand and invited me in. "I was here when she called. I'm Marcus Franklin."

"I know."

He raised an eyebrow at me, and Wally rushed to greet me as soon as I was through the door.

"Down, Wally," Franklin said. Wally immediately dropped all paws to the floor.

"Marcus, how do you do that?"

I looked up and saw Emma sitting alone in the kitchen.

Her voice had that flat quality common to people under stress. She looked fragile, her eyes dark and lost. Her worry simmered beneath the surface, as tangible as a pot boiling on the stove.

"Any news about Blaine?" I asked. Emma shook her head. I bit my bottom lip. My feelings were hurt. She should have called me the second it happened, and it took all of my self-control not to ask her why she hadn't.

Missing teenagers are the trickiest. There's usually a fight. The parents are angry and hurt and on the defensive. And in protect mode. They might want to kill their children in private, but they want to protect them in public. The problem with that is the legal issue. Report it to the police, and the child officially becomes a runaway. Don't report it, and you're a negligent parent.

Marcus Franklin sat next to Emma at the table. I noticed that he was wearing bedroom slippers. He did not seem to be here in a professional capacity.

"Emma, I need to know what happened. How long Blaine's been gone, why she left. You have to trust me with everything." I realized I was still on my feet, and took a seat across from them at the table.

"She's been gone since the day before yesterday. In the morning," Franklin said.

"Why did you wait to call me?" It had slipped right out. So much for self-control. I knew from Emma Marsden's face that I had just added another layer of guilt to the weight on her shoulders.

They both started to talk, but Franklin pulled back and let Emma tell it.

"We had a big fight. I was driving her to school because she hates to take the bus. And she jumped out of the car and ran away."

"What did you fight about?"

"It was stupid, nothing big. I wouldn't let her have one of her friends spend the night, and she just blew up. Got totally hysterical, and I . . . I pulled to the side of the road so she and I could talk sensibly, and she jumped out of the car and ran away."

I waited.

Emma looked down at the table. "I pulled over to the side of the road because my little girl was beating me up."

Marcus took her hand. Emma cried silently and the morning light trickled into the kitchen.

"My daughter has been gone two days. She hasn't called. None of her friends know where she is, or if they do, they won't tell me." Emma held her arms out.

There were bruises on her arms, finger marks on her skin the blue black of ripe Concord grapes. She lifted her chin so I could see the scratches on her neck that had bled and scabbed over, and the muscle area in her upper arm looked like the sky before a thunderstorm. Blaine had evidently driven her fist in hard, over and over. I noticed Emma winced when she moved.

She wore no makeup, and her face was round and pale, the way your face looks when you have cried yourself out and haven't slept. She was wearing comfort clothes—an old pair of Levi's, quite loose, and a French blue T-shirt that was worn soft but not quite threadbare. Her feet were bundled in clean white socks, thick and soft.

Emma put her arms back down. She seemed to me like a bird that has flown into a window and lies stunned and bewildered on the pavement below. We sat quietly. A breeze ruffled through the open window, making the blinds sway and clack. Emma held a cup of hot coffee in a bright yellow ceramic mug. She did not drink the coffee; she simply held the cup.

None of us spoke of the litany of horrors that can befall an angry and foolish teenage girl out on her own, but the knowledge was heavy around us, like a fog.

Emma hiccuped and then laughed. "I'm sitting here wondering how many calories you burn when you cry."

Franklin shook his head at us, but Emma and I both laughed,

and I grinned at her, because only another woman could possibly understand the thought.

"Emma, you have to make a police report. For your own protection, if nothing else." The only way to deal with the police was to work within expected parameters. Too many people were arrested because they didn't act like they were supposed to act. And once the police think you're guilty of something, you might as well be. Behavior outside of the norm, like having sex in a car on the anniversary of your son's death, had already gotten Emma in enough trouble.

"I did already; Marcus took me." Emma squeezed his hand but looked at me. "But won't that get her in trouble? Won't it cause her to have a record?"

"Emma, there are so many kids that run away, your problem will be getting police attention, not fending it off."

Marcus was nodding. "That's what I told her."

Emma folded her arms and began rocking gently in her chair. "Do you know what it's like to be talked down to by a little girl with a blond ponytail in a police uniform? To have her tell you that any teenager who beats on her own mother has problems? That if I don't get it under control now, she'll kill me one day? Blaine? This policewoman wasn't even old enough to *have* a child, much less tell me about mine. And you know what? They weren't the least bit worried about Blaine. They were worried about *me.* They took pictures of my bruises. They wanted to know if I wanted to swear out a warrant for her arrest."

I looked over Emma's head at Marcus Franklin. He was watching me. He shook his head slightly, but I didn't need him to tell me that now wasn't the time to tell Emma Marsden that the little girl in uniform had been right. Franklin, who had no doubt done his share of autopsies in the ebb and flow of family discord, seemed to be walking into the life of Emma and Blaine Marsden with his eyes open. But here he was, right there in the kitchen when Emma needed him. I liked that.

Emma blew her nose on a napkin. Her voice took on the tone of a mother making excuses for her child. "We've had a pretty tough couple of years, you know? You can't explain something like this to someone who doesn't have children."

My own feeling was that you could. But this time I kept my thoughts to myself.

Emma shoved the napkin into her jeans pocket. "God, I feel weird. Like I'm walking through water on the bottom of the ocean."

"It's the sedative I gave you," Marcus said. He glanced over at me. "I've gone over the medical records of Emma's son. I persuaded Dr. Tundridge to share some tissue samples, and I ran some of my own tests, put some skates on the results."

"Lena, do you want some coffee?" Emma asked.

"That would be great." I looked over at Franklin. "Go on."

"There were definitive traces—"

"You take cream, don't you?" Emma asked me.

I stood up. "Emma, excuse us, just for one minute. Dr. Franklin?"

I headed into the living room, and he followed. We stood between the couches.

"Emma is—"

"I get it. Tell me what you know."

"Ned Marsden was poisoned."

I caught my breath. "What are you saying? That it was intentional?"

"I don't know that. His system was full of—"

"Put it in layman's terms, Dr. Franklin."

"Okay. He was chock-full of mold toxins. The kind of toxins you find in nuts or grains. He had to be ingesting them continually. He had too many attacks spaced too far apart for it to be something isolated. Eventually his system weakened, was overloaded, and he died."

"You said nuts? Does that include peanuts or not?"

"Peanuts are legumes, but yes, the mold could definitely start there."

"Could it be grown there? On purpose? How hard would it be?"

"It's a problem farmers contend with all the time. And it would be pretty easy to contaminate peanuts."

"How could you be sure they were contaminated?"

"There are simple tests that measure it. Farmers use them all the time. Their problem is volume—it's financially ruinous to throw out an entire barn full of grain when only a small segment is contaminated. But if you were *intentionally* contaminating a small sample, it would be very doable. But I'm telling you right now that Emma didn't do it."

I put a hand on his arm. "No, of course she didn't. But I think I may know who did."

"Peanut butter?" Emma stood in the doorway, holding a cup of coffee. She looked at me, walked across the room, and handed me the cup. "Could it be in homemade peanut butter?" She looked at Franklin. "Amaryllis Burton gave us homemade peanut butter. Ned loved it, and I gave it to him. It was really good, and he liked it so much I saved it *all* for him. I ate the store-bought stuff. Blaine doesn't like peanut butter. But then, when Ned died, I started eating it. And I've been getting sick."

Marcus Franklin nudged her to sit on the couch and he sat beside her. "When you say sick, Emma, what were your symptoms?"

"Pain, right here." She pointed to her midsection. "And violent vomiting. It's like an attack. It lasts about three hours. The pain is incredible, and the vomiting is violent. Like nothing I've ever had before. I get chills—"

"Why didn't you say something?"

Emma looked over at me.

"She couldn't," I said. "Of course she couldn't. She's been accused of Munchausen's. If she starts coming up with the same symptoms, then they're going to say she's poisoning *herself* now. And if they couldn't find out what was making Ned sick, there's not much chance they're going to figure out what's making Emma sick. Right?"

She nodded. Franklin sat beside her and put his arms around her. "What a nightmare."

I perched on the arm of the recliner, too antsy to sit. "You got the peanut butter from Amaryllis Burton, right, Emma?"

She nodded. "But we had it tested. It turned out okay."

I thought of the jars I had found in Amaryllis Burton's desk. Some labeled with a flower sticker. Some not.

"The jar you had tested was okay. That doesn't mean they all were," I said.

Emma shook her head. "There's no way she could have poisoned it. She wouldn't do something like that. Her own son . . ."

We were all quiet.

"That's right," I said. "Her own son. And not her only child to die."

Emma caught her breath. "She had other children?"

"Yes. As it turns out. Two other children, both died as infants. That's a total of three dead children. I've done background on her, Emma. She's a licensed practical nurse, an LPN, but she does reception work for Tundridge, not nursing. She's worked in the pediatric wards of two hospitals that I know of, and been fired from both. Look, Emma, when I first started working this case, I didn't believe in Munchausen's. But now I'm not so sure. I'm thinking about Amaryllis Burton. It's been my experience that some people accuse other people of what they themselves are doing."

"But Amaryllis didn't accuse me. She believed in me. She was the only one on my side."

"How do you know that?"

"Because she was here—you met her. She comes over, she's kind, she brings me—"

"Homemade peanut butter. Poisoned homemade peanut butter."

"Oh my God. I feel like Snow White."

I looked over at Franklin. "Did Tundridge tell you why he suspected Emma of Munchausen's?"

Franklin shook his head. "We didn't get into it. I wanted him to share tissue samples, and that's tricky territory. I didn't want to say anything to spook him."

"So the question is, does Amaryllis Burton work for Tundridge? Does he know the children are being poisoned?"

"Not a chance," Franklin said.

"Why? Because he's a fellow doctor, and you don't want to believe it?"

Franklin frowned. "Maybe. But there's no way he's going to share samples with me if he's guilty."

He had a point.

I stood up. "Franklin, run some tests on Emma. See what you can find in the way of toxins. Do you have any of that peanut butter left?"

Emma nodded. "Half a jar."

"I've got two other jars I took from the clinic."

"How—"

"Don't ask, because there's no way I'll tell you. One thing at a time, folks. Right now I need to find Blaine."

"I don't understand why she hasn't called me," Emma said.

Neither did I, but I kept my mouth shut.

"I'm scared for her. And I also want to beat the ever-living crap out of her."

"Let's get her home first. Listen, Emma, do you have a picture of Blaine that I can have?"

"Sure. In the bedroom."

"Go get it, will you?" I waited until Emma was out of earshot, then turned to Franklin.

"I know," he said. "I've got feelers out, in case something bad turns up."

"What do you think, Dr. Franklin, does Blaine do drugs? Was it that kind of thing? How well do you know Blaine?"

"I've been around her a lot lately. She's a great kid. I think the world of her. I do suspect she smokes pot, and I don't think Emma knows. But it's not like her to disappear and not call her mother. They're close, she and Emma. I've given her my cell and office numbers, and I've told her she can always call me. But we're still new, Emma and I. So I don't know if she'd feel awkward about calling me."

Emma came in carrying a picture, which she handed me while looking at both me and Franklin. "What's going on?"

"Emma, is there any chance Blaine might have called Clayton?" I asked.

Emma shook her head no. "She didn't call him, I've already talked to him three times."

"Okay. Tell me exactly where you were when she got out of the car. I need to know what she was wearing and what she had with her. Backpack, purse?"

"She didn't have anything. She left it all. And she was wearing a long skirt and platform shoes."

"Not planned then. That's good." Good and bad, I thought. Good she hadn't planned it, bad she hadn't shown up. "Emma, I want you to sit down and come up with a list of Blaine's friends."

"I've already called all of them."

"Call them again. Have Dr. Franklin call them. Talk to their parents. Kids hide each other, I've seen it a million times, and some of the parents let it slide. Pound away. Tell them that even if Blaine won't talk to you, you have to know if she's safe. You'll have to use your own judgment about when to get tough and bring up the cops, and when to be soft about it. You got a cell phone, Dr. Franklin?"

"Yes."

"Write the number down for me, that's how we'll stay in touch. All other lines stay open in case Blaine decides to call."

CHAPTER TWENTY-FIVE

I found tire marks at the side of the road where Emma said Blaine had jumped out of the car. The tread was fresh, and it looked like the tires on a Wrangler. Not that I was sure, but sure enough. The ground was still muddy and soft, and I saw little footprints leading into the woods, the kind you would make in platform shoes, which Emma said her daughter had been wearing.

The ground in the woods was dry. I didn't find any strands of hair in any tree branches, but I spent some time roaming around, watching where I walked. I wanted to know if Blaine had ever even come out of the woods and back to the road. Likely, but I wanted to make sure.

I stuck to the edge of the tree line, where Blaine could watch her mother and stay hidden. I didn't find anything, like threads or lost buttons, but about a hundred yards farther up the road, I found another small footprint. Looked just like the ones near the Jeep tracks. It looked like Blaine had come out of the woods there, and walked back out on the road.

The footprints pointed to the highway, and most likely she had crossed the road to walk on the asphalt walkway that ran along the lake on the other side. I crossed right where I found the footprint and walked for a while. I didn't see anybody. It was early, there wasn't much traffic. Blaine Marsden had picked an isolated spot, and she was a very pretty teenage girl.

I checked my watch. Eleven AM, my hungry time, but I had no appetite today.

Blaine was smart. That much was clear from meeting her the other afternoon, and from everything that Emma Madsen had said about her. She struck me as sensible. She'd moved around a lot, which would give her some street smarts, and she was very self-possessed for a fifteen-year-old.

She'd walk along the road, looking for a phone. That was the most likely thing. But she hadn't called her mother. So either she hadn't found a phone, or she had called someone else.

Unless Emma Marsden was lying and trying to cover up something. Parents, in the way of spouses, are always suspect number one. But I didn't think so, and the footprints bore me out.

I got in the car and drove slowly, looking left to right. I saw two other cars. I supposed Blaine might have tried to hitchhike, in which case Franklin would likely know what had happened to her before I did.

Three miles down the road I found a Texaco station and food mart. I pulled up next to the curb in front of stacks of canned Coca-Cola on sale for three ninety-nine for twelve, and went inside.

I waited for a woman wearing uncomfortably tight blue jeans to pay for gas and a package of M&M's. I usually have a hard time resisting M&M's, and just seeing someone buy a pack would usually trigger me to buy one myself. Today I was not tempted.

The guy behind the counter was in his early thirties, long, lean, eyes set close together and lips thin and tight.

"Help you?" he asked.

"Yes, I'm looking for a missing girl." I took out the picture and handed it to him. "I wonder if she came in here day before yesterday in the morning, some time around eight-thirty, nine o'clock."

The guy spent a long time looking at the picture, and the way he looked at it made me put him on my list of people to check out.

"I didn't work that day."

He held on to the picture, and I held my hand out. He passed it over.

"Can you tell me who did?"

He shook his head. "Company policy. We can't give out the names of our employees."

"You can tell me or the cops."

"I'll tell the cops."

"Excuse me, miss?"

I turned. An old man in a dirty corduroy coat came from behind an aisle where he'd been looking at the Little Debbie Snack Cakes.

"You mind if I take a look at that picher?"

I handed it to him. More thumbprints.

"I seen her."

I looked at him. He met my gaze and held steady, nodding his head.

"I was in here a couple days ago, buying my smokes. And this little missy comes in limping and needing the phone."

As soon as he said limping, I believed him. Blaine Marsden had walked over three miles in platform shoes.

"Did she use the phone then?"

"Oh, yes, Belinda was working here, 'cause him yonder didn't show up for work."

I had to resist turning and looking at "him yonder." But I was glad that he hadn't shown up for work.

"Now Belinda, she's just the sweetest woman ever live. She sets that little missy up to sitting on the stool, gets her some hot chocolate and some little doughnuts, and tells her to go on ahead and use the phone all she want. And after a while, some lady come and pick her up."

"You saw the lady who picked her up?"

"Nope, 'cause she didn't get out the car."

"But you saw the car?"

"Yes, ma'am. Was one of them old Chevy Novas."

"What color was it?"

He squinted. "Not quite sure. Green, maybe? Is the little missy okay? Din she go home? She said she was a-wanting to call her mama, but there weren't nobody home. Belinda tol' her to call a fam'ly friend."

"I don't know if she's okay or not, sir. But I'd like your name and number if I need to get in touch."

"Don't got no phone, but I live right up yonder there on the hill. White trailer."

"Thank you, sir. You've been a lot of help."

"I hope she is okay. Such a polite little thing. Sayin yes ma'am and all. Belinda took a shine to her."

"I really appreciate your help."

"Ma'am, I don' want to hold you up. But you think you could drop back by here and let us know when she turns up? Belinda and me would be happy to know she's okay."

I promised him that I would, and exchanged glares with the guy behind the counter as I headed to my car.

Amaryllis Burton drove a turquoise Chevy Nova.

CHAPTER TWENTY-SIX

I knew where Mr. French had his office, so I made it past reception at the Tundridge Children's Clinic without being seen. I had checked every car in the lot. The Chevy Nova wasn't there, and the car in Dr. Tundridge's parking spot was a RAV4, not the Volvo that had been there before.

I heard the shouting before I got to the door. Mr. French and a woman. No point knocking and giving them a chance to say no.

Mr. French was standing up next to his desk, and a woman was sitting in his chair, computer screen pulled close.

"—I *sign* those tax returns, I'll remind you of that." The woman was furious, and she turned to me with a frown.

"Who are you?" she asked.

"She's that detective," Mr. French said, and to me, "And I'll be calling the police."

"You go right ahead," I told him. "Because Emma Marsden's daughter is missing, and someone on your staff is involved. While you're at it, call the FBI."

"*Detective?* Mr. French, what is this?"

"It's nothing you need to worry about."

256

"Do I need to remind you that I'm a major stockholder in the clinic corporation, and that you answer to me?"

He looked at her and blinked.

"Sit down," she ordered. He sat in the chair that had been pulled up close to the desk. She turned to me, and held out a hand for me to shake, which made me like her. "I'm Syd Tundridge."

"The doctor's wife."

She looked expensive. The hair, the nails, the casually thrown-on slacks that had a designer tag in the back. I knew because I'd seen Judith wear a pair just like them, and she told me they cost her over three hundred dollars.

"That's right, I'm Ted's wife. Who exactly are you?"

"This woman came in last week," Mr. French said. "She's working for Emma Marsden. Her client's son was Ned Marsden, one of the patients who died."

"Yes, I know exactly who Emma Marsden is. Her son was barely over two years old. Liver failure, over a year ago, wasn't it?"

"That's right," I said. "About three months ago someone from this office called my client and said that Ned had been buried without all his internal organs."

Syd Tundridge leaned closer. She looked grim, but not surprised. "Go on."

"My client wasn't aware that anything had been . . . kept back. She thought she'd buried her son completely intact."

She looked at Mr. French. "The permissions again."

He shook his head. "I know, Syd, I've tried, but what can I do? You know what he's like."

She cut him off with a wave of her hand. "Then what?"

"Then my client came here and found that her son's heart and various other parts were preserved as samples downstairs in your chamber of horrors."

"It's a pathology lab," Mr. French said.

"Quiet," Syd told him.

"She objected, and soon after Dr. Tundridge accused her of

Munchausen by proxy. None of this is news to you, is it, Mrs. Tundridge?"

"No, it's not."

"You've seen the videotape?"

"I'm the one who insisted we send it to the police."

"Then I'll tell you to your face, I think someone on your staff here had something to do with it."

Syd Tundridge shook her head. "Not a chance. We have better things to do."

But she looked like she felt guilty about something.

She tapped a finger on the desk. "What about the missing girl? What did you mean when you said somebody who works here was involved?"

"You have a woman on your staff named Amaryllis Burton?"

"Not anymore," Mr. French said.

"I fired her day before yesterday. Why?"

"Emma Marsden's daughter has disappeared, and she was last seen getting into a car with Amaryllis Burton."

"Amaryllis and Emma Marsden are friends, as I understand it," Mr. French said.

"Are you aware that Ms. Burton is a licensed practical nurse?"

Something in his eyes. "Only recently. Not when we hired her."

"Think that's odd?"

Syd frowned. "Amaryllis is an LPN?"

"Not licensed anymore," I said. "Tell me why you fired her."

Syd shook her head. "I can't do that." She looked at Mr. French, who threw up his hands.

"Syd, I think you better."

Syd Tundridge sat and thought, rocking from side to side in her chair. She closed her eyes for a minute and took a breath.

I lifted my chin. "Maybe I can help you. Are you aware that your husband patented genetic material from the blood of Ned

Marsden and is in the process of selling this patent to a pharmaceutical company?"

Syd Tundridge opened her mouth, then closed it. "Not until yesterday, no. I didn't know the patient was Ned Marsden, I just knew it was one of the patients who had died. But the patent is already sold, for the price of four-point-eight million dollars."

She braced her arms on the desk. "Amaryllis dropped by my house several days ago. Bringing me some of the accounting statements. I don't like Amaryllis, and she knows it. It's mutual. I couldn't figure out why she dropped the statements off, but I figured she was trying to cause trouble. Messing with people is one of her favorite pastimes."

"She had no business with that paperwork," Mr. French said. "She took it right off my desk."

"I'm aware," Syd said. "Obviously something was up. I started going back over the books. I found this million-dollar slush fund—" She glared at French, who winced. "I think that's what Amaryllis wanted me to find. She knew it would cause problems between me and Ted. But I also found out that Amaryllis has been buying medical supplies on our account. Not using our money—we would have caught that. Just going to Scotties and buying things with our discount and authorization codes, and paying for it herself. That's why it took us a while to track it down.

"Day before yesterday, I came in to fire her. I had talked to Mr. French by phone, and we both agreed she had to go."

"Long overdue," Mr. French said.

"She didn't seem all that upset," Syd said, frowning. "I was braced for this big emotional scene. But she just smiled at me, really nasty, and said okay. I asked her what she was using the supplies for, and she said she was setting up her own little business down in Tennessee."

"Tennessee?" I said. "Why Tennessee?"

"She's from there. From Gatlinburg. She's got a house down

there she inherited with her brother. She spends a lot of week-ends down there."

"That's why she's been calling in sick all the time," Mr. French said. "She's been setting herself up in business."

"What kind of business?" I asked.

"She didn't say." Syd pushed hair out of her eyes. "And then, she gets this really sickening little smile, and says maybe I should ask my husband about the millions he's made selling patents to the drug companies. If she hadn't told me that, I don't know how long it would have taken me to catch on." She looked over at Mr. French. "You didn't do such a bad job of hiding it, but you shouldn't have paid off those loans."

"I was under orders, Syd," French said.

"Then what?" I asked.

"Then Janet comes in and says that Amaryllis had a phone call, and that's the last time I saw her. I cut her a check for two weeks' pay and went to find her, but she'd gone. Didn't even clean out her desk."

"It wasn't her desk," French said.

"Don't pick at things, Mr. French, it might not have been her official desk, but she used it."

"What time did the call come through?" I asked.

"I don't know, after nine, maybe nine-thirty. Why?"

"Can you get Janet in here?"

Syd inclined her head to French, and he picked up the phone and spoke softly. His shoulders slumped, and he rubbed a palm across his forehead.

Janet was quick. No doubt she had overheard the shouting, because she looked tense and wide-eyed.

Syd smiled at her. "Janet, do you remember when you came in here the day before yesterday and told me that Amaryllis Burton had a phone call?"

Janet nodded.

"Do you know who it was?" I asked.

"They didn't say."

"Female?" I asked.

Janet nodded. "It sounded like a young girl. It was some-body Amaryllis knew because she called her honey and was really sweet to her, which was weird because I knew she just got fired. I thought she would have been all upset, but it didn't seem like it."

"Did they talk long?"

"No. But she did say something about she'd come and pick somebody up. And then she walked right out."

"Do you have caller ID?"

She nodded. "Yes, and I looked, but the call came from a gas station in Athens."

I took a deep breath. "Thank you."

Syd looked at me, but waited to speak until Janet left the room. "What is it? Amaryllis was friends with the Marsdens."

"Maybe," I said. "If you think someone like Amaryllis Burton is friends with anyone. But Blaine Marsden went missing day before yesterday, in the morning, after she had a fight with her mother. It's pretty clear Amaryllis Burton picked her up. And she hasn't called Emma to let her know that Blaine is okay or that she has her."

"What would Amaryllis want with Emma Marsden's daughter?"

Mr. French sat down and put his head in his hands. "*Oh, blessed Jesus.*"

Syd looked at him. "Does this have something to do with Ted leaving a clinic full of patients today?"

Mr. French's voice had gone thin. "An e-mail came into the clinic late last night. On the private address, the one we use for . . . for the pharmaceutical companies. It offered to sell us blood samples, samples that contained the specific genetic mate-rials that had been present in Ned Marsden's blood. The message said a sample would be left at a certain place, and that Dr. Tundridge should take it and see if it was what he wanted. And if it was, then he should get his checkbook ready, and they would be in touch."

Syd stared at him. "Are you kidding me? That's where Ted is right now?"

French nodded.

I picked up the phone and slammed it down in front of Syd Tundridge. "Call your husband. Now. Call him on his mobile and stop him. Then we call the police."

"But—"

"Look. Amaryllis Burton has kidnapped Emma Marsden's daughter. There's two reasons you don't want your husband anywhere near Amaryllis right now. One, she's dangerous. And very unpredictable. Two, she's our lead to Blaine Marsden."

"Amaryllis?"

"She's had three children, Mrs. Tundridge. Every single one of them are dead."

She looked from me to Mr. French, then picked up the phone.

Chapter Twenty-seven

It was funny the way she had fallen instantly asleep right there in the mess on the floor. The second the pain had stopped, she had gone to sleep. Blaine was afraid to move, afraid she would feel that pain again. Last time it had gone away completely. This time it was still there, more in the background but definitely there. She did not know how long she had been asleep, but she thought maybe a long time. It was light outside now. It felt like morning. The house was quiet.

She crawled out of the bathroom, moving slowly, pleased to find that the pain had receded to the point that crawling was comfortable enough, pleased that just moving that little bit did not bring back the nausea.

The bedroom was cold, the window was open. Blaine heard something rustling outside. Probably a cow. The house backed right up to a farm; she had noticed the rolls of hay in the field, the sagging barbed-wire fence, the white-and-brown cows who were sometimes there and sometimes not. Wally would have wiggled right under that fence. Wally was extraordinarily gentle with other animals, and often lay on her belly to play with smaller dogs so they would not be intimidated, but even Wally would bark at cows.

Blaine really really really missed her dog. Wally liked to sleep right in the doorway of her bedroom—that way she could protect Blaine and keep an eye on the rest of the house, and make herself available for snacking on any food that might be prepared in the kitchen after Blaine went to bed. Wally would eat anything. Wally would even like the peanut butter that Blaine could still taste in the back of her throat.

It occurred to Blaine that she had eaten nothing but peanut butter since she'd been here, and she'd gotten sicker and sicker. She knew that her mother ate that peanut butter sometimes. At home, Blaine turned her nose up at peanut butter, even the homemade kind. It was her least favorite thing, and her mother usually had better things to eat around the kitchen. She'd eaten it here because that's what she had been served, and she had been raised too well to complain, question, or ask for anything else. Maybe there was something wrong with the peanut butter. Maybe that was what was making her sick, and her mom sick. And Ned? The Nedster had eaten that peanut butter too.

The night Marcus had talked to her and her mom about what had killed Ned, he had said there were some kind of toxins in his system that eventually caused him to die. Blaine had a lot of questions that night, and Marcus had answered them adult to adult. It was obvious, too, that he was really smart. And he didn't flinch, no matter what she asked. Her mom had finally had to go out of the room. But Marcus had said that the toxin that Ned had was found in animal feeds, like corn, and grains, and also in nuts. He had said almonds, but he'd also said peanuts, which weren't really nuts but legumes.

And Ned had eaten peanut butter. He was crazy for it. Mom had kept food diaries, and they had thought about the peanut butter, but he didn't get sick every time he ate it, just sometimes, so it was hard to tell. But Ned ate the peanut butter, and Ned got sick. And she knew her mom ate the peanut butter, she ate it on wheat bread for breakfast. And her mom got sick. And Blaine didn't get sick, and she didn't eat the peanut butter. Except now. She'd eaten Amaryllis Burton's peanut butter, and she was sick.

Blaine had thought she was cried out, but the thought of little Nederick being in the kind of pain she had been in last night, and him only a little bitty guy . . . and all because of that idiot woman's peanut butter? It was like botulism in homemade canned vegetables. Stupid, stupid bitch. Suzy Homemaker bitch. Could they get her put in jail for that? For involuntary manslaughter or something? Negligent homicide? Marcus would know. No matter if this stupid woman hadn't meant to make them all sick, after a night of agony and lying weakly in her own vomit, Blaine wanted Amaryllis put in jail for the rest of her life. Let her make peanut butter for the other inmates.

And then Blaine caught her breath. Maybe it was all on purpose. The more she thought about it, the more it made sense. The baskets the woman brought to the house. Poisoning them. Because why?

Blaine didn't have a problem figuring why. Not after what she'd seen of Amaryllis Burton. Because she was a jealous, weird, crazy woman, that was why.

She needed to get away.

The wind stirred the leaves. Blaine thought of climbing out the window. It was just as well that Wally wasn't there, because Wally could not climb out of a second-story window, and Wally would have definitely eaten the peanut butter, and Wally was way too heavy for Blaine to carry even when she felt good. Right now she wasn't even sure she could walk to the window, much less climb out and make it to the ground in one piece.

Of course, out the front door would be better.

Blaine was shaking, but she got out of bed and tried the door. Locked in. She turned on the lamp, trying to stay quiet, and looked at the door. She had thought it had no lock, but the hardware had been put on backward, and the lock was on the outside, not the inside. It would have to be the window.

The doorbell rang.

Blaine felt her heart jump. Maybe it was Mom there, come to take her home. She listened. She could hear someone moving around in the kitchen. Amaryllis, she guessed. The doorbell rang again. Could it be her mother?

She raised herself on one elbow. The pain was there, but not as bad. She slammed the bedroom door hard with her fists. It made a good noise, a thin hollow cheap door, and she pounded on it till it vibrated in the frame.

"Open . . . the fucking . . . door. Now. Open it, you bitch, open it."

She stopped pounding for a minute. Heard the doorbell again. And then a slam, from the other side of the door, and Blaine jumped back. Someone had hit the door, hard. Blaine knew that it had to be Amaryllis; she could smell her, the perfume and old-lady smell she had.

"Be quiet in there, or I'll make you sorry."

Amaryllis. In that hideous little voice.

Blaine felt the air stir on the back of her neck and the nerves tingle at the small of her back. And part of her was even a little bit relieved, because it was out in the open between them, mortal enemies.

"I'll fucking kill *you* before *you* kill me." Blaine said it in the lowest, deadliest voice she could make. She wasn't her mother's daughter for nothing.

The doorbell had stopped ringing. Blaine went to the open window, hit the screen hard with her fist, and it popped out of the frame and slid to the grass below.

"Help. Please help me now. Call the police, please, call my mother. Help help help help help—"

Amaryllis was slamming her fist against the door. "Shut up, you brat, shut up right now. Shut up shut up shut up or I'll *make you shut up.*"

And Blaine pulled her head inside the window for one minute. "I'm not eating any more of your goddamn peanut butter, so stop trying to poison me." Then she stuck her head back out the window to scream.

"Okay, up there, hang on, I'm a-coming."

A man's voice, and then Blaine saw him, a big guy, her hero. He wore beige Dockers, a navy blue Polo shirt, a braided brown leather belt, slip-on loafers. Everything he wore was reassuringly normal; everything about him told Blaine that he was someone from the world she was used to. He was black and had a little bit of a belly, but he was well muscled and had big shoulders, and Blaine thought maybe at one time in his life he'd been some kind of an athlete. He had a certain grace and stiffness in his bearing, like he was proud of who he was.

"You wouldn't by any chance be the famous Blaine Marsden, now, would you?"

She liked his voice. Deep and reassuring. His confidence gave her confidence.

"Yes, oh, God, yes, I'm Blaine Marsden."

"I'll be damned. You don't look too good. You all right?"

"*Fuck no,* I'm not all right. I'm being held prisoner here. And don't believe the crazy woman who lives here, she'll tell you I'm an alcoholic or a drug addict—she said the same thing about my mom. She is a lying bitch."

"I don't know about that, little sailor-mouth, but I admit she's not very good at answering the door. You sure she's there?"

"She's right out here in the hallway. How'd you find me?"

"Twyla sent me."

"Oh, my God. Twyla. Is she here?"

"No, she's in school where she should be. And where you should be too."

"I would love to be in school." Blaine felt a sob overwhelm her.

"How about your mom? You getting along okay with your mom? She treat you all right? You want to go home?"

"Of course I do. But I don't think she knows where I am. Have you talked to her? Did she send you?"

"I called your house once, but your mama wasn't home. I did hear that message she left you on the answering machine though. I liked the sound of it."

Blaine licked a tear that ran down the side of her cheek.

"I thought I better get on down here. Your little friend Twyla said you were in a weird situation with your mom and you wanted to come home. I promised her I would check it out."

Blaine laughed, a relieved sound. "Twyla, I can't believe it. Oh, God, it's a long story. See—"

"That's okay, little sailor. I'll be coming inside, and you can tell me then. Now, you go tell that lady to open the door and let me in, or I'm calling the cops. Then come on back to the window."

"Did you hear that, you bitch?" Blaine shrieked. "Open the front door, or he's calling the cops." She noticed that Amaryliis had stopped beating on the door. She crossed the room, her stomach hurt, hurt bad actually, but she went and listened. And just as she put her ear to the door, the fist slammed again, making the wood jump in the frame, and Blaine ran back to the window.

"She's beating on the door. She just keeps beating on the door."

"Don't be scared. I've got my cell phone, I'm calling the police as we speak. Oh, hell, what's . . . no service."

"She keeps beating the door."

"Don't panic, honey, I'm coming in one way or another."

He jammed the cell phone back in his pants and ran around the house.

The beating against the door stopped. Blaine heard noise from the hall bathroom, running water, the rattling of glass or something under the sink. The doorbell was ringing again, ringing, ringing, and someone was slamming a shoulder against it, and then quiet. She couldn't hear for sure, but Blaine thought that Amaryllis had opened the front door. Voices in the hallway, the man's and Amaryllis Burton, sounding breathless and little-girlish and very, very angry.

And then she was throwing up again, and running for the bathroom. She thought maybe she heard the front door slam. She flushed the toilet, stepped over the dried vomit in the bathroom, and went to the door. Listening, listening. But nothing, no sound.

"Hello? Are you out there? Help?"

But her voice was smaller now, she was feeling so bad, and she was afraid because it was so quiet. She hesitated, then slammed her fists on the door. No one came. She called and called, but no one came. And after a while, she had to lie down.

CHAPTER TWENTY-EIGHT

Charlie didn't like leaving the little girl behind, but he needed help, and he was still trying to get a handle on what he was dealing with. His thigh ached where Amaryllis Burton had injected him; his heart was pumping hard.

He took her by the arm and dragged her to the door.

"Where are you taking me?"

"I don't know what the hell was in that injection, lady, but you and I are headed for the emergency room, where you can tell the doctor and the cops what was in the syringe."

"I won't," she said.

Her eyes were round and disturbing, and he knew he was dealing with a certified nut. He still felt okay, though, he just didn't know for how long. Damn, his hands were shaking. It was shock, of course. He'd had no idea what he was walking into. Leave it to Twyla to land him in the middle of something bizarre.

"Let me go, you jerk."

Jerk? he thought. That little girl back there, that Blaine, could have come up with a lot worse. Kid cussed like a marine. Her mother ought to have a word with her. Charlie didn't like a potty mouth, not on little girls. But he supposed he'd cuss too if he'd been locked up in a house with this crazy lady. And a part of him admired the child. She'd been mad as hell and ready to fight. Make a good marine.

She wasn't all that strong, this woman, this Amaryllis Burton, and she kicked him but he was big and well trained, and he kept her arms pinned and wrestled her down the front steps and over to his car. He kept an eye out, hoping some neighbor might come out of their house and object to a large black man overpowering the white lady who lived right across the street, but either Amaryllis Burton was not popular with her neighbors or there was nobody home. He would have been grateful for some concerned citizen deciding to get involved, or at least call the local sheriff.

He got the jumper cables out of the trunk, keeping the woman pinned with one hand. It was sad, really, how easy it was for a man to overpower a woman. But damn lucky for him.

He tied her into the front seat with the jumper cables, making sure she was in her seat belt, more to keep her strapped in place than safe, and she bit him like a rabid bunny, on the wrist and the back of his arm. If they did have a car accident and she got hurt, no doubt she would sue the state of Kentucky. Not that it would do her any good. Kentucky had passed enough state laws making it illegal for people to sue them. Sovereign immunity.

God, his mind was wandering.

He heard the little girl crying. *Be brave,* he thought, but he didn't say anything, because he was starting to have a rather severe pain under his rib cage that made it hard to talk. He checked the cell phone. Still no service.

"You're going to die," Amaryllis Burton told him. Her voice was whispery and babyish.

Charlie slid into the front seat beside her and started the car. He pulled out of the little horseshoe street where Amaryllis Burton lived, onto one of the main arteries of the neighborhood.

He wasn't sure where the hospital was, but the main thing was to get out of the neighborhood, and then onto the main roads where he could find help, and a phone to call the local cops for help. There was a BP station right on Dolly Parton Parkway, no more than three minutes away. He'd go there. He was feeling bad. Really bad. He wasn't sure he would make it to a hospital, and it wasn't like Amaryllis Burton was going to give him directions. Right now he'd settle for another human being who registered comfortably high on the *normal* scale.

The nausea hit with a violence that rocked him. He pulled to the side of the road and opened the car door, vomiting on the pavement. *This is not good,* was all he could think. He knew she was watching him, but all he could do was hang his head out the door and empty his stomach, keeping his right foot on the brake so the car would not roll.

He could not stop throwing up. Everything he had eaten in the last twenty-four hours came up, heavily, smelling strong and making him regret he'd eaten anything at all, but then it got down to yellow bile, and after that, he still didn't stop throwing up, although now it was nothing more than flaky white froth. The pain over the top of his stomach made it impossible for him to talk or do much of anything, even though he was aware that the woman was struggling with the jumper cables. A really ineffective way of tying her up, and he was aware when she put the car in park, but he still kept his foot on the brake. He couldn't think clearly. Should he take his foot off the brake? If the car rolled, he knew he would not be able to break his fall. He heard the front passenger door opening and closing. Amaryllis Burton put her little rabbit face close to his just for a moment. She pulled the lever to pop the trunk.

Hazy as he was, he was aware of her pulling him out of the car, skidding a little in the vomit, putting her shoulder under his. He knew he should do something, he just didn't know what. Maybe she would just leave him there by the side of the road and someone would come along to help. Maybe she was just stealing his car. He could crawl to one of the houses, there were at least ten of them right on this street, they hadn't even made it out of the neighborhood.

She walked him around the car, bumped him suddenly, and he knew then what she was up to. She was going to put him into the trunk.

That focused him. He pushed her away hard, and she stumbled backward and onto the curb. He slammed the trunk down, the sound of the latch clicking into place a monumental relief. He could see out of the corner of his eye that she was opening the back door, left-hand side.

Another bad idea. He had to get out of the street and onto the sidewalk, crawl if he had to, find a house where someone was home and would call for help.

He realized that he was either going to pass out or throw up again, and he wondered which would happen first, and which he would prefer. It was funny the way your vision went just before you lost consciousness, like the world was a tunnel and then a little pinpoint of light.

She had him. He felt her arms around his midsection, pushing him. He groaned, rigid with the pain in his middle. Then the feel of the upholstery on his left cheek, and he collapsed in the backseat of the car.

Stupid way to die, he thought. If he did ever wake up again, he would snap the damn woman's little rabbit neck with one hand, even if it meant prison for the rest of his natural life.

Chapter Twenty-nine

She slept. Not for long, but it impressed her that she had actually fallen asleep. Let her know how sick she was. She was getting worse. Weaker. Whatever it was she had, whatever it was in that peanut butter, there was enough of it that even after throwing everything up, it was in her system, and shutting her down.

She had gone through every drawer in the room, and through everything in the closet, and then under the sink, finding the kind of skanky stuff people keep in bathroom cabinets—Windex, and dirty rags, and a toilet brush. A can of peach shave cream, some nubs of scummy green soap, an open box of maxi pads. Ick. Her treasure was a huge toenail clipper. Blaine had never seen one so big, and she figured it was a guy clipper, and probably belonged to Stanley the Manly. The nail file on that end could be used like a flat-head screwdriver, and she sat cross-legged at the door, taking the screws out of the round faux brass plate that held the doorknob on. Going out the window was her backup plan, but it was a second-story window, and there wasn't really anything to grab onto except the surface of the brick. She'd have preferred the window—there was no chance of running into

274

Amaryllis that way. But there was a good chance she would get hurt, weak as she was. And the thought of Amaryllis dragging her back into the house, only this time her with a broken leg or something . . . she'd never get away. She had listened for a long time. Screamed and beat on the door. No one had answered. No one had come and hit back at the door. She got the empty-house feeling. She had the impression the front door had slammed shut while she was being sick earlier. And she felt pretty sure that if Amaryllis had been there, she would not have stayed so quiet, that she would have hit back against the door like earlier. Blaine had tried screaming out that back window, but this time no one had come. Who was that guy . . . Charlie? Where was he? Thank God for Twyla. The kid next door must have kept his promise and called her. She wondered if he was still over there. She wondered if he had heard her scream.

Her biggest fear was that Amaryllis was out there, still in the house, waiting quietly. It didn't make sense, but just the image of that woman, waiting, breathing quietly, made her afraid to leave the bedroom. But she was leaving. If she did go out there and find Amaryllis, she would stab her with the damn nail file. She would punch her and hit her and run out the door; go to a neighbor and call for help. All she had to do was get across the street. And it was no more than thirty feet, max, to the next house. She just had to get out of the house.

Even when her side of the doorknob came off, the locking mechanism was still in place. Still, she unlatched it pretty quickly, peering out the hole in the door down the dark hallway. Her hands shook, and her legs trembled so much it was hard to walk. She had gotten very afraid of Amaryllis when the woman had beat back against the door. It had been so weird, so angry.

Blaine moved quietly down the hall, using the wall as a support, pushing her way along with her hands. No noises, except the ones she made; no sound of anything or anyone but herself. Everything dim in the afternoon gloom. The sun was already going down, another day in this god-awful house, another day out of school and away from home, and God please she did not spend another night here.

Phone first, or just get out?

Out, of course. Get the hell away.

No one in the living room. No sign of that Charlie. Where had he gone?

The front door had a dead bolt. She twisted it free and turned the knob and opened the door. She was surprised. It was almost too easy. She headed down the steps of the porch and ran across the street. Oh, God, to be out of the house. She looked over her shoulder. She'd left the door wide open. It was awful and weird, the compulsion she felt to go back and shut it.

The people in the house across the street had a dog, a little one—Blaine could see the top of the dog's head as it jumped and jumped, could see the dog through the frosted window beside the door. She rang the bell. The dog jumped and barked, but no one came. Nobody home. Next door, no one home. The next two houses were empty, rentals between families.

She was sick again, and threw up right there in the road, falling to her knees, vomiting up air and white froth. Even with nothing to expel, her body jerked and convulsed with a frantic strength, trying to survive whatever it was in that peanut butter. Blaine was in pain again. But even in pain she could walk fast, if not run. Which way? The road, or cut through the backyards?

No lights in the backs of those houses. Nobody home any-more these days. A neighborhood was never more deserted than during the hours of broad daylight, where every adult in the household had to work and the kids had to be warehoused away from home.

Blaine decided on the road. More chance to flag down a car or something.

She couldn't run, and her walk was a halfway stumble, but she was making progress. There were several vacant lots in this neighborhood, and the houses backed up onto farmland, but today even the cows were gone.

She stumbled and fell right by the curb, and hit her cheekbone against the concrete. It hurt bad enough that she thought it might be broken, and she cried, and lay in the road, but she knew that help was not that far. There were lots more houses on the next block, and surely, in one of those houses, someone would be home. Someone would call the police, someone would call her mother. She was minutes, literally minutes, away from help. She was out of the house. She could do this. She just needed to get up and get on the move.

Blaine pushed up and got to her feet. She tasted blood in her mouth. Her cheek felt like it was getting bigger and bigger; she felt it swell and even go a little numb on the skin, but the ache was bad and competed with the pain in her side for her attention.

And then the sound of a car.

She looked up, and the car flashed its lights. A silver Nissan. Thank God. Blaine raised an arm and waved, but could not quite get up. For a minute she was afraid the car would hit her, then she heard the sputter of gravel as the tires ground to a stop, a car door open, and a sound like a trunk popping up.

The blow took her by surprise, a backhand across the top of her head that knocked her temple into the pavement. She felt the hands lift her, and smelled Amaryllis before she actually saw her, those unshaven fat little legs sticking out of the denim farm-lady jumper, the nasty Birkenstocks on her bare feet, the thick yellowed toenails.

Get a fucking pedicure, Blaine thought, and tried to slap the woman's hands off her.

"Shitty little brat," the woman said, and somehow it was the cursing that shocked her, even more than the sensation of being lifted into the air. Just as she realized she'd been slapped into the trunk of this silver Nissan, the lid came down, hard, and the latch clicked solidly in place.

Blaine screamed. The car moved forward, but went only a little way. She felt the turn, then another sharp turn directly after. Heard the noise of the garage door going up and knew that she was back in the house, right back where she started from, except this time she was locked in a trunk.

She still had the nail file. Amaryllis had taken her by surprise, but she still had the nail file, and if nothing else, she could hurt this woman. She would slash her eyes out.

The garage door closed. She heard footsteps, and the car rocked, like someone was taking things out of the backseat. The car door slammed, and the door to the house opened and closed, slammed again, and then the garage was dead quiet, except for the metallic tink of the cooling engine.

And Blaine, still in the trunk, still grasping the nail clipper with the nail file out and ready to slash the woman's eyes, realized that Amaryllis was going to leave her in the trunk.

CHAPTER THIRTY

The drive to Tennessee was an awkward convoy—Joel and I ahead of the pack in the BMW, Emma Marsden and Marcus Franklin behind us, and trailing behind, Syd and Theodore Tundridge and Mr. French in a silver RAV4. Syd Tundridge had brought her two dogs, sizable golden retrievers.

There was a car show in town, and few hotel rooms to be had close to Pigeon Forge and Gatlinburg, so we were all staying at the Clarion on Highway 66, on the outskirts of Sevierville.

Joel had insisted on exploring while we waited for the FBI. Exploring meant driving up and down the four-lane highway, and I knew he was trying to keep me distracted. I wanted to go straight to confront Amaryllis Burton, but I knew it was best to let the FBI handle it.

So I let him distract me; I watched the scenery.

If Amaryllis Burton wanted to pick an area where she could live cheaply, drive to Lexington on half a tank of gas, and pretty much go unnoticed, she had chosen wisely.

The Gatlinburg/Pigeon Forge/Sevierville area survived on the tourists. The traffic was bad, bumper-to-bumper, most of it comprised of gigantic RVs, all inching their way up and down a four-lane highway that stretched between all three cities. It was impossible to tell which city you were in unless you knew the order, which was one, Sevierville, two, Pigeon Forge, and three, Gatlinburg.

It was an area that offered the kind of vacation no one admits they actually take—a vacation of mini golf, Wal-Mart, Ripley's Believe It or Not, and pancakes. If you figured that the locals made a living by giving people what they wanted, then I took the optimistic view that Americans weren't as spoiled as people say they are, since so many of them seemed perfectly content to come and stay here.

Each of the three towns had its own flavor. Sevierville was a town devoted to the locals, though it allowed for the seasonal influx of tourists. Sevierville had the most normal things—a movie theater, a Kroger's, and a Golden Corral Restaurant. Pigeon Forge was wall-to-wall souvenir shops—my personal favorite the one advertising SWIMSUITS, LEATHER, FUDGE & KNIVES. Something for everyone. Gatlinburg defined cute, tucked away at the bottom of the Smoky Mountains. If you followed the narrow and climbing Ski Mountain Road, you would find chalets and a ski lodge, and perhaps the occasional bear.

We passed outlet malls, Hillbilly Golf, horseback riding stables (including one where you could get married in the saddle), and Dolly Parton's Splash Country. Most of the hotel rooms advertised rates from twenty-nine ninety-nine a night all the way up to fifty dollars. Some of the marquees claimed that their rooms were newly renovated, and I pictured worn hotel rooms that smelled of industrial-strength cleanser and embedded cigarette smoke.

The trio of towns was surrounded by mountains and farmland. I was struck by the way the locals adhered to truth in advertising. All of the people filling the tour buses and driving the RVs knew exactly what to expect. The signs were very specific. COME AND SEE THE LEAVES. And they did have leaves, lots of them, on and off the trees. COME AND SEE THE CHRISTMAS LIGHTS. We were months from Christmas, yet the lights were up everywhere, all over all three towns. I counted three Christmas stores. The residents landed on the high-end slope of genius. They invited the world to visit and enjoy what they had, leaves and lights and mountains, and made a living in a town with few natural resources and little industry. Everyone was happy—the tourists, who got what they came for, and the locals, who did not have to move away from their beautiful mountains to make a living. I felt a certain admiration.

The area clearly had one industry, and that was marriage. It was Hillbilly Vegas and the Poconos—southern style—with chapel after chapel, jewelry stores that promised one-hour wedding ring sizing, and boutiques that sold wedding dresses at half price. The little motels showed heart-shaped Jacuzzi tubs on their signs.

A new segment of the highway funneled traffic directly into the expansive parking lot of Dollywood, and billboards proclaimed an assortment of local shows that included The Dixie Stampede, Country Tonight, and The Black Bear Jamboree. There were pancake houses on every block, sometimes more than one, and signs for the Gatlinburg artists' community that included a world-renowned chain-saw carver and a boutique called Treasures from Around the World.

Joel and I were intrigued by the sign promising a real English pub, the Fox and Parrot, which seemed an odd thing to find in the middle of the Tennessee mountains.

"Do you think they have real English beer at that pub?" I asked Joel.

We were stuck behind another RV, this one from Wisconsin. It amazed me that someone would drive here all the way from Wisconsin, though I had only the vaguest idea how far that was. Far.

"Let's put it on our list of things to do. Going to an English pub in Tennessee."

"Not everybody can say they did that."

"See that chapel back there?" Joel said.

I turned and looked over my shoulder. I saw three. I wondered which one he meant.

"It's a drive-through. Like Vegas."

"How come you haven't asked me to marry you?"

The cab of the car flooded with tension. Joel did not answer, just kept driving. I watched the scenery go past. Another wedding chapel, and then a welcome center. It seemed to go welcome center, wedding chapel, pancake house, then start all over again.

"Are you going to do that thing where you pretend you don't hear me?" I asked.

"I heard," Joel said.

"Because I asked you why you haven't asked me to marry you."

"I figure we'll get married one of these days."

"One of these days?" I pulled my hand, which he happened to be holding, out of his.

He gave me a sideways look, and then checked the rearview mirror and both side-view mirrors. I'm not sure what he was looking for. Help, maybe.

He took my hand back. "We can get married if you want to."

"If *I* want to? Like, against your will?"

"I wouldn't marry you if it was against my will."

"When?"

"When what?"

"When do you want to get married?"

He shifted his weight and frowned. The serious frown that made me worry. "Give it a couple more years, and we'll see."

"What do you need a couple more years for? What exactly are you waiting to see? We've been living together for a year."

He didn't say anything. Neither did I.

"You hungry?" he asked.

"No."

"Are you mad?"

"Nope."

He looked at me. I was still holding his hand and had not moved to my own side of the front seat, which is what I do when I'm mad. And the truth was, I wasn't mad. You can't fault a man if he doesn't want to get married. I wouldn't want a man who didn't want me.

"Joel. You should know that I have definitely decided that I want to get married."

"Okay."

"You should also know that it doesn't necessarily have to be to you."

"Lena—"

"That's all I have to say, right now."

Because my feeling is that while you certainly cannot blame a man if he does not want to get married, you cannot blame a woman if she does.

Joel's mobile rang. He answered quickly, his mobile his lifeline, muttering so that I could not hear what he said. He pulled into the left lane and made an illegal U-turn.

"Time," he said.

We drove in silence. I counted welcome centers. I was at sixteen by the time we made it back to the Sevierville courthouse, where we were meeting up with the FBI.

The head FBI agent, McKay, waited for us outside in the parking lot. He was stocky and about five-ten—not the tall and perfect physical specimen you see on television—and he wore round spectacles that reminded me of the granny glasses John Lennon used to wear way back when. He was nicely pulled together, in the way of FBI agents, with brownish blondish hair gelled and sprayed back. I could smell the aftershave he used. He wore his deep black suit coat and crisp white shirt with flair. This is the mark of an FBI agent, this little bit of style. It separates them from the Secret Service (studied dullness) and the ATF (individualists, as much as one can be on the federal payroll). Of course, my favorite ATF agent, Wilson McCoy, had a lot of style, but he was from Los Angeles, so you can't judge by that. Also, last I heard, he was out of ATF and running a restaurant at the beach in Marina Del Rey.

McKay gave Joel a nod and a smile that had a hint of warmth. They seemed friendly enough, for mortal enemies.

"Joel."

"Booker." Joel waved a hand in my direction. "This is my fiancée, Lena Padget."

My mouth opened, but I managed to say hello.

Booker McKay shook my hand, and then actually grinned at Joel. "Congratulations," he said. "I hadn't heard you were getting married."

I hadn't either. Wasn't there supposed to be a proposal or something? Or had I actually done the proposing myself, as far as Joel was concerned?

"When are you doing the deed?" McKay asked.

I looked over at Joel. I wanted to know too.

"Next week," Joel said.

McKay looked down at me. "You guys could always stop off here at one of the chapels."

I waited to hear if Joel had made any specific plan, but McKay's cell phone rang, ending the flow of information.

McKay glanced at his watch, then nodded at Joel. "War room's ready. Local sheriff's department set us up. We'll brief everybody in twenty minutes. Before we go in there, though—" He looked over at me.

"Am I a problem?" I asked.

"No, no. But here's the thing. We've got a lot of civilians here—you, and the girl's mother, Emma Marsden. Dr. Tundridge and his wife. Everybody's anxious, and everybody wants to be involved. And I'm glad everybody is here, on hand, in case I need to consult with somebody. But I've still got a job to do."

I folded my arms. "I'm listening."

"I've set up a spare conference room for the families. I'd like you to be the liaison."

"You mean the babysitter," I said.

"I mean the babysitter," he said.

I pointed at Joel. "What about him?"

McKay raised an eyebrow. "He gets to choose. He can come with me or stay with you."

I nodded. "Okay. Whatever I can do to help."

"Good," he said. He headed toward the door. Joel hung back and looked at me.

"You want me to go with him and report to you?" Joel said.

"You know me well."

He kissed me, just a quick brush of the lips. "I'll tell you what I want you to know."

"I'd like it better if you'd tell me what I want me to know."

He winked and walked away.

CHAPTER THIRTY-ONE

Joel swore afterward that it had been a mistake, but he almost smiled when he said it, so I've never been sure. He called me ten minutes after we'd parted in the parking lot, told me the FBI had just gotten moving on their plan and were calling it Operation Angel. Then he said something muffled that sounded like good-bye, except he did not hang up. I heard voices. I heard McKay arguing with someone, and I put my mobile on speaker phone and set it down in the center of the table where I sat with Emma Marsden, Marcus Franklin, Syd and Theodore Tundridge, and Mr. French. The newest member of our group, Janine Russell, sat near Emma. They had hit it off. Janine was the wife of Charlie Russell, a social worker from Lexington who had gone out to visit Amaryllis Burton this morning and never returned. Charlie Russell had been looking for Blaine, unofficially for a friend, according to his wife. He was not there "officially," as in with the knowledge of the Office of Child Protective Services, because, as she told me privately, out of earshot of Tundridge, he thought that Emma Marsden was being railroaded.

They'd put us in a small room on the second floor, off a courtroom, and it had a faux wood table and twelve folding

chairs. I had been worried that Dr. Tundridge would recognize
me from the night I had met him in the pathology lab, but evidently cleaning crews were invisible. He shook my hand when I
introduced myself, nodded curtly at Emma Marsden, and immediately engaged Marcus Franklin in technical conversation.
Although he sat next to his wife, they seemed miles apart.

It was not a congenial grouping. The Tundridges sat with
Mr. French on one side of the table, and Janine Russell, Emma,
and Marcus Franklin sat on the other side. I didn't sit at all.

From the noise of chairs scraping the floor and random
coughing, it sounded like McKay was addressing a full house. I
listened while he introduced everyone—a six-person FBI team,
my future husband, Joel, and three sheriff's deputies. I had met
the deputies in the hallway. They wore beige uniforms, and
were friendly. They did not seem inclined to turf wars, and in
fact were low-key and professional. One was female. I was
impressed.

I heard a tapping noise, like someone was using a pointer,
then McKay's voice.

"This is the subject, Amaryllis Burton. We've had agents
researching Ms. Burton's background, and we've had somebody
talk to the husband." This was the value of the agency. They
could send people out literally all over the country, everybody
pursuing his one piece of the puzzle, and reporting back in a
matter of hours.

"She was born here in Sevierville, got a nursing degree in
Louisville, Kentucky, and worked as an LPN for about ten years.
During that time she was employed by three hospitals, one rehabilitation center, and a doctor's office, where she was employed
until early this week. She left under shady circumstances in every
work situation; usually she was fired, or about to be fired. She is
manipulative and twisted. Do not underestimate this woman.
People around Ms. Burton tend to get very sick with liver ail-
ments. The second hospital she worked for was pretty sure she

was poisoning patients, and she worked in the pediatric unit with children. In every work situation, she's been involved either with infants or young children."

Emma Marsden sobbed. I looked at Marcus Franklin. We might have to take her out of the room.

"Agents have searched her home in Lexington. The toothbrush, shampoo, things you'd need every day, are all gone. Clearly, she packed up and left. She told a neighbor, who saw her packing things into her car, that she was taking a leave of absence from work and would not be back for a few weeks. She stopped her mail.

"We talked to the husband. He is employed as a mortgage portfolio analyst, and at best is home three weekends out of the month. He says there are no problems in the marriage."

Someone in the back of the room laughed cynically.

"Mr. Burton says that he and Amaryllis had three children, total, none living. The first two died of SIDS as infants—one at two months, one at five. Both girls. Their third child, a male, lived to the age of eight, but was sick off and on most of his childhood. Mr. Burton said that doctors thought the boy had some kind of rare and congenital liver defect. Mr. Burton said that he got a vasectomy after the birth of the third child, much against his wife's wishes. She has reportedly never forgiven him, and has several times looked into adoption and foster care, but has always been turned down."

"For once the system worked," Janine Russell said softly.

Dr. Tundridge gave her a look, and I thought for a moment that he was going to shush her. But the look she gave him across the table made him change his mind. I realized I was holding my breath. McKay should have given me one of those deputies.

McKay was still talking. "Deputy Sheriff Krupp says that the local police had a call three hours ago from a Janine Russell, wife of Charlie Russell, a social worker with the Department of Child Protective Services in Lexington, Kentucky. Mr. Russell and his wife arrived in Gatlinburg early this morning, rented a hotel room, and split up. His wife went shopping, and Mr. Russell went to check on Blaine Marsden, who was reportedly at the home of Amaryllis Burton. Mr. Russell was working unofficially on information provided to him by one of his charges. One of Blaine Marsden's friends from school called Mr. Russell, who is her social worker, and said that her friend Blaine had called for help, and that she was staying at the home of Amaryllis Burton. It was unclear whether or not she was there against her will. Mr. Russell went to the Burton home this morning to check the situation out, and has not returned. We had an agent do one drive-by in front of the house. Lights are on, someone is home. Mr. Russell drove a silver Nissan, and that car is nowhere in sight. The local police and deputies have had an APB out, but so far, there's been no sign of Mr. Russell or his car. His wife is extremely concerned and says there is no way he would not have called her by now. He does not answer his cell phone.

"We have reason to believe that Ms. Burton is holding Blaine Marsden in order to sell her blood."

There was a murmur in the room, but McKay held up a hand.

"I know, I know. But Blaine Marsden is the half-sister of Ned Marsden, who was a patient of the clinic where Ms. Burton worked. The boy's blood had unusual genetic materials that were patented for over four million dollars by the doctor who employed Ms. Burton."

Someone muttered something, but I did not look up. I did not want to see them glaring at each other across the conference table.

Some of McKay's people were whispering. McKay kept talking.

"This doctor, Theodore Tundridge, received an e-mail offering to sell him blood that contained the same genetic material for research purposes. Doctor Tundridge did retrieve this blood sample, and had done so before we caught up with him. We have established that the offer was not some kind of hoax, and Dr. Tundridge is cooperating fully with this investigation."

And that lets you off the hook, I thought, giving him a look.

"The theory," McKay said, "is that the blood sample was left by Amaryllis Burton, who is assuming that Blaine Marsden's blood will contain the same material as her half-brother's. We think that's why she's holding the girl."

The tapping noises again. McKay probably had a diagram he was pointing to—*X*'s and *O*'s, like football strategy. Their plan was simple. The FBI would surround the house, one of the agents would ring the doorbell, and they'd swarm, heavily armed and ready for anything. They would take Amaryllis Burton by surprise to avoid any kind of a hostage standoff. They were set to leave in twenty minutes. Were there any questions?

"I've got a question," Janine Russell said.

I turned the cell phone off.

Russell was looking at the doctor. She was small and slender, hair severe in a French knot. "What made you accuse this woman here of Munchausen by proxy? Just what kind of evidence did you have? Because from what I know, and I know a lot, you don't have a shred of proof."

"Who exactly are you, anyway?" Tundridge said.

Janine Russell leaned across the table. "You know exactly who I am—you heard the man in there. I'm Charlie Russell's wife. And I happen to know that Emma Marsden here isn't the only person you've made accusations against. And what I want to know is why."

"That kind of information is confidential. And frankly, I don't care what you want."

Syd Tundridge looked at her husband. "Well, I want to know, Ted. Do you really have anything on Emma Marsden?"

"Would you all please not talk about me like I'm not in the room? I'm right here at the table."

Mr. French held up a hand. "I'll tell you exactly what evidence we have. We have the evidence fed to us by Amaryllis Burton. Who told us, Ms. Marsden, that you had had two children who'd died of SIDS, and that you were using your son's illness to try and get the boy's father to marry you. She told us that you had confided in her. That you'd told everyone you and Mr. Roubideaux were married to pressure him into actually marrying you."

Emma opened her mouth, but Franklin patted her shoulder and told her just to listen.

"And then the video arrived in our office. Of you in the parking lot. And it seemed—"

"Don't go into that," I said. "We get it. Basically, Amaryllis Burton accused Emma of what she herself was doing. Was Amaryllis involved in the other accusations?"

French looked at Tundridge.

"Was she?" I asked.

"He won't answer that," Syd said flatly. "He's worried about lawsuits."

"He'd better worry," Emma said.

Janine squeezed her hand.

I went to the conference room door and opened it. Spoke to the deputy posted right outside. "Can we get some food brought in? Lots of carbohydrates, coffee, and maybe a few tranquilizers?"

CHAPTER THIRTY-TWO

They brought us hamburgers and sandwiches from Virgil's Restaurant, including cardboard cartons of the best little skinny french fries I'd ever eaten. I made sure everyone had food in front of them before I picked up a can of Coke. Dr. Tundridge was opening a bottle of water, but he put it down and looked at Emma Marsden.

"For what it's worth, Ms. Marsden, I'm sorry."

"Dr. Tundridge, you made four million dollars off my son, and then you accused me of killing him. Drink your water, eat your hamburger, and do not the fuck talk to me again."

I had a chicken salad sandwich. I tried to concentrate on that. We were short catsup packets, so I ate my fries without. I was going to strangle McKay next time I saw him.

We all watched the clock on the wall. The sweep of the second hand was mesmerizing.

Two hours and five minutes after I turned off the cell phone, it rang. Everyone jumped, and I flipped it open.

"Joel?"

"We've got the wrong house," Joel said.

"What?"

"It's the wrong house. Amaryllis Burton owns this house, but evidently she's rented it out to someone else. She's not here."

"Shit," I said. "Where are you?"

"Some place in Pigeon Forge. Venetian Way. I'll get back to you when I know something else. Got to go."

I looked up at the faces around the table.

"They've got the wrong house," I said.

Everybody started talking, but Janine Russell was the loudest.

"What's the name of the street they're on?" she asked me.

"Venetian Way."

"That's not it. It was Country Place. Country Place Way. Charlie asked me to look it up on MapQuest for him. It was in Sevierville, not Pigeon Forge."

Syd Tundridge shook her head. "No, Amaryllis told me her house was in Pigeon Forge."

Janine raised her voice. "Charlie told me he was going to Country Place."

I held up a hand. "Quiet, for God's sake. Look, the house Amaryllis Burton owns is in Pigeon Forge, but it's been rented out. She's not there. She must be at that Country Place Way." I looked at Janine. "Do you by any chance—"

"Let me think, let me think. Yeah, yeah. Twenty-seven twenty."

I picked up the phone. Joel didn't answer.

Janine stood up. "I'm out of here."

"Oh, no, you don't," I said.

"Oh, yes, I do. My husband has been gone all day. Something is really wrong with him, and don't ask me how I know, I just know. You go on ahead and call the FBI, but I'm going there, and I know the way."

"I'm going with you," Emma said.

"I'll go." Tundridge stood up. "I can reason with Amaryllis. She . . . respects me."

Syd rolled her eyes. "He's right, though. She'll listen to him."

"*Nobody's going,*" I said. But I was wrong. We all went. Even the dogs.

Amaryllis lived in a subdivision that had the river on one side, and the mountains on the other. Some of the houses had big lots and great views, and the ones on the periphery backed up to farmland. Some of the homes already had Christmas lights. Definitely a local thing.

There were streetlights, but we were a ways out of the city, and the darkness seemed heavy. At the very end of the subdivision was a small horseshoe of houses with tiny yards and half driveways. Amaryllis Burton's house was on the far corner. Her turquoise Nova was in the driveway.

The FBI was on the way, but they were stuck in traffic behind all the RVs. We were supposed to sit tight and stay put. Instead, we'd come up with our own plan.

While I walked to the front door, Mr. French and Marcus Franklin were heading around to the back of the house. Emma and Janine had flattened themselves up against the side of the house near the street. There were no windows there. Syd stayed at the cars with the dogs—our FBI liaison. Dr. Tundridge walked just a step behind me, as we'd planned.

The house was a split foyer. There were no bedroom lights on, and the living room light was off, but there was a glow from the back. Probably the kitchen.

I looked up and down the street. Lots of lights on in most of the houses. People were home from work, having dinner. I could see the bluish flicker and glow of television screens.

Amaryllis Burton had a flowerpot on her front porch, sprouting dead petunias, but no welcome mat. Tundridge followed me up the five front steps and rang the doorbell. I could hear it echo through the house.

No one came. I looked around while I waited. There were two garage doors with no windows, and someone had run into the one on the right and left a big dent. There was no sign of Charlie Russell's silver Nissan. I looked at Tundridge. He took a breath and patted me on the shoulder.

"We'll be fine," he said. The bedside manner.

The front door opened suddenly. There was no screen door, and Amaryllis Burton stood no more than six inches away. It was so weird to see her, after everything that I'd found out, that I caught my breath. She frowned when she saw us. I was a shock to her too.

"*Dr. Tundridge?*"

"Hello," I said. "Lena Padget—you remember me, don't you? The lady detective?"

"Of course," she said. She was holding a dish towel down by her side, and she fumbled with the top button of her denim jumper. "What are you doing here?"

"My dear Amaryllis, the sample you left me was perfect." Tundridge sounded smooth. He was right. She more than respected him.

I smiled. "You've got what we want, Amaryllis. We've come to negotiate."

For a minute I thought she was going to block me, but she changed her mind and moved back a little, and Tundridge and I went past her into a tiny foyer that had a staircase that led up to the living room and down toward the garage. I went up. The house seemed strangely quiet. No television. No music.

"Nice house," I said. "Oh, I see you're working in the kitchen. You want to go there, or should we sit in the living room?"

I flicked the light switch on. That was the signal to everyone outside. Amaryllis Burton was in.

I sat down on the couch. "Well, Amaryllis. You have what Dr. Tundridge wants."

Amaryllis sat down across from me in a recliner. "But why are you here?"

"Dr. Tundridge has talked to Emma Marsden, and they've worked out a deal."

Tundridge sat in a rocking chair, facing Amaryllis. "Ms. Marsden has agreed to give me . . . access to her daughter in exchange for dropping the Munchausen's accusation."

I crossed my legs. "I'm here representing Emma's interest, Amaryllis. We know you've got Blaine here with you. I wanted to go straight to the cops. Dr. Tundridge has convinced me that it would be better for everyone if we don't involve the police. It looks like we all have something to lose if things get official. You'll go to jail for kidnapping, Emma will have to deal with Child Protective Services, and Tundridge will get a shitload of bad publicity."

Amaryllis Burton blinked. "Dr. Tundridge, you and *I* have a deal."

He smiled at her. "So it was you, then, who sent me the e-mail and the sample?"

Amaryllis frowned. "I—I think you should both leave now."

Dr. Tundridge looked gravely at Amaryllis. "You must know how important my research is. I'm willing to agree to terms, Amaryllis. But it will have to be a one-time thing. One payment, then we all go our separate ways."

"I want half of what you got from the pharmaceutical company," Amaryllis said. The pupils of her eyes looked huge. "Two million dollars."

"I don't have it," Tundridge said. "I paid off the loans on the clinic. But I did bring one hundred thousand dollars in cash, and I have it with me in my car."

Amaryllis stood up suddenly and looked out the window.

"I'm in the RAV, not the Volvo," Tundridge said. "The money is in the front seat."

"It's not enough," Amaryllis said. "It won't last. You got *millions.*"

"That's for research," Tundridge told her.

"Give her your house," I suggested. Syd had filled me in on the way over, about how much Amaryllis hated her, how much she envied her.

Tundridge glared at me. "That's ridiculous."

I wasn't sure if he was acting or annoyed. "I don't think it's ridiculous. She's got a point. You made four million dollars, and I'm not going to let you put my client's daughter at risk because you're cheap. Give her the house in Heartland and your car, and make it legal. Put them in her name, and pay them off first—" I glanced over at Amaryllis. "You don't want any liens. Amaryllis, you get the house in Heartland and the Volvo and the cash."

Tundridge winced. "Okay. The house, the cash, and my wife's car. I'm keeping the Volvo."

"She gets the Volvo," I said.

"No. I want Syd's car." Amaryllis stood up. "Go get the cash and the title. Right now, as good faith."

"Then we get Blaine," I said.

Amaryllis didn't answer. I wondered if Blaine was still alive. I did not like the feeling I got in this house.

"Do you mind if I use your bathroom?" I jumped up and headed down the hallway, moving fast. I heard the recliner creak and Amaryllis moving behind me. I noted a bathroom off the hallway but kept on going, and behind me, the hall light went on.

There were three bedrooms. The doors were shut on all except the one on the left, the master. I took it in immediately, the doorknob and plate unscrewed, the door swinging open.

"Don't—"

I turned on the light. The bed was unmade. The window was open, the screen popped out. The bedclothes were tangled. It smelled as if someone had been sick in here. I saw vomit on the floor. And shoes. Two muddy platform shoes.

Amaryllis faced me from the hallway. "What are you doing?"

The sound of the front door slamming open made both of us jump. Footsteps beat like drumrolls in the hallway, and the room was suddenly swarming with large men and women bulked out in navy blue flak jackets that had "FBI" stenciled on the back. Amaryllis raised her right hand suddenly. The agent who grabbed her thought she had a gun, but when she dropped the towel, I saw that it was a syringe. It hit the floor and rolled under the bed.

I heard the sound of garage doors going up, the thundering of more feet on the stairs. Amaryllis had gone very limp, rag-dollish, weirdly smiling.

I looked up and saw Joel in the doorway.

"I left you a message," I said.

Joel led me out into the hall, but it was crowded with agents. "This way," he said, pointing. He bent close to my ear, whispering. "You should have seen them all trying to cram through the front door."

We heard the ambulance, and two minutes later saw the pulse of light from the window. It was followed by police cars, and the small street began to fill with neighbors. I followed Joel out of the back kitchen door, and around to the front of the house.

The garage doors were open.

Charlie Russell's silver Nissan was parked on the left-hand side, trunk open. Blaine Marsden was on her feet, wrapped in a blanket and enveloped in hugs from Emma and Marcus Franklin. One of them was crying, maybe both.

The ambulance crew was bringing out a stretcher, and they bypassed Blaine Marsden and headed straight for the open back door of the car.

Janine Russell was crying. McKay bent close to her; he looked like he was reassuring her.

"Janine?" I said.

She heard me and looked up. "He's unconscious, but alive." She brushed tears away and gave me the thumbs-up.

McKay pointed a finger at me. "Stick around. You and I need to talk."

"You can thank me later," I said, and looked at Joel. "I don't like his tone."

"How about I take you home?" Joel said.

"Sounds good."

"We just need to make one quick stop, if you're not too tired."

"What, are we out of milk?"

"No. But I saw a jewelry store on the way in that has one-hour sizing. And then I thought we might go celebrate at the Fox and Parrot. McKay can find us there, if he wants to talk."

CHAPTER THIRTY-THREE

I watched the court listings for months but never saw any sign of a divorce filing between Syd and Theodore Tundridge. The last time I passed the Tundridge Clinic, they were building a new addition.

Charlie Russell and Blaine Marsden made full recoveries with the assistance and care of Dr. Theodore Tundridge, who was, after all, an expert on liver toxins. Marcus Franklin moved in with Emma and Blaine in the house in Athens and planned to commute to his job in Frankfort until Blaine graduated from high school. The last time I talked to Emma Marsden, she and Franklin were planning a wedding and trying to talk Great-Aunt Jodina into living with them.

Judith said yes to Rick, and they flew to Jamaica and got married on the beach. They showed up at our door with their big news and were incensed to learn that we had beaten them to the altar.

Four days after we got back from Tennessee, just after dark, Joel and I drove into the Kentucky countryside near Versailles to the Pisgah Presbyterian Church on Old Frankfort Pike. Someone had lit candles, and I could see them flickering in the windows when we drove up.

The minister was young and broad-shouldered, and he had a friend with him—a girlfriend, I thought, from the way they smiled at each other. She was there to witness the ceremony and sign our marriage license. She sat in the front pew, until we invited her up to the pulpit with us. The girlfriend turned the sanctuary lights off so we could have the ceremony by candlelight.

I wore a white sheath silk wedding dress, elegant and simple, and Joel wore his best suit. We'd stopped at a florist to buy roses just that afternoon, and the girl behind the counter had put together a spur-of-the-moment bouquet.

The minister had a nice voice, and he was unhurried and clearly pleased to be marrying us. Joel and I said our vows in the flickering candlelight, and in just a few minutes we were man and wife.